EVA CHASE

SINISTER WIZARDRY

ROYALS OF VILLAIN ACADEMY

Sinister Wizardry

Book 3 in the Royals of Villain Academy series

First Digital Edition, 2019

Copyright © 2019 Eva Chase

Cover design: Christian Bentulan, Covers by Christian

Ebook ISBN: 978-1-989096-44-4

Paperback ISBN: 978-1-989096-45-1

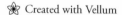 Created with Vellum

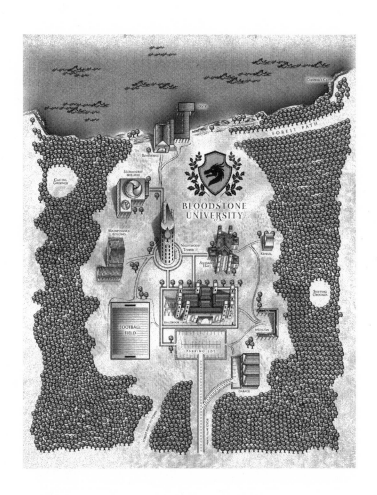

CHAPTER ONE

Rory

The main Bloodstone residence couldn't have been more different from the family home I'd done most of my growing up in. I'd heard the building described as a "big foreboding stone mansion," and that was right on the mark. It loomed over the forested Maine landscape—not so much manor house or castle like the buildings back on campus, but more a fortress of weathered limestone. The windows I could see, narrow and arched, held only darkness. I half expected to catch a glimpse of a medieval warrior standing by one with a crossbow at the ready.

I'd never missed my bright and airy house in California more.

The pang of homesickness and grief echoed through me as I peered through the car window. My hand rose instinctively to the glass dragon charm on the silver chain around my neck—the last remnant from a bracelet made up of years of birthday gifts.

The chauffeur, on staff with the company that had been tending to the Bloodstone properties since my birth parents' death and my disappearance, drove us past the stretch of mossy stone wall and came up on the wrought-iron gate. Someone had clearly been waiting for us. He didn't make any movement, but a second later the gate whirred open to admit us.

The chauffeur cleared his throat as he pulled into the property. "Your grandfather—the former baron—left strict instructions for the care of this property before his death. Everyone who's worked here was carefully vetted. But if you have any concerns about the valuables, there's a list at the bank of what should be present. Your grandfather packed away the more personal items in a locked room in the basement that no one has touched at all. That's the third key on the ring they gave you." He made a sideways nod in my direction.

"Got it," I said, and touched the side of my purse where I'd tucked that keyring away.

As one of the ruling entities among the fearmancers, my birth family had several properties across the Northeast, but this was the oldest and the largest. I was still getting used to the fact that I'd gone from owning not much more than some clothes and art supplies to having an immense bank account and extensive real estate.

Of course, if I could have reversed the trade and gotten back my *real* family, I'd have taken that deal in an instant. I didn't know a lot about my birth family, since I'd only been two when my parents had been killed, but I knew enough to make a few basic judgments. The fearmancer authorities had viciously murdered the people I thought of as Mom and Dad in front of me. The heirs of the other ruling families and a whole lot of the other young fearmancers had made my life hell when I'd first arrived at the fearmancer university to learn how to use my powers.

And just a few days ago, I'd watched one of the few professors who'd seemed to give a damn about me fatally stab himself to cut off the effects of a spell compelling him to attack me. A spell he'd told me had been cast by the older barons as well as "the reapers," whatever that meant.

The mages who ruled over fearmancer society, the ones I was supposed to rule alongside when I finished my education, had attempted to batter my magic out of me. That was the world I'd been thrown back into—a world where fear meant might, and might ruled over any ideas of human decency. I'd seen enough to realize the joymancers I'd left behind in California weren't perfect, but at least they didn't thrive on violence and destruction. Powering your magic through happiness made for very different attitudes than powering it through terror did.

The car pulled to a stop in the curve of the drive just outside the imposing front door. "The staff inside will show you around," the chauffeur said. "They'll be glad to have a Bloodstone in residence again. The work's more fulfilling when there's someone to appreciate it." He shot me a quick smile.

"Thank you for the drive." I bobbed my head in return

and eased the car door open. It might be summer now, but the Maine air wafted damp and a little cool around me, the sun partly blotted by thin gray clouds. The clover scent that reached my nose was pleasant enough, at least. I dragged in a deep breath of it and started up the steps.

My mouse familiar dug her claws a little more deeply into the shoulder of my blouse. Her small white head swiveled as she took in our new accommodations, and her dry voice trickled into my head. *Plenty of atmosphere, I'll give it that.*

Most mages' familiars couldn't outright talk to them, only pass on vague impressions through the magical bond. Deborah wasn't just a mouse, though. The Enclave that ruled over the joymancers had arranged for the spirit of one of their mages, a woman who'd been dying of cancer, to be placed into the animal's body.

The opportunity had meant a second life for her—and a way for them to monitor me. The more of the story I'd managed to get out of her, the more it'd become clear that the joymancers had been very worried about my fear-based powers emerging despite the steps they'd taken to suppress them.

I couldn't reply to her telepathically, unfortunately, and saying much to her out loud wasn't a good idea in front of witnesses. The fearmancers had no idea I'd brought one of their enemies into their midst in mouse form, and if they found out, I had no doubt Deborah's second life would be cut much shorter than her first had.

The door to the mansion opened just as I reached the top step. A middle-aged woman beamed at me. She welcomed me in with a sweep of her arm, her black hair, piled high on her head, gleaming with a purple tint.

"Welcome home, Miss Bloodstone," she said in a measured but friendly voice. "I'm Eloise, the house manager. I'll see to it that everything remains in order during your stay."

"Thanks," I said, and then anything I might have added was lost with my breath as I took in the vast front hall on the other side of the doorway.

A brocade rug covered the tiled floor, and another ran up the grand staircase ahead of me. Oil paintings with gilded frames hung on the walls between mahogany side tables with porcelain vases and bejeweled boxes. A young woman in a maid uniform was just setting a bouquet of lilies into one of the vases. A faint perfume drifted off them. The space was airier than I'd have expected from its imposing exterior.

I must have spent a lot of time here in the first two years of my life. I didn't have the faintest memory of any of it. Eloise had welcomed me home, but this didn't feel like home at all, more like a well-kept museum dedicated to strangers. What did any of this tell me about my birth parents other than they'd had old-money aesthetic tastes like most other fearmancers seemed to?

Maybe I'd get a better sense of them going through these "personal" items my grandfather Bloodstone had apparently stashed away.

The shifting of Deborah's body on my shoulder reminded me of one thing I needed to have "in order" from the start. I caught the house manager's eye and motioned to the mouse.

"This is my familiar," I said. "I'd like to give her free run of the property while we're here. All the staff need to know to be careful of her."

If Eloise thought it was strange for a fearmancer to have a mouse for a familiar rather than the predatory animals that most preferred, she didn't let it show. "Absolutely, I'll make that exceptionally clear to everyone on staff."

She led me through the ground floor, which included a sitting room, a music room, a ballroom, a parlor, a dining room that could have accommodated fifty people, and then the kitchen, which was unexpectedly open and modern-looking compared to the rest of the furnishings, if still at least a decade out of date. My grandfather Bloodstone would still have lived here until his death, presumably. I guessed the family had appreciated modern amenities over style where it mattered most.

A skinny man with angular limbs and a round head that made me think of a grasshopper was perched on a stool by one of the gleaming counters. He hopped up at our arrival.

"This is Claude, your chef," Eloise said.

The man offered me a little bow. "At your service. Perhaps you could tell me what you'd be interested in having for your meals today? We have enough ingredients on hand to manage a simple lunch, but if you wanted anything more complicated—for dinner as well—it would be good to know ahead of time so I can get everything I need."

My mind went blank. I'd known a lot of my classmates had family chefs preparing and sending their school meals, but I'd been managing to feed myself just fine, and I'd assumed it'd be the same here. "I, um… I hadn't given it much thought. I'm not very picky. Would it be a problem if I said you can make whatever you think would taste good?"

He blinked, and then the corners of his mouth curled upward. "It would be my pleasure. If you do think of anything in particular you'd like during your time here, don't hesitate to make a request, of course."

I wasn't sure how long I was going to be here. Bloodstone University—or Villain Academy, as the joymancers called it, which was a pretty accurate nickname —was closed for two weeks, but then it would open again for an optional summer term. I'd gathered that only the senior students attended, and usually only the stronger talents among those, to compete in some sort of special project.

I didn't like the idea of spending any more time on campus, surrounded by peers who mostly saw me as either a tool or a target, but I'd accomplish a lot more there than I could here. My mentor, Professor Banefield, had given me a key just before he'd died, one that mattered a lot more to me than any on the ring in my purse. He'd seemed to think it would lead me to something that would help me against my enemies.

My hand came to rest on my purse, where I'd stashed

that key too. I needed to figure out what the hell it opened... and I also needed to continue finding out everything I could about the school so I'd be able to see through my plan to bring the place down.

Bloodstone University taught young fearmancers to turn into the sadistic murderers so many of the adults were. Deborah had told me the joymancers had been trying to put a stop to those teachings for years, but the wards had stopped them from even locating the university. If I could bring them the information they needed to tackle that part of fearmancer society, they'd *have* to see that my magic didn't mean I'd turn out as cruel as my heritage would suggest. I'd get vengeance for Mom and Dad and for Professor Banefield, and I'd be able to return to my real home.

And with my enemies ramping up their efforts to take *me* down, I might not have much time left to accomplish that.

Upstairs, Eloise showed me to the master bedroom, my childhood bedroom, and several guest rooms. Even my birth parents' most private space didn't give much sense of who they'd been as people. A framed photograph of the two of them hung on the wall—the woman dark-haired and eyed like me with an elegant bearing, the man a little lighter in coloring and slightly awkward in his tallness—but everything else was more posh, old-fashioned furniture and antiques.

The room with the crib had been stripped of all but a few well-preserved stuffed animals and basic furniture. I tried to imagine the man and woman from the photograph moving through this space, tending to and playing with a younger version of me. No memories stirred. I couldn't even bring them to life in my mind.

Both places left my skin prickling with discomfort. I picked a guest bedroom somewhat at random and told Eloise, "I think I'll sleep in here. I don't want to disturb my parents' room yet."

She nodded as if she understood. I reached for my purse again, thinking of the chauffeur's comment about other rooms I hadn't yet seen. "I was told there's a storage room in the basement with the things my grandfather wanted to keep particularly secure. Can you show me where that is?"

If I was going to unravel any mysteries within my former home, I might as well get started now.

"Of course," Eloise said. "Right this way."

CHAPTER TWO

Rory

The Bloodstones certainly had a lot of things they wanted to hide away, Deborah remarked from where she was perched on my knee.

I sighed and shoved aside the plastic bin I'd been sorting through. "I'm not sure it's so much hiding as normal security. Even regular Naries don't want people they don't know digging through their financial records."

That was mostly what I'd found in the basement storage room across the last two days—bins and bins of receipts and invoices and statements, most of which didn't look especially significant to me. I'd looked at every bit of paper in those things, though, and there were dozens more boxes in the large room around me. It was brightly lit, at least, with beaming florescent bulbs across the ceiling, but the artificial brightness and the extra layer of chill in the air didn't let me forget I was underground.

Looking at the stacks I still hadn't touched, my heart sank. I forced myself to reach for another box.

This one was on the smaller side, and the contents jostled in a way that didn't sound at all papery when I lifted it. Maybe I'd get a change of pace. I set it on the floor, popped off the lid, and froze.

I'd unearthed a box of baby memorabilia. A tiny gold-cast shoe sat right at the top—the rich people equivalent of bronzing? Underneath it lay lacy dresses that couldn't have fit any child older than an infant, a board book that appeared to have teeth marks around the edge, a plastic bag with a lock of dark brown hair... My hair, obviously.

My chest clenched. My birth parents had kept all this stuff after I'd grown into a toddler. I couldn't have asked for clearer evidence that whatever they'd been like, whatever fearmancer horrors they'd been party to, they'd seen me as more than a necessary heir. They'd loved me.

I didn't know what to do with that knowledge, especially with it staring me in the face so blatantly.

Lorelei? Deborah said tentatively.

Before I could find the wherewithal to answer her, footsteps tapped down the hall outside the storage room. They paused before they reached the doorway, respectful of the private nature of the room. Eloise's voice carried to me.

"Miss Bloodstone, there's someone here to see you. A Lillian Ravenguard from the blacksuits. She says she's hoping the two of you can have a word."

Someone from the blacksuits? My body went rigid. The blacksuits were the fearmancer version of law enforcement. It'd been blacksuits who'd stormed into Mom and Dad's house and killed them in front of me. What did this woman want to talk to me about now?

The obvious answer came to me a second later: Professor Banefield's murder. If they'd even figured out it was a murder and not simply a delusion brought on by a natural illness. I didn't trust these people not to be under the barons' thumbs, but maybe I'd learn something useful from her. I got up, scooping Deborah into my hand.

"Okay, I'll come up," I said. "You can let her in."

"I'll show her to the sitting room."

I think I'd better keep my distance from this guest of yours, my familiar said as Eloise bustled off. *We don't know how finely honed her skills are. I'll find a covert place to watch from.*

"Good thinking," I said. A blacksuit was a lot more likely to ask questions about my familiar than my family's hired staff was.

When I reached the top of the stairs, I set Deborah down so she could scurry to a safe vantage point and headed into the sitting room myself. I still hadn't figured out how it was any different in purpose from the parlor. Eloise escorted my visitor in a moment later.

The woman who strode into the room was tall, broad-shouldered, and well-muscled but with enough poise to give a svelte impression over her toughness. With her short, silver-flecked tawny hair and wide-set eyes, she made me think of a lioness on the prowl. She wasn't wearing the usual black outfit of her job but fitted jeans and a modest silk blouse.

"Persephone," she said in a commanding voice that rolled through the room. "It's so good to finally see you again."

Again? "I, er— I'm actually going by Rory," I said quickly. "It's the name I grew up with. Whenever anyone mentions 'Persephone' I feel like they're talking about someone else."

The woman paused and then nodded, studying me with what felt like professional precision. Then she smiled with more warmth than I'd been prepared for. "I'm sorry. I'm sure this has all been overwhelming for you. I'm hoping I can help make the transition easier. Your mother and I were good friends—I did everything I could to locate you so we could bring you back. If I hadn't been on assignment overseas at the time, I'd have been there to retrieve you."

I restrained a shudder at the memory of my bloody "retrieval." So, this wasn't an official visit after all. I groped for something to say as I sat down on one of the stiff armchairs. Was I supposed to thank her for her contribution to wrenching me from the life I'd loved and the slaughter of my parents?

"Thank you for coming by," I settled on. I could say that without wincing. "Was there anything specific you wanted to talk about, Ms. Ravenguard?"

She made a dismissive wave as she sat across from me. "Please, you can call me Lillian. I just wanted to see how you've been doing. Have you been coping with the changes all right? Is there anything you're still confused about?"

How so many of you can be such total assholes and not even seem to realize it? I thought, and bit my tongue. Not all of the fearmancers were awful all of the time, and so far this one was being kind.

"Not really," I said. "I mean, it's kind of weird… I don't remember any of this." I motioned to the house around me. "I still don't have a very good sense of what my family was like. But I think I'm getting along pretty well with everything at school. That seems to be what's most important right now." *That, and making sure the other royal families don't destroy me.*

Lillian made a humming sound. "Of course. I think I might have…" Her gaze sharpened. "You must still be shaken by what happened with your mentor at the university. I can assure you that the blacksuits are working hard on that case to determine why his illness caused him to take his life in that way—and to ensure any contagion doesn't spread."

I could have told them it wasn't a contagion but a purposeful spell, if I'd trusted any of them enough to relay what Banefield had told me. I didn't trust them, though—not even this woman in front of me. I'd known her for all of five minutes, no matter how much presence she claimed to have had in my family's life before.

"That's good to hear," I said. "It was horrible. He was a good mentor—he helped me a lot in adjusting."

"No matter how long it takes, we always get to the bottom of a situation eventually," Lillian said.

I found that a little hard to believe given the number

of crimes I'd already heard of fearmancers getting away with, but I wasn't going to argue with her.

She switched topics with a smooth grace, mentioning a few shops, restaurants, and other attractions nearby I might want to visit while I was home, and I replied as well as I could. She must have sensed my uncertainty about the whole conversation, because she didn't try to sustain it very long.

"The main reason I stopped by was to let you know you can call on me at any time, anything you need," she said, scooting forward on her chair. She handed me a business card with her name, phone number, and email address in stark print. "If you don't get me, you'll get my assistant, Maggie, who can connect you to me right away if necessary. Don't hesitate to get in touch. I mean it. Your mother was my best friend, and watching over you is the best way I can honor her memory."

The vehemence in her voice sent a pang through me, a longing to be able to believe and trust in someone who'd say that. My fingers closed around the card. "Thank you. It means a lot."

"It's no problem at all. I can already tell you've grown up to be an impressive young woman."

After Eloise had shown Lillian out, I went up to my room to save her number in my phone. It definitely couldn't hurt to have a blacksuit on call just in case, right? Maybe she'd end up being on my side like Professor Banefield had.

I'd just added her into my contacts when the phone

rang in my hand. The number that came up on the screen was Jude Killbrook's.

My pulse hiccupped. For a second, I sat there frozen.

Jude was one of my fellow scions, heir to the Killbrook barony. He'd also been one of my main tormenters when I'd first arrived at the school, but after I'd proven my magical abilities, he'd appeared to have a change of heart. He'd put a hell of a lot of effort into making amends and winning me over, and I had to admit it'd worked… until I'd gotten a chilling reminder of how strategic his kindness could be.

He'd been sweet to me, sure, but at the same time he'd happily been planning pranks to torment the nonmagical —Nary—students the university took in on scholarship. The most recent of those tricks had ended with my dormmate and friend Shelby fracturing her wrist and losing the spot in the music department that had meant everything to her.

Jude hadn't even felt bad about destroying her dream. He'd tried to justify it—he'd expected me to be *impressed* by his stunt.

Remembering the last real conversation we'd had, which had ended with me forcing him out of my car and leaving him on the side of the road, sent a twist of nausea through my gut. That'd been a couple weeks ago though, and I hadn't really talked to him since. I should probably at least find out what he wanted.

I raised the phone to my ear. "Hello?" I said warily.

"Hello, Ice Queen," Jude said in his usual languidly

wry tone. "You're having quite the busy social life at the family home, aren't you?"

"What are you talking about?"

"I was just coming up on the place, and there's someone leaving. Who've you been entertaining already?"

"I don't think that's any of your business," I said automatically, and then the rest of what he'd said caught up. "You were just coming up on *what* place?"

Jude chuckled. "The Bloodstone mansion, Rory. I'm right outside the gate. Will you let me in so we can talk? I promise not to bite unless you ask nicely."

I rolled my eyes, but at the same time I was springing to my feet. I hurried across the hall to one of the rooms with a view of the front yard.

Indeed, a red Mercedes was parked beyond the wrought-iron bars. As I watched, Jude's lanky figure emerged from the driver's side. He shut the door and propped himself against it, looking toward the house, the sunlight gleaming off his dark copper hair. I was standing far enough back that I doubted he could see me, but he must have suspected I'd come take a look, because he aimed a cheeky wave toward the house.

Did he figure if he ignored our argument for long enough, the conflict would disappear?

"What, you just happened to be in the neighborhood?" I said. Was the Killbrook home in Maine too?

He shrugged. "You could say that, only I took about a four-hour detour to get into the neighborhood. It was a very scenic drive. Although the only thing I'm really interested in seeing is you."

He did know how to lay on the charm. And, fuck, he'd driven four hours just to pay me this visit without any idea of how I'd respond?

"You really should have called *before* you headed over."

"Ah, but it's much harder to turn me away when I'm already here, isn't it?" He grinned wide enough that I could see the flash of his teeth. "Come on, Rory. I'm not asking for much. Just to talk for a bit face to face."

"I'm not sure that's a good idea," I said. Especially since his cajoling was already working its way under my skin.

The times I'd spent with Jude before we'd fallen out had been among the few bright spots in my new life. He'd made me laugh. His kiss, his touch, had lit me up from the inside out. He'd expressed such unwavering devotion —and proven it in front of the other students—that I couldn't believe it'd been a sham or that he'd had any part in his father's plans as baron. He'd had way too many chances where he could have hurt me but hadn't.

Maybe now that he'd had some time to think over what I'd said...

"You know I can make it good," he teased, and then his voice turned more serious. "I'm sorry about what happened, all right? I didn't set out to hurt anyone, and if I'd known that Nary was your friend, I'd have been a lot more careful of her—I swear it."

The hope that had been rising inside me snapped away

in an instant. I swallowed thickly. With those few words, he'd put the problem on full display.

"You still don't get it," I said. "That's not the point. It shouldn't matter whether any of them are my friends or not. If I hadn't known who she was, it'd still be a horrible thing to leave her injured and cost her the spot at school over some stupid prank."

"It's not as if I did that on purpose. We can't tiptoe around them all the time."

"There's a big difference between tiptoeing around them and just avoiding pointless pranks that'll totally freak them out," I said before he could keep going. My stomach was full-out churning now. "I don't want to talk about this anymore. We obviously think about it too differently."

"Rory, please…"

I closed my eyes and gathered my resolve. "Look, I'm not furious with you like I was before. I understand that you didn't think you were doing anything wrong. But I can't trust someone who has such a different perspective on… well, everything. When we're back at school, we can be classmates and colleagues, but that's it. That's as far as it can go. All right?"

He was silent for a moment. "You're really not letting me in."

"No. I'm sorry about the drive."

"Well, that was my own damn fault, wasn't it?" He laughed, a little tightly. Then his tone relaxed again. "It's fine. I'll try again another day, another way."

I trusted he meant *that*, regardless of my other doubts. A question tumbled out. "Why does being with me matter so much to you? You know we can never have anything serious."

I was the last living Bloodstone. Any guy I married, on the off-chance I stuck around here long enough for that to happen, would automatically become a Bloodstone too. Jude and I couldn't have a real future together, even if his attitudes had lined up with mine, unless he gave up the barony. I wasn't sure he even could—if there was anyone to inherit it in his place. He didn't have any siblings.

"Don't you worry about that," Jude said without missing a beat. "I will find a way to convince you to give me another chance, I promise you. Just wait and see."

CHAPTER THREE

Declan

Malcolm leaned back in the lounge chair, rotating his beer bottle lazily between his fingers. "You know," he said, "this isn't bad at all."

The July sun beamed over the back deck with just enough heat to be pleasant but not searing, and the breeze rustled through the trees that framed the lawn beyond. It was a perfect summer day, really.

Some of the prominent fearmancers looked a little horrified when they first saw the large modern sunroom and wooden deck Dad had arranged to be built off the back of the old Ashgrave mansion. If I looked at it with an outsider's eye, I could admit the addition did clash with the stone walls and gothic styling of the rest of the place. But it was around back where only family and guests saw it, and I'd take the enjoyment of it over maintaining appearances any day.

I downed a gulp from my beer. "I'm glad you could come over. It seems like a shame to have this spot and no one to hang out with back here."

The deck had gone in last summer, and all four of us scions had gotten together a couple times back then to relax and shoot the breeze. Considering how tense things had become between Malcolm and the other two, I'd figured a group hang-out wasn't the best move right now.

Besides, I'd wanted the chance to talk to each of them one-on-one. There were some subjects sensitive enough that it was hard enough feeling my way to a real answer without an audience.

I'd talked to Connar and Jude earlier this week. It'd been obvious pretty quickly that neither of them had any information about what the barons were up to beyond what I knew. But then, Jude had always seemed antagonistic toward his dad, and Connar avoided talking about his mother as much as possible, so I didn't think much political gossip got passed around in their homes.

Malcolm, on the other hand, had been doing his best to follow his father's footsteps and become part of the most senior baron's plans for as long as I'd known him.

"You're going back for the summer project?" I said, to shoot the breeze a little more before I got to the subject that really mattered to me.

Malcolm snorted, because it *was* a rather stupid question. "We've got a reputation to maintain, don't we? Can't look like we're shirking the chance for extra practice." He cracked his knuckles. "I wonder which of the profs got to pick the assignment this time. Hopefully it'll be better than Sinleigh's lame project last year."

I let that jab slide past me. *I'd* won last year's summer competition, partly because Professor Sinleigh had naturally picked a task that revolved around Insight. Which was also Malcolm's weakest area of magic. Malcolm's comment had been said casually enough, though—only a bit of mild posturing to remind me that he considered himself king of the scions even if I was nearly full baron now. I was used to that.

"I can't compete since I'm an aide now, so you'll have it a little easier," I said, giving him a light kick to the ankle.

He laughed and shook his head, relaxing into his chair. Malcolm held onto his authority rigidly with most fearmancers, but he liked it when the three of us pushed back. He'd never said it in so many words, but I got the impression it made him feel better to think he'd be ruling alongside friends he could also consider equals.

Of course, even scions could push back too much. I didn't even know exactly what line Jude or Connar had crossed, but they'd clearly pissed him off somehow or other. One of the—increasingly many—downsides of the teacher's aide gig was how much less time I'd been able to spend with the other guys at school.

"I suppose there's Rory to contend with this year, though," I added.

Malcolm's shoulders tensed just slightly, but he kept the same nonchalant tone. "I'd imagine five years of practice with three strengths will still beat out three months of practice with four."

It wasn't all about magical power, though. Even when there were scions attending the university like now, the records I'd seen indicated that regular students still won at least half of the time. Any good project included a bunch of plain old strategizing.

"She might have some trouble focusing anyway," I said. "The professor who died—did you know he was her mentor?"

Malcolm's head jerked around at that. He could keep a good poker face, but I didn't think he was a good enough actor to fake that startled response. "Seriously?"

I nodded. "I've been wondering if that fact isn't at least part of the reason he's dead now."

"Everyone's saying he had some awful illness."

"Well, it's not as if magic can't make someone sick. How many illnesses do you know that'd make someone stab himself?"

"So you think… someone might have killed him. Because it'd hurt her. Who—" Malcolm stiffened much more obviously than before, straightening up in his chair. His eyes darkened. "If you're trying to hint that *I* would have resorted to—to murdering a fucking professor just to make a point, then—"

"Hey!" I raised my hands, cutting him off before he could go any further. I couldn't blame Malcolm for getting upset about the possible insinuation, but an angry Malcolm Nightwood was pretty unnerving to be around.

"That's not what I was implying, not at all. I know you're not a psychopath."

His dad I was less sure of. The barons hadn't mentioned Professor Banefield's death at our most recent meeting, but there was plenty they didn't bother to loop me in on. They hadn't made any secret of the fact that they wanted Rory as helpless as they could get her so they could mold her to their whims—for some higher purpose they also hadn't shared with me. A bad sign, since it meant that purpose was probably something I'd disagree with.

Malcolm's shoulders came down, but his expression stayed stormy. "Then you think someone *else* had a big enough beef with Glinda the Good Witch to start offing her support system? It's one thing to duel it out with someone you have an issue with directly. Going around killing random bystanders... that's just wanton brutality. Why the hell would anyone come down on her that hard?"

"I'm not sure," I said carefully. I wasn't supposed to reveal anything that was discussed in the baron meetings with anyone outside that pentacle, and I didn't really *want* to place the burden of all the things I'd learned about the other scions' parents on their shoulders yet. I'd had to grow up way too fast out of necessity. No need to drag them along with me before they were ready. "That's what I'm trying to figure out. You've been pretty... focused on her since she turned up. Have you seen anything odd?"

Malcolm frowned. He appeared to give the question genuine thought. "Nothing anywhere near murderous," he said. "For fuck's sake. Are you *sure* it wasn't some other kind of feud that had nothing to do with her? Who knows what this Banefield guy got up to. Everyone says he cracked up a little after his wife died."

I hadn't heard anyone say that, so I'd be willing to bet "everyone" in this case was Malcolm's parents. Interesting. A broken mage was easier to use than a strong one. But Malcolm wasn't showing any sign of knowing about this specific plan. Time to let it drop.

"I was just speculating," I said with a wave of my hand. "You're right—it could be something totally unrelated. It could even have been a natural illness after all. Still hard for her, though." I paused and couldn't help adding, "Maybe it's not the best time to keep going at her the way you have been, while she's recovering from that? She had to watch him die—I think we could cut her a break."

Malcolm's mouth shifted into a grimace. "She's the one who made the rules here. She's the one who threw our generosity in our faces. I've just been re-establishing the status quo."

"It has been going on for quite a while."

"I *tried* to give her a way out, and she wouldn't take it." He took a swig from his beer and glowered at the trees. "If she wants to survive in this society, she's got to learn that decisions have consequences."

I was pretty sure Rory had already figured that out. It wasn't a lack of learning—it was that she was just as stubborn as Malcolm was and just as dedicated to her own principles.

But after his refusal, a brooding expression came over

the Nightwood scion's face, as if maybe he was thinking through what I'd said in a little more depth after all. I decided to leave it there for now.

Malcolm wasn't any real threat to Rory, not compared to the barons and whoever else they might have roped into their scheming.

We chatted some more and one of the staff brought us lunch out on the deck, and then we whiled away a good part of the afternoon playing a magically-modified version of basketball Malcolm had invented some ten years ago. It wasn't quite the same with just the two of us, but my brother and one of his friends ended up joining in. There was a relief in just goofing around without thinking about all the pressures looming over me.

After Malcolm and my brother's friend left, Noah sat down on the front steps next to me with a satisfied sigh. He'd stopped getting taller a few years ago, topping out at just an inch shorter than me, but every time he came home from the fearmancer college in Paris, he seemed to have aged at least a year. He was only seventeen still, but it was getting harder to see him as a kid.

He still needed his big brother's protection, though. I was the only thing standing between him and our aunt's ambitions for the barony. Get rid of me and then him, and the authority would be all Aunt Ambrosia's.

"That was fun," he said, swiping his sweat-damp hair away from his eyes. "We should do that more often."

"Yeah." Guilt pinched my gut. "I guess I haven't been able to hang out as much as we used to lately, huh?"

He elbowed me teasingly. "I know you've got all your

important baron stuff to take care of. Just don't get too self-important."

I had to laugh. "It's a period of transition," I said. "Things should settle down once I'm finished with school and can focus just on the barony." At least I damn well hoped they would.

"Like I said, it's okay. I'm not some little kid who's going to expect you to drop everything the second I'm back home."

"You're liking the school over there still?" I asked.

"Oh, yeah. It's great. The fearmancers over there seem a little more... relaxed than people here. And I get to be an exotic foreign student." He waggled his eyebrows.

"Be sure to use those powers for good and not evil," I teased.

He gave me a mock salute and then turned his gaze toward the driveway. "I was actually going to ask you... I know the plan was that I'd start attending Blood U once you graduated, but I think I'd like to go all the way through in Paris, if that's okay. I realize I don't know how expensive it is or whatever..."

"Hey, we can afford it. The money's no issue." I studied him with an affectionate twinge. I'd hoped sending him to school overseas would help broaden his horizons even if Dad and I weren't there as much for guidance. It'd worked—and he was hungry for more. "You get your education wherever you're happiest, Noah. That's what matters the most to me."

Maybe there was a bit of envy in that twinge too. I hadn't

let myself stray very far from my territory here out of fear of what moves Aunt Ambrosia or the older barons might make if I were an ocean away for any significant length of time, but I couldn't deny that part of me itched to see more of the world. To experience more of the people and cultures in it, outside this often suffocating cycle of struggles for domination.

That sacrifice was made worth it by the relieved smile Noah shot me. I stayed here and shouldered the responsibilities of our family name so he could have some kind of freedom.

His smile turned a little sly. "So, what's new with the pentacle of barons? Any unexpected new power plays or big events in the works?"

Noah had always been curious about the work of the barony—more than I really preferred. He wouldn't have been half as enthusiastic if he'd had any idea what it really involved or how much danger came with it.

"You know I can't talk about anything that's not already public knowledge," I said.

"Hey, I can keep a secret! I've got to be ready as next in line, right?" He gave me another teasing jab of his elbow with no idea how sharply that remark hit me right through the chest. God forbid it ever came to that.

Before I had to answer, Dad appeared at the door, his brow furrowed.

"Declan," he said. "Someone's called for you on the home line. They wouldn't tell me what it's about."

That was odd. I conducted all my business, both barony- and school-related, through my own phone. I headed in, with a sudden leap of my heart that it might somehow be Rory.

My heart shouldn't be leaping about anything to do with Rory, even if she was the fiercest and yet the most compassionate girl I'd ever met. Even if the one intimate afternoon we'd indulged in had become my favorite memory.

I couldn't be with her without dumping the responsibilities of the barony on Noah's shoulders. If anyone found out she and I had slept together while I was working as an aide and she was a student, my position would come into question regardless. So that moment had to stay just a fond memory, and it was hands and heart off from here on.

Especially because the two of us weren't the only people who remembered what had happened between us.

"Mr. Ashgrave," a voice cooed over the line when I picked up the phone. "It's Stella Evergrist. We met recently at my granddaughter's country home."

Every inch of my body tensed. By the most awful luck, Rory's paternal grandparents had caught us leaving her country property together. They hadn't seen anything *that* incriminating, but I had been holding Rory's hand, and we had come all the way out there just the two of us… It'd been obvious they assumed something more than friendly was going on.

"Yes," I said evenly. "I remember. What can I help you with, Mrs. Evergrist?"

"Oh, mostly I just wondered if Persephone is there.

The two of you did seem quite close, and we haven't heard from her as soon as we were hoping."

It wasn't difficult to figure out why. They'd tried to glom onto Rory from the first second they'd seen her, without any apparent sense of the fact that to her they were strangers— and horribly pushy ones at that. I'd heard the other barons make occasional disparaging remarks about the family that had most recently mingled with the Bloodstones. The Evergrists were known for being grasping and power-hungry with little self-moderation. Not a pleasant combination.

"I'm afraid Rory and I aren't actually in frequent contact," I said. "Our trip to her property was a one-time occasion, something she needed help with out there. I haven't seen her since school let out."

Mrs. Evergrist let out a soft guffaw that told me she hadn't bought into my lie in the slightest. Well, it'd been worth a try. "Now, now," she said. "I understand why you're so cautious. Got yourself set up as a teacher's aide, they tell me. Can't have it getting out if you've taken a student too far under your wing, hmmm?"

I kept my voice as emotionless as possible. "I can't say I know what you're talking about, Mrs. Evergrist."

"No, of course not. Well, when you do talk to Rory again, remind her that we're dearly looking forward to reconnecting. Oh, and there was one other thing."

I braced myself. "Yes?"

The wheedling note came back into her voice. "My husband and I have an interest in a business venture that's been put before the pentacle. It should come up for consideration soon… I hope, in recognition for our discretion, you'll help nudge it along?"

Shit. There it was. I lowered my head, my jaw clenching at the blatant blackmail.

I couldn't completely shut her down. If I could keep her thinking I was playing along until I finished the aide gig—it'd just be a few more months—the situation would be much less precarious. The consequences wouldn't be as harsh if they made a claim after I no longer had authority over any students anyway.

"I'll see what I can do," I said.

As she babbled on about the details of the venture, Dad and Noah meandered down the hall past the sitting room where I was taking the call. Noah was gesturing wildly with the story he was telling, and Dad was chuckling, glowing with fatherly joy. My stomach knotted.

If I was under threat, then they were too, just as much. I *had* to play this right, or I could be screwing over my entire family.

CHAPTER FOUR

Rory

"The bitch of Bloodstone returns," Victory Blighthaven said in an undertone the moment I walked into the dorm. She was standing by the dining table with her besties, Cressida and Sinclair. The queen bee of Villain Academy looked as pretty and polished as ever, her auburn hair falling in sculpted waves and her silk summer dress perfectly tailored to her hourglass figure, but her personality clearly hadn't gotten any less ugly.

I'd spent most of the last few months ignoring Victory's jabs. Her dislike seemed incredibly petty, based mainly on the fact that the administration had given me the corner bedroom with a view that she'd once claimed—and that she adored Malcolm Nightwood and I very openly did not. I'd had bigger things to worry about, like mages who'd outright kill to screw with me. But as I tugged the strap of my purse higher on my shoulder, I found I'd completely run out of fucks when it came to keeping the peace.

The rulers of the fearmancer world were out to destroy me. If Victory thought I was going to be scared of *her*, she could forget it.

"Takes one to know one," I said breezily, and headed across the room without waiting for her reaction. From the corner of my eye, I saw her expression darken.

"You know," she said with forced sweetness, "it's just you, the three of us, and your good friend Imogen here for the summer. Keep that in mind before you start picking fights."

Sinclair, who'd been especially pissed off at me ever since Jude had declared his affection for me, let out a sharp snicker. Cressida tossed the tail of her ever-present French braid over her shoulder.

Oh, wonderful. Imogen and I *had* been becoming good friends until Victory had manipulated her into betraying me. Since then, I'd held her at a wary distance. None of the other girls in our dorm had ever stood up for me against Victory and her crew, but they'd at least been a small moderating influence. I had to assume there were things Victory wouldn't have openly said or done in front of them. Now I didn't even have that buffer.

"Thanks for the heads up," I said. As I reached my bedroom, my gaze slid down the line of doors to the one that had been Shelby's. A lump of guilt rose in my throat.

She might have been the dorm's one Nary student, but Shelby had been the only person at Blood U I could still call a real friend, even if I hadn't been able to talk to her about the magical side of my existence. The Naries were brought into the university so the mage students got practice at being careful with their magical practice in regular society—and to give them easy targets for stirring up fear. But Shelby had loved it here despite the bullying she'd faced. She'd keep going to classes even when she was falling over with a fever. The opportunities she'd get with her musical career after finishing the program mattered that much to her.

And with one stupid trick, Jude had stolen the future she'd dreamed of away from her. If I hadn't been distracted by Malcolm's harassment, maybe I could have helped her, stopped her injury from happening...

So many things to look forward to being back on campus. I restrained a grimace and went into my room, shutting the door firmly behind me. Who knew how many new dangers might be lurking around me this term?

Deborah crept out from where she'd been hiding beneath my hair at the back of my neck. I let her run down my arm to hop onto the bedspread. *So lovely to be back*, she said in a tone dry as dust.

"No kidding," I murmured.

Nothing in my room appeared to have changed during the last two weeks. The cleaning staff must have come through, their efforts leaving a faint lemony scent in the air. Between the double bed, the wardrobe, and the desk and chair set by the window, the space was pretty full. Beyond the window stretched the north end of campus, across the green and the wilder fields to the glinting water of the lake.

I tugged the window open to let in the warm breeze and sat on the edge of the bed. Deborah set her front paws on my leg.

What's the plan now?

"I have to find out what this summer project is about and work around that," I said. "There's an assembly in about half an hour that's supposed to explain it. Then I've got to figure out some way to uncover what Professor Banefield wanted to tell me."

You be careful, Lorelei. I don't trust a single person in this place. They've shown just how vicious they're willing to be. I'll keep watch around your dorm as well as I can—and you let me know if there are any other ways I can help.

"Thank you." I stroked a finger over her fur.

I didn't feel entirely safe even in my bedroom, knowing Victory and company were hanging around on the other side of the door. I flopped down on the bed to relax for a few minutes, but then restlessness had me back on my feet. A little meander around outside would give me some idea who'd come back for the summer session, anyway.

I cast my protective wards before I even opened the door, not wanting to give Victory any chance to observe my strategies. Magic tickled up from behind my collarbone, gathered there from my walk through the forest after the chauffeur had dropped me off in town and from the few students I'd encountered on my way to the dorm building who gave off jolts of fear just at the sight of the newest scion. I still didn't exactly *like* the idea that my mere presence could inspire terror, but it did come in handy for building up my power.

Victory's trio kept murmuring and giggling amongst themselves when I came out. They weren't quite finished with me, though. I caught the extra shine on the floor ahead of me a split-second before my shoe came down on the conjured slickness. I stiffened my leg just in time that I only wobbled a little. Without a backward glance, I dodged the rest of the spot meant to toss me on my ass and strode out.

Nice try, sorry to disappoint.

The area of trimmed grass between the university's three main buildings—Killbrook Hall, which held the junior residences and the staff quarters; Ashgrave Hall, home to the senior dorms and the library; and Nightwood Tower, with all the classrooms—was definitely emptier than usual. Normally during class hours, there might have been dozens of students and teachers ambling across it and more in view farther afield.

But the junior fearmancers didn't take part in the summer session at all, and I'd heard only about half of the seniors attended. A handful were already setting off toward the Stormhurst Building closer to the lake, where the assembly was being held, and a few small clusters stood around the fringes of the green catching up after their time away. I didn't see anyone I knew all that well. No one I could be sure wasn't a threat, but no one who definitely *was* either.

Too bad it couldn't have stayed that way. I was just

starting toward the Stormhurst Building at a leisurely pace when an all-too-familiar voice rang out.

"Couldn't wait to leap back into the fray, huh, Glinda?"

Malcolm Nightwood had just come around Killbrook Hall, his posture confident, his tone cocky. As often before, I was struck by the unfairness that a guy who could be such an asshole was so stunning to look at. His golden-brown hair with its hint of curl framed his face perfectly, his features such a perfect mix of sly and sweet that I'd thought of him as a divine devil when I'd first seen him.

The conversations around the green quieted at his arrival. The scions ruled this school, and Malcolm had set himself up as king of the scions.

I tensed as he approached, focusing twice as much magic on my mental shields. Malcolm's primary strength was Persuasion, and he'd gotten a lot of mileage out of inflicting that talent on me. I'd been getting better at shutting him out of my head, though.

How complicit in the barons' plans was he? It'd seemed like he and his dad were pretty tight.

"I was under the impression participating in the summer project was a matter of honor," I said with forced calm.

"Not much honor in it if you've got no hope of winning," Malcolm replied.

"I wouldn't count me out yet. I led my league to a win, didn't I?"

He made a scoffing sound, but it *had* been my approach that had allowed the Insight league to come out on top in last term's competition. Each student joined a league when they discovered or decided on their main area of magic, and the professors assigned credit throughout each full term based on spells cast in that area. The league with the most credit at the end of the term got to have the other three leagues cook and serve them an epic feast. Insight, not being a particularly flashy sort of magic, rarely won.

"You won't have a whole team behind you this time," Malcolm said. The remark didn't sound as threatening as I'd have expected the heir of Nightwood to make it. He was studying me, but his attention felt less aggressive than I was used to from him, as if he was evaluating me in a broader way rather than simply as a target.

Of course, I didn't want this guy evaluating me in any way at all. Any weaknesses he thought he'd spotted, it was fearmancer nature to exploit—and Malcolm seemed to enjoy exploiting weaknesses as often as he could. He'd messed with me way too many times and in too many horrible ways in the past for me to patiently wait around to find out what he was up to now.

"I'll remind you of that when you're eating my dust," I shot back. "For now, how about you make things easier for yourself and just fuck off."

I spun on my heel, hearing his sharp intake of breath behind me, half hoping that might be the end of it for now but knowing it probably wouldn't be. A second later, he spat out one of his casting words.

Advanced mages made up strings of syllables or contradictory phrases to direct their spells so that their target and anyone observing wouldn't be able to anticipate the effect. I knew exactly what Malcolm had tried to throw at me in an instant, though. He'd hurled a general insight spell at me like a spear aimed straight at my mental shields.

I hadn't been prepared for him to try insight. The wall around my mind could fend off a fair bit of magic in general, but I'd been focusing on the idea of preventing persuasive castings. The sharp edge of Malcolm's spell split a small crack in the barrier that made me wince. I murmured under my breath to tighten the layer of protection against that kind of intrusion.

Which was exactly what the Nightwood scion must have wanted. The second I'd shifted my focus, he threw out another comment, this one with the eerie lilt of magical compulsion.

"*Stop walking.*"

The persuasion spell pierced through my momentarily scattered defenses like a needle, finding the tiniest gap to stab into my brain. My feet jarred to a halt under me. Shit.

I heaved power into my shields. He'd only told me to stop. I wasn't letting him get in another command.

"Nice try," I said. "That's as much as you're going to get. And you know what, I bet I can make it to the Stormhurst Building without doing any walking at all."

Malcolm let out a quiet growl. "Lift," I murmured to my feet, and with a jerk I propelled myself an inch off the ground. "Float."

It took enough energy that sweat started to trickle

down my back, but I drifted slowly along the path the way I'd meant to go.

"*Come back here,*" Malcolm ordered, but the persuasion spell bounced off my defenses this time. His feet thumped against the path as he strode after me. He tossed out another nonsensical casting word—and an invisible wall slammed my shoulder, spinning me around. We were switching to Physicality now, were we?

I glared at him as I caught my balance and opened my mouth to shatter the force that had hit me—and a brawny figure hurtled into my field of view, straight toward Malcolm.

"Leave her *alone,*" Connar Stormhurst barked, and shoved the guy he'd once called his best friend so hard Malcolm stumbled right off the path.

Malcolm whipped around. "What the fuck are you doing?" he snapped, staring at the Stormhurst scion. His face had flushed to an angry red hue.

I was staring at Connar too. The most physically intimidating of the scions had also proven to be the kindest for a little while. Connar and I had ended up bonding—in, er, ways both emotional and physical— during secret talks in his favorite clifftop spot away from the rest of campus. But he'd proven where his real loyalties lay by tearing me down on Malcolm's behalf not long after.

He'd said something to me about making up for it the last time I'd seen him, the night of the League feast. I'd been shell-shocked from Professor Banefield's murder, so my memory of that moment was blurry. I hadn't really considered whether or how he'd follow through on that promise.

Apparently he'd meant it—even more than I'd have imagined. He stepped between Malcolm and me, glowering at his friend, his entire muscular frame tensed. I'd seen him come at people who threatened the other scions before, but I'd never seen him turn physical aggression on anyone within the pentacle.

Neither had anyone else, from the expressions our spectators around the green were sporting. I had a feeling every mage on campus would hear about this confrontation by the end of the day.

"You've been waging this war long enough," Connar said to Malcolm. "It's time for it to stop. And since you didn't listen to me when I told you that, I'll just have to *make* you stop."

The spell that had pushed me around had faded. As I let my feet touch the ground, I realized the effect of Malcolm's persuasive spell had wisped away too. He might have been able to jab it through my shields, but not very deeply. I shifted my feet, and they moved just fine.

"I'm okay," I said cautiously. "I just want to get to the assembly."

Connar eased over to stand beside me. Malcolm stepped back onto the path, rage and betrayal etched all over his face. "I've been there for you through *everything*," he started.

"Right," Connar said before he could go on. "Because that's what we're supposed to do—look out for the other scions. Not tear them down. The pentacle shouldn't be divided, and it's not Rory who's dividing us. It's *you*."

He turned to me. "Let's go."

I nodded, a little stunned, and we turned our backs on Malcolm, who for once in his life was completely speechless. But as I set off for the Stormhurst Building, I couldn't help wondering if what Connar had just done had ended the war—or pushed it to an entirely new level.

CHAPTER FIVE

Rory

My altercation with Malcolm had sapped away most of the time before the assembly. Now that there was no spectacle to watch, a whole bunch of students were making their way to the Stormhurst Building. Connar walked steadily beside me, his jaw still tight, the muscles in his arms flexed.

I had no idea what to say to him. The history between us had gotten so messy.

"Thank you." That seemed like a reasonable place to start. But I also had to add, "You didn't have to jump in. I can handle Malcolm."

"I know," Connar said in his low voice, which was no longer taut with anger. "But I meant what I said. This feud has gone on too long, and I know you never wanted a war in the first place. Malcolm's just..." He sighed. "Maybe if enough of us put our foot down, it'll snap him out of the mindset he's gotten into."

He paused and ducked his head. "I'm sorry. I should have spoken up to him sooner—I obviously never should have lashed out at you the way I did. All I can say is… he has been there for me in an awful lot of ways for an awfully long time, and I'd gotten into the habit of trusting his judgment over my own. I didn't want to be the kind of guy who'd betray his best friend. I don't think I *am*, though. He needs to hear this. He needs to know it's gotten to be too much."

The pain in his expression made my chest ache in spite of everything. "Well, I'm still not happy about how horrible you were to me, and I wish you'd had this change of heart sooner, but… I am glad that you're seeing things that way now."

"I'm sure it'll take time for you to trust me again," he said. "I don't want to be pushy. You should just know that I'm on your side, officially." He glanced around at our fellow students, many of whom were continuing to shoot curious glances our way. "And very publicly, apparently. If you ever do feel you can turn to me and need to, I'll be there."

"Okay," I said, with a little relief that he wasn't pressing me to sort out my feelings or grant full forgiveness right this second. "I'll keep that in mind. And, just so you know, I really did mean that 'Thank you.' I get that it must be hard to stand up to him after being friends that long."

Imogen waved to me as I came into the gym where the assembly was being held, and as I headed over, Connar drifted away. He was keeping his word about giving me space, at least.

The forty or so students already in the space were buzzing with anticipatory chatter. I spotted Declan standing with several of the professors and a few other teacher's aides by the small platform that'd been set up, but he wasn't looking my way. I swallowed hard.

Things had gotten messy between him and me too, and that was mostly my fault. The trip to my family's country property near here should have been just a brief interlude away from the pressures of the school and everything else he was dealing with. A thank you for everything he'd been doing to protect me from larger forces that wanted to manipulate me behind the scenes—and, as it'd turned out, a chance to act on the attraction we'd held in check up until then.

And now that moment of indulgence could screw up everything he'd worked for. He'd helped me so much, but he had to keep his distance from here on. *I* had to make sure I didn't show our relationship had become anything beyond student and aide. I owed him that much.

"Do you have any idea what the project is going to be?" I asked Imogen as I came up beside her.

She shook her head, one of her usual silver clips flashing in her blond hair—a sparrow today. "No idea. They never let anything slip until the official announcement. Oh, there's Ms. Grimsworth. She'll deliver the news."

She rocked on her feet in anticipation. A few last students trickled in after the headmistress's entrance, a familiar head of floppy copper hair among them. I tensed at the sight of Jude, wondering if he was planning on making good on his promise to find some way to win me over before the assembly started, but before he'd looked my way, Ms. Grimsworth had gone up to the podium and picked up the microphone.

"Hello to our senior students who are participating in this year's summer project," she said in her cool voice. She looked prim as ever in her navy dress suit with her graying hair pulled into its tight coil at the back of her head. Her beady eyes skimmed over the crowd in the gym. "I know you're all eager to get started, so I won't keep you waiting. This year's project was proposed by Professor Crowford, although I expect it will involve many talents other than Persuasion."

The Persuasion professor tipped his head to her where he was standing by the edge of the platform with the other teachers. I thought the black streaks in his silver hair had gotten thinner since the last time I'd seen him.

Ms. Grimsworth leaned over the podium. "We'll have fifteen Nary students on campus for the summer session. Each of you will be assigned one as your target. You must come up with a specific outcome you wish to achieve with that student—an action you'd like to see them take, a habit formed—the larger and harder the impact earning you a higher score, naturally. Over the course of the next six weeks, you'll attempt to sway your target along your chosen course."

What? A wave of cold horror swept through me. It was bad enough that the administration brought in the nonmagical students to be used in more subtle ways without them knowing, but to instruct us to actively set out to alter their lives in some major way...

The headmistress wasn't even finished. "As you can probably determine, there are many more of you than there are Nary students. Your target will have three or perhaps even four other mages also trying to influence their behavior. If your opponents are careful, you won't even know who you're competing against. So you will not only need to affect your target if you wish to win, but offset the effects of other magic as well."

I glanced at Imogen, but she appeared to be taking this assignment in stride. Of course, she'd always been a little hesitant about including Shelby in any friendly activities. To her—to everyone in the room other than me, by the looks of things—there was nothing odd about this proposal at all.

"Throughout all this, you must remember the policies of Bloodstone University," Ms. Grimsworth added. "If you are careless enough that your target or any other Nary realizes that you're working a supernatural influence on them, you'll be immediately disqualified. Slow and steady will win the day here. Now come up and receive your assigned student."

She read out our names one by one, in alphabetical order by last name. That meant I was the third student called. Professor Crowford had stepped up in front of the podium to distribute the envelopes. He gave me a small smile as he handed mine to me. "I hope to see great things from you during your first summer project, Miss Bloodstone."

Apparently the disgust twisting my stomach wasn't printed all over my face. I slipped away to the wall and opened my envelope.

"My" Nary was a senior student in the architecture program, which I hadn't even known was one of the scholarship offerings. Benjamin Alvarez, twenty years old, with a shock of black hair and an intent expression in the photograph that came with the brief information sheet, which also told me he was staying in dorm A4. The second paper held his class schedule for the summer. The other blanks in my knowledge about him, I guessed I was supposed to fill in myself.

I scanned the gym as others went up to grab their envelopes. At least two other students had also been assigned Benjamin. What were they going to try to change about him?

What was *I* going to do to him?

The queasiness in my belly expanded. Would it be enough just to set out to stop him from being affected by any other magic? I should be able to manage that if I worked hard enough.

That wouldn't help the fourteen other Naries my fellow fearmancers would be bending to their will, though.

The last of the envelopes must have been handed out. Ms. Grimsworth started talking again.

"The Nary students will be arriving tomorrow. By the end of that day, you must turn in a paper with your mission statement, which I will hold onto. This allows us to confirm that whatever effects you achieve line up with your goals. And of course, there's the matter of the prize. As usual, the winner can request any object in their possession to be enchanted to the purpose of their choice by the professor of their choice. You could have one of these experts' skills at your disposal. Let's see who's up to the challenge. May the best mage win!"

It took a moment after I knocked on Ms. Grimsworth's office door before the headmistress answered. She peered at me, her expression puzzled before she schooled it to be impassive. I guessed she hadn't expected anyone to come calling quite this soon after the assembly. I'd let my feelings stew for about twenty minutes and then been unable to do anything other than march over here.

"Miss Bloodstone," she said. "Come in. Is there something I can help you with?"

I eased inside and waited until she'd shut the door. Nothing was burning on the shelves that lined her office walls, but a powdery whiff of incense smoke lingered in the air. I shifted on my feet on the thick rug.

"I hope so," I said. "I—I wanted to raise an objection to the focus of the summer project."

The headmistress's eyebrows jumped up. "And what objection is that?"

I clasped my hands together in front of me to stop them from fidgeting. "The Nary students come here without realizing anyone might be using magic on them. I already have a problem with the pranks and so on that get played on them during the rest of the school year. But this is encouraging us to yank them around and change them to our whims... It just isn't *right*."

"Mages have always needed to manipulate the nonmagical population in order to maneuver around them."

"But this isn't for survival," I protested. "This is going out of our way to treat them like puppets. Isn't that the opposite of learning how to live productively alongside them?"

Ms. Grimsworth's mouth had tightened. "I believe this assignment will actually stretch all of our students' abilities in that area—to help you learn the limits of how far you can extend your magic without tipping off the Naries to a supernatural presence."

"But—"

"Miss Bloodstone," she said firmly. "The project has already been decided. The professors take turns choosing on the content, and Professor Crowford's submission meets our guidelines. I don't expect the Nary students will come to any major harm. If they do, then please make that known to me. In the meantime, you may approach the project however you'd like, but the project itself stands."

She wasn't budging. I wasn't sure how much hope I'd really had that she would, but my spirits deflated anyway.

"Is that all?" she asked.

I couldn't think of any argument that would overcome her last statement. "Yes. But I might be back."

Did the corner of her mouth twitch upward just for a second? I might have imagined that. "And if you do, I'll be happy to hear your further concerns." She paused. "Have you been well during your break? I understand it may have taken some time to recover from recent... events."

From watching my former mentor stab himself to death in front of me? Yeah, that had been an event all right. I suppressed a cringe.

"I'm still upset about what happened, obviously," I said. "But I don't think it'll get in the way of my work here. I suppose... Professor Viceport is still my mentor now?"

I'd have rejoiced if the headmistress had corrected me. Viceport, whose specialty was Physicality, held some kind of a grudge against me that I hadn't figured out, other than she seemed to dislike the fact that I was a Bloodstone at all.

But Ms. Grimsworth was nodding. "You'll continue to meet with her once a week to discuss any concerns. We'll be distributing the new schedules later today. Classes continue during the summer in a modified form to directly tackle aspects of your project."

Wonderful. I managed not to groan and made my escape.

In the hall, I tipped my head back against the wall and closed my eyes to gather myself. Okay, so it didn't appear I could get this project cancelled. I'd just have to think until I came up with a strategy I could live with.

And if it was a strategy that would win me that prize, even better. There were a heck of a lot of uses I could think of for an object enchanted by one of the experts on staff—many of which could end up making the difference between whether I survived my time here or not.

CHAPTER SIX

Jude

My Nary target was a slip of a girl who wandered around campus in frilly dresses with hair that looked as if it hadn't been brushed since she got up. According to my project package, she was sixteen, but she didn't look much older than twelve. She basically embodied the word "feeb."

I couldn't say I felt any burning desire to make her acquaintance, but a certain amount of pity stirred as I watched her meander toward Killbrook Hall. It wasn't hard to imagine why Rory had been peeved about this assignment.

From the glimpse I'd caught of her face as Ms. Grimsworth had announced it, maybe "infuriated" was a more accurate word. It was a good thing I didn't really give a shit about winning this competition, because I sure as hell couldn't put in a solid effort without making the Bloodstone scion even more pissed off with me.

So I'd throw this game. No big deal. I cared a lot more about getting back into Rory's good graces than pleasing the professors. She was probably already coming up with some scheme to turn this project around. I'd give her a little longer for her initial fury to cool off, and then I'd come around offering my assistance, and we'd see if that didn't gain me some ground.

Just as the feeb disappeared into the hall bearing my family's name, Connar came ambling out. At the sight of my fellow scion, a prickle ran down my back. I had a few things to say to him right now.

I caught up with him halfway across the green and fell into step beside him, our footsteps rapping against the ground together, my slim shadow looking rather feeble itself next to his bulky one in the warm mid-morning sunlight.

"Mr. Stormhurst," I said with forced brightness. "I hear you've set yourself up as our Bloodstone scion's white knight."

Connar's expression twitched, but he had to have realized that a display that public would get talked about. He drew his chin up, his mouth firming. "She doesn't need a 'knight,' but it was about time someone stood up for the pentacle."

I guffawed. "Oh, this is all about scion solidarity, is it? And not at all because you'll champion your way into her bed?"

I hadn't really been sure whether attraction factored into Connar's motives, but the faint flush that crept up his neck gave me all the confirmation I needed. The guy could be a blockhead, but he had *eyes*. Rory was gorgeous no matter how you felt about her attitude, although personally it was her spirit I liked best. Even if her stubbornness was making achieving my aims difficult at the moment.

"That's not the point," Connar said. "She might not want anything like that after the way I treated her. And if she does, then it won't be any of your business, will it?"

"I just thought you might have forgotten that you can't offer her much of anything. Seeing as you're the only remaining Stormhurst heir, thanks to various violent takeovers."

That might have been a lower blow than was absolutely necessary. Some of that violence had come from the guy beside me. Connar's stance tensed, and his voice came out just barely above a growl. "That isn't how I wanted things to be. And *you* are in pretty much the same position, but that didn't stop you from chasing after her last term, did it? You weren't what she wanted, though, it seems like. Whatever she does now, it's up to her, not either of us."

"Of course," I said, letting my tone lighten again. I didn't really want Connar pissed off at me too. He was not a guy whose bad side you wanted to get on—and it actually did take quite a bit for him to hold a grudge, to be fair. He just needed to realize he couldn't expect to slide right into Rory's heart easy as pie. "But I intend to make her choice very easy. So don't get your hopes up."

I veered off as he reached Nightwood Tower, where he must have had class. I wasn't due anywhere until the afternoon, so I meandered vaguely in the direction of the lake, turning over possible grand gestures in my mind.

Driving all the way over to pay her a visit hadn't swayed her. Well, it might have if I hadn't somehow said the absolute wrong thing all over again. Just showing up on her doorstep now and saying I wanted to help might not cut it.

I could do better than that anyway. Scheming was my forte. How could we best turn this project on its head with maximum enjoyment along the way? If I came to her with a plan already worked out, or even in motion…

My mind was spinning through the possibilities so intently I almost ignored the jangle of my ringtone. It cut through my concentration, though—and there was a *tiny* chance it could be Rory, taking me up on my promise to win her over of her own accord. I fished the phone out of my pocket and grimaced when I saw it was my home line.

"Hi, Mom," I said when I picked up, because my father never called me. He barely spoke to me when I was in the same room as him, let alone a whole state away.

"Darling," my mother said, in a simpering tone that set my nerves on edge in an instant. It was the voice she used on my father when she had to give him news she expected him to react badly to—her walking-on-eggshells voice, I'd always thought of it as. She generally hadn't felt the need to use it on me. "How are you doing?"

"About the same as before I left home two days ago," I said breezily, staying wary underneath. "We got our summer project. Lots of work ahead. The usual crowd came for the session. Not much else to report."

"Well, at least there hasn't been any trouble." She let out a twitter of a laugh, which also sounded nervous. What the fuck was going on? Had Dad made a big to-do about something to do with me, and she was looking for me to smooth things over with him, as if it were my fault?

"Did you expect there to be trouble?" I asked. "What are you calling about, Mom?"

"Oh, I just—I would have told you while you were here, but there's so much uncertainty, especially at my age —I didn't want to bring it up until we were sure everything was progressing as it should, and now you might not be home for over a month..."

All her rambling was only making my skin tighten more. "*What* are you going to tell me?" I said. "You don't have to explain all that other stuff." *Just spit it out.* Before I broke the phone with how hard I was gripping it.

She sucked in a breath and gave another twittering laugh. "I'm sure this will be a surprise—it was to us—but we are so happy. You're going to have a little sister."

I stopped dead in my tracks where I'd still been moseying along the path, my heart plummeting to my stomach. One sharp word slipped out before I could control my reaction. "*What?*"

"I'm three months along now. We just got the results from genetics testing to make sure she's healthy —and the report gave us the gender too. Isn't it wonderful? Not that you weren't enough, of course, never think that, but we always did hope for two, and for it to happen after all this time..." Her laugh sounded genuinely joyful now. "Honestly I've had trouble believing it."

The strength in my legs wavered. I'd have leaned against something if I hadn't been in the middle of a damned field. Instead I let myself lower to the grass a few feet from the path. My heart still seemed to be pummeling my stomach with its thudding beat. The world around me had numbed.

"I guess Dad must be happy too," I managed to say. There was no way I could ask the question I really wanted to—but I already knew the answer to that, didn't I? I'd heard the way he talked about me. This pregnancy wouldn't have happened unless it was the way he'd have wanted. The way he'd wanted all along.

Fuck, fuck, fuck. I was screwed. Completely and utterly screwed, so much more than even before.

But Mom had no idea I knew about any of that. She babbled on about her due date in the new year and possible names and, like a knife to my chest, how thrilled Dad was, yes, completely.

As her voice washed over me, I thought back to the last two weeks at home. Dad had been his usual standoffish self... but I *had* thought once or twice that he'd seemed more affectionate toward her than he usually was, hadn't I? And maybe her spirits had been slightly more buoyant. The first signs had been there. I just never would have put the pieces together like this. She'd turned forty-five this year.

But it happened, especially when you had fearmancer

doctors using magic to help things along. After all this fucking time…

I registered that she'd paused, presumably waiting for me to say something a little more meaningful than, "Huh," or "Great." I fumbled for my words. Generally I was rather good with them. At this particular moment, they careened around my head in total chaos.

If I gave away what I knew, I'd be in even deeper shit than I already was. I had to react like she'd expect me to.

"I'm so happy for you," I said, injecting as much warmth into my voice as I could summon. "And I'm looking forward to meeting her."

After I hung up, my hand dropped to my lap. I couldn't find the wherewithal to even return my phone to my pocket. I could barely focus on the scenery ahead of me as anything more than a greenish blur.

Six months. I'd thought I'd have years, maybe even decades, but now it was six months until my life completely imploded.

CHAPTER SEVEN

Rory

Benjamin Alvarez and his friends had obviously gotten wise during their years at Blood U. The four architecture students who were studying here over the summer had come onto the field behind Ashgrave Hall to work on sketches, and they positioned themselves back-to-back in a rough circle. As far as I could tell, it made conversation awkward, but it also meant no harassing fearmancer could sneak up on them.

Which meant that spying on them was a little tricky as well. I'd spotted them when I'd come out of the kennel farther up the field, after paying Malcolm's familiar a little visit. The Nightwood scion might have warned me off from Shadow, but the eager lift of the wolf's head when it'd heard my voice had been enough confirmation that in its opinion, I was perfectly welcome.

When I'd seen Benjamin with the others, I'd wandered

into the forest that bordered the campus grounds and picked my way along through the cool shadows until I was as close as I could get while staying concealed. I'd still had to brainstorm my way into working out a sound amplifying spell so I could hear what the Naries were saying. It was halfway through the afternoon, and I still wasn't sure what I was submitting as my project goal. Maybe my subject would give me some inspiration.

So far they hadn't talked very much, just brief comments of encouragement when one or another had shown off a sketch. Watching them, my fingers itched to create something myself. Back home, I'd sketched and then transformed those images into little sculptures all the time. Now, with magic, I could do way more way faster. I just hadn't had much time or energy to exercise my artistic side.

One of the two girls had brought a plastic grocery bag out with her. She'd been eating an apple when I'd first spotted them. Then she'd gnawed through a granola bar. Now she'd moved on to mini powdered donuts that required her to regularly wipe her fingers on the grass before she started drawing again.

As she started on her third of those, the other girl glanced over at her with a frown. "Are you okay?" she said, her voice turned tinny by my spell as it traveled to my ears. "We just had lunch a couple hours ago. Are you that hungry still?"

The girl's hand paused halfway to her mouth, and her cheeks reddened. "I know. I just—my stomach keeps feeling empty. I should probably stop now." She gulped down the rest of the donut and nudged the bag farther away.

My gut twisted. She didn't look like someone who regularly overate—she was pretty slim, really. And her friend obviously wasn't used to her snacking that much. I lifted my gaze to scan the area around the field.

My eyes caught on a figure propped against the side of Ashgrave Hall, mostly hidden in the building's shade. I couldn't recognize the guy at that distance—he wasn't anyone I knew well—but I could tell from his slick clothes that he was almost certainly a fearmancer, not another Nary. And I'd be willing to wager half the Bloodstone properties that he'd already picked his goal for his summer project target. He was trying to make her stuff herself... so she'd get fat? *That* was his big plan?

The girl was glancing at the grocery bag again, hunger pangs apparently still bothering her. I set my jaw and murmured a warding spell that I directed her way. It would cut off any magic flowing toward her, at least for now.

After a moment, the tension in her face relaxed. She went back to her sketching, no more longing looks at her snack stash.

I got a little relief from seeing that, if not much satisfaction. I'd protected her for now, but I couldn't follow every Nary on campus around, warding them constantly as my magic faded. It wasn't all that easy to cast a long-term spell on a living being to begin with.

Benjamin held up his latest sketch of a sweeping modern structure, and an idea tickled up from the back of my head. I couldn't make all of campus safe for the Naries, and none of it was really safe for them right now. Their dorms were shared with several fearmancers, and they had no magic to lock their bedroom doors.

What if they had a space here that was just for them, like we mages had the warded areas the Naries weren't allowed to know even existed? A building they could retreat to if the other students' aggression got to be too much. One spot would be much easier to ward. And I'd be playing to the strengths of my "target."

The inspiration came with an exhilarated rush. I watched the group for a few minutes longer as more and more pieces clicked into place in my mind, and then I hustled across the field, giving them a wide berth, so I could get writing.

When I came into my dorm room, Victory and Sinclair were lounging on one of the couches. Imogen was just clearing her dishes from the table after a late lunch. My nemesis ignored me, but Imogen caught my eye as I crossed the room and pulled a quick grimace that served as a warning.

The girls had been up to something. I braced myself as I opened my bedroom door.

For the first few seconds, I just blinked, my mind taking a moment to process the scene in front of me. They'd… turned all of my furniture upside down. The desk wouldn't have been that hard, but the bed tipped at an angle from its thick wooden headboard, the wardrobe with its knobby feet sticking up by the ceiling—that would have taken some effort. And I didn't want to think about the mess my clothes would be in when I managed to right it.

It'd have taken even more effort to break through the protections I'd cast on my door. I'd put a lot of energy into them... but Victory was one of the top students here at Villain Academy, and she'd had at least one helper. How long had they spent on this prank?

I didn't have time to worry about that. I closed the door without giving the girls the enjoyment of seeing my reaction and heaved the desk and chair over with just a quick punch of magic for help. I'd fix the rest later. Right now I needed to get this project statement written.

But as I sat at the desk with my back to my upside-down bed, the uncomfortable sense crept over me that even *I*, scion and nearly baron, didn't have any place on campus I could really call safe. I didn't even know who I could count on and who I needed to protect myself from.

Well, that wasn't entirely true. There was one person I was sure of. I'd just have to draw on some of that creativity of mine if I wanted to talk to him again.

By daylight, this plan had seemed pretty solid—and a little amusing too. Now, as I peered out my bedroom window toward the one below through the darkness just before midnight, I was starting to feel it might be full-out ridiculous.

It'd been the best option I could come up with, though. I'd be leaving no evidence like a text or a phone call would. There should be no chance of being interrupted in that one private space. I knew I could cast an illusion strong enough to hide a person.

Just go for it, I told myself as the cooling night air washed over me. I had to do something. If there was anything I was becoming convinced of by my time here at Blood U, it was that I wasn't likely to survive fearmancer society very long if I tried to go it alone.

I tested the length of hunting rope I'd been able to buy at a store in town. It held firm where I'd tied a knot to the leg of my now right-side-up bed, doubly secured with magic. I looked down the building toward the open window below mine again and murmured the words to reinforce the illusion I'd already cast. No one looking this way should see anything other than empty windows and a blank wall.

Clutching the rope, I clambered out the window. The taut material bit into my palms as I adjusted my weight so I was balancing between my grip on the rope and my feet braced against the stone wall. Then, with a shaky breath, I started walking my way down. I kept one hand tight around the rope at any given moment, moving one and then the other.

There was a five-story drop below me. I wasn't sure any mage had enough magic to heal me if I fell.

An ache spread through my fingers and then across my shoulders. My heel hit the window frame a moment later. It hadn't been that far a climb.

This was the tricky part, though. I eased myself to the left of the window and descended until I was level with it.

Then I took a little jump and swung right through, tugging the rope with me.

Thankfully, the furniture layout in all the dorm rooms was essentially the same. I landed on a desk identical to my own, scattering a few papers that'd been left on it. At the thump of my arrival, the form under the bed covers jerked and shoved into a sitting position.

Declan squinted at me in the darkness of the room, his defensive posture relaxing as he recognized me. He didn't look exactly happy, though.

"What are you *doing*?" he said in an urgent whisper.

"Sorry." I slid off the side of the desk to plant my feet on the floor as quietly as I could. "Cast one of those silence spells?"

I knew he could manage it—he'd done it once before when he'd ended up stuck in my bedroom above while Victory and her cronies chatted outside. The Ashgrave scion's brow stayed furrowed, but he said something with a wave of his hand and let out a sigh.

He ran a hand through his black hair, the smooth strands adorably rumpled from his interrupted sleep. The whole room smelled like him—that warm and dryly sweet scent like cedar wood. My pounding heart started to slow as I soaked it in.

"Okay," he said, still quietly but no longer at a whisper. "Now are you going to tell me what you're doing here?"

I ducked to pick up the papers I'd scattered and set them back on the desk. "You don't have to worry. I cast an illusion spell so no one would see me coming down. It just

—I needed to talk to you, and it was the only way I could think of that seemed totally, er, covert."

His eyebrows arched slightly. "Well, it was definitely that."

I shot him a mock glower for the teasing note in his voice, but my gaze couldn't help dropping over the slim but solid muscles that defined his bare chest. The covers were pooled on his lap—I couldn't tell whether he slept in pajama pants or boxers or… maybe totally naked?

A weird but giddy little thrill raced through me. When I raised my eyes to meet Declan's again, even in the dim moonlight, I could see the smolder that had lit there. And suddenly there was one thing that I absolutely had to do before we got to the talking part.

I stepped around the desk to the edge of the bed and leaned in, my hand rising to his cheek. I was half afraid Declan would pull away, but he shifted forward to catch my mouth with his. His fingers slipped into my hair, tracing trails of pleasure over my scalp as we kissed, and God, I wished we didn't ever have to stop. Why couldn't my life be just this?

When he did draw back, it was only a couple inches, his hand falling to my shoulder. His voice came out a little hoarse. "You know I don't like having to act as distant as I've been with you. If I could stand right there by your side—but with everything that's at stake—"

Affection for him, for everything he was trying to do and how hard he fought to hold it together, squeezed my chest. "I do know," I said. "Why do you think I went to all these lengths to arrange the stealthiest possible meeting?"

He laughed under his breath, and then he was tugging me to him again. He kissed me so hard my knees wobbled with the rush of pleasure. When he let me go, it took me a moment to catch my breath.

"I'm sorry," he said. "We shouldn't even— We *definitely* can't do anything else. Even this room isn't totally secure from intrusion."

Yes, there were more compromising positions that would be much harder to explain away than me simply being in his room. "Of course," I said. "But you don't have to apologize."

Before I ended up kissing him again, I sat down on the bed a few feet away, leaving what felt like a reasonable space. Declan scooted closer to the edge so that I only had to turn partway to look at him. "What's going on?" he said. "It must have been pretty important for you to go to all those lengths."

He had that lightly teasing tone again, but what I could see of his expression was serious. I swallowed hard. I had no doubt that I'd come to the right person, but discussing this still wasn't going to be fun.

"You heard what happened to Professor Banefield," I said.

Declan's mouth twisted. "He attacked you and then stabbed himself in some kind of delirium from his illness. Although I've been assuming there's more to the story than that."

"Yeah. That's just the official version. I didn't know how much to tell anyone else. I didn't know who I could trust." I looked down at my lap. "Someone made him sick

—magically. I know because I was able to dispel the curse. But they left a failsafe in, one that meant he'd try to hurt me, to make it so I couldn't use my magic anymore. He killed himself to stop himself from doing that."

Declan sucked in a sharp breath. "God." He reached for my hand, and I let him twine his fingers with mine. His grip steadied me. "Did you find out anything about who cast those spells?"

I nodded. "He managed to tell me a little. He said... He said it was the older barons and someone called 'the reapers'."

"The barons." Declan's voice darkened. "I wondered, but they haven't said anything to me. They haven't even hinted... I knew they'd been making plans without looping me in. They don't totally trust me. Fuck." He paused. "And... the reapers?"

"That doesn't mean anything to you?" I asked. "I have no idea what he meant. And I didn't get a chance to ask for clarification."

"No. I've never heard anyone use that term to refer to anyone in the community. But I can do some digging and see if I can turn anything up. It's hard to keep something totally secret from a person who knows what they're looking for." He squeezed my hand tighter, and his expression shifted. "Speaking of which... your grandparents called on me."

Shit. I stiffened. "What did they say?"

"Well, they seemed upset that you hadn't gotten in touch with them yet, so it might be a good idea to do that soon if you can bear it. They made insinuations about our relationship—which of course I denied as blandly as I could—and then prodded me about helping them with some business deal that's being put to the barons."

"I'm so sorry."

"Not your fault. I can handle them."

"But anything I can do to convince them they've got nothing to hold over your head, the better." I bit my lip. "I'll give it my best shot. What do you think I should do about— We might not know who these 'reapers' are, but the barons aren't a secret. Is there something I should watch out for, some way I can defend myself better?"

Declan frowned. "I don't know. They shouldn't be meddling like this in the first place. If we had solid proof, it could cost whoever cast the spell or gave the order the barony. But that's exactly why they'll have been incredibly careful. It's impressive Professor Banefield was able to tell you as much as he did."

My poor mentor. "He did his best. He gave me a key, too, that he implied would lead somewhere important, but I have no idea what it's for."

"I can't help you there, but if you can find it, it might help a lot. I can pay extra attention to the barons' activities. It'd be hard for them to come onto campus without anyone noticing."

"They got to Banefield when he took a trip off-campus, I think," I said.

"That makes sense. So I'd be extra careful of any staff if you find out they've taken time off—or anyone new on campus who you haven't seen around before. And just watch for changes in behavior in general. That's where your skill in Insight will help you the most." He grazed his fingertips over my temple. "I'll keep an eye on the staff and students too. Between the two of us, hopefully we can pick up on any ill intentions before it turns serious."

I could take a little comfort from that solidarity, anyway. "Do you think—if the other barons haven't even told *you* what they're doing, will they have mentioned it to the other scions?"

The emphatic shake of Declan's head put that one worry to rest. "I talked with each of them to feel them out during the break. I can't promise they'll all be on good behavior, but everything I saw convinced me that none of them had a clue about a plot among the barons. They didn't even realize the professor who died had any connection to you."

"Well, I guess that's something." I groaned. "It's so hard not knowing who to trust."

"Hey." He waited until I met his eyes again. "I might not be able to offer you very much, but I can offer you this: I'll have your back in every way I can, no matter what happens. You can trust in that. I don't want to be standing in the pentacle of barons unless you're going to be standing there beside me."

My throat tightened as I smiled back at him, closing around the one secret I couldn't reveal even to him: that I didn't intend to stay among fearmancers long enough to take on the barony in the first place. But either way, I did still have to survive first.

I clasped his hand. "Let's hope we make it that far, then."

CHAPTER EIGHT

Rory

Malcolm must have been waiting for me to come down from my dorm. As I stepped out of the stairwell into the hall, he peeled himself off the wall across from me, his dark brown eyes fixed on me with a cool glower.

"Bloodstone," he said, "we need to talk."

I tensed automatically from head to toe—shields up, casting words at the ready, alert to any move he might make. But apparently he really did just want to talk. He tipped his golden head toward the far end of the hall and started ambling over as if he expected me to follow him.

I did, just a short ways, keeping a careful distance and trying to figure out what he was leading me to. I came around the bend to see him reaching for the door to the scions' basement lounge, and stopped in my tracks.

"If you want to talk, we can talk up here," I said. I had

no interest at all in being alone in an enclosed space with this guy.

He stopped and folded his arms over his chest. He might not have been quite as brawny as Connar, but the pose still highlighted the ample muscle in his chest and arms. "I think it's best to keep scion business between scions, don't you think?"

I couldn't hold back my laugh. "Oh, like you've kept your issues with me so very private in the past? What's different this time? Are you starting to realize that you don't actually come off looking as impressive as you assumed you would when you try to push me around?"

His jaw tightened, and he took a step toward me. His gaze darted across the hallway and came back to rest on me. This end of the hall was decently secluded. If I yelled, there were plenty of people in the library and coming and going from the dorms who'd have heard, but speaking at normal volume, we wouldn't draw any notice.

Maybe I didn't want to be totally alone with the Nightwood scion, but I wasn't itching for an audience either. Having spectators seemed to add extra fuel to Malcolm's spite.

"I thought you were so big on conscience, Glinda," he said, his voice searingly cold. "Now seducing my friends so you can use them against me is fair play in your book?"

I blinked at him. "'Seducing' your friends? Excuse me? Who exactly are you talking about?"

"Connar didn't get it into his head to come to your rescue out of nowhere. He wouldn't throw away more than a decade of friendship over some girl out of nowhere. You might have picked insight, but somehow I suspect you've been honing your persuasive skills as well."

For a second I could only sputter, my throat was so choked with indignation. "Are you fucking kidding me? Maybe he just happens to think that you're wrong without any outside influence at all. I didn't even *ask* him to do anything, let alone magic him into jumping in."

Malcolm's glower came back. "Do you really expect me to believe that, especially when you've somehow convinced Jude to trot at your heels for weeks now too?"

I just about exploded then, but the murmur of voices carrying from around the bend brought me back to caution just in time. I schooled my voice as low as I could without diminishing the bite of anger. "I didn't *want* Jude's attentions. I've been telling him to leave me alone. You know, you really should spend some time paying attention to what's actually going on around you instead of making up stories in your head. I'm not the villain in this story to *anyone* but you."

"I can see perfectly fine," he snapped, his hands dropping to his sides as he shifted closer. His gaze didn't leave my face for a second. "And if you think casting a couple of love spells is going to make me go easier on you—"

"I didn't cast any spells," I shot back. "And you know what? Even if I was happily welcoming every guy in this school into my life and, hell, into my bed, it wouldn't be any of your business. Or do you think being king of the school means you get to decide who your friends date too?"

Malcolm's jaw clenched. "It's not dating if you're brainwashing them into it." But even though the words came out taut, I caught a flicker of some emotion other than anger in his devilishly divine face. Something that had come out when I'd mentioned taking guys into my bed. Something as hot and hungry as the way Declan had looked at me when I'd appeared at *his* bedside last night.

I'd have expected to recoil at the idea that Malcolm had any interest in me that way. Instead, the recognition sent a triumphant shiver through me. The magic that coiled behind my collarbone, born of others' fears and weaknesses, hummed in harmony.

There was a chink in Malcolm's armor. There was a way of dueling that I hadn't tried yet, one where I now knew I had the upper hand. Maybe a way to stop us going in more and more of these stupid vicious circles and put him off from hassling me for good.

And fuck, it would feel so good to win one real victory here.

I didn't question the impulse. It rose up in me like an instinct I'd always had, and I let it propel me forward. Close enough to jab my finger against Malcolm's well-built chest and watch the spark light in the back of his eyes.

"You know what?" My voice fell into a silkily cool murmur I hadn't known I had in me. "I don't think even you really believe all these stories about me working voodoo on your friends. I think you're just jealous that I'd even consider giving them the time of day when I can't imagine ever wanting anything to do with *you*."

Malcolm's stance went rigid. "What the fuck are you talking about? That's the last thing I—"

"No?" I said, cutting him off, and bobbed up the last short distance between us to brush my lips against his.

At least, it was supposed to be just a brush, the faintest whisper of a kiss to kindle a reaction. But oh boy, did he react. The second my mouth grazed his, he caught my jaw and tugged me closer, turning the kiss into a branding.

It wouldn't have mattered. He was proving me right. The problem was in an instant I wasn't so sure I had the upper hand here after all. The heat of his mouth blazed through me right down to my toes—fuck, the guy knew how to kiss—and a whole lot of other parts of me woke up with tingling attention.

I didn't *want* to want him, but apparently a significant portion of me did despite myself.

I jerked back, willing my breath to stay calm and the flush to retreat from my cheeks. With what remained of my composure, I managed to swipe the back of my hand across my mouth as if the kiss had been so distasteful I couldn't wait to wipe all trace of it away. Malcolm stared at me, his gaze outright scorching now, his stance momentarily hesitant.

Thank God for that brief hesitation. "I think I've made my point," I said with all the tartness I could summon from the whirl of emotions racing through me, and strode off before he might try to pay me back in kind.

What the fuck had I been thinking?

It was over. I'd kept up my front of being unaffected. The gambit might have worked, regardless of how I'd felt

about it. No matter what else he felt about me, Malcolm
wanted me, and he knew I knew it. That meant I had one
thing over him I hadn't had before.

I could at least be thankful that my summer project target
was predictable. Benjamin and his three architecture
program friends took to what appeared to be their favorite
spot in the field nearly every day in the early afternoon
and stayed there for a couple hours as long as the weather
was pleasant. Today, no one was lurking beside Ashgrave
Hall watching them—until I took up that post myself,
anyway.

Naries didn't have any mental shields, with no magic
to generate them and no knowledge that they'd need to. I
guessed that was part of what made them such appealing
targets in general. I fixed my eyes on Benjamin's forehead
from across the field and murmured my casting word for a
general insight spell—the word that honored the family
that had raised me to care about how others saw the
world: "Franco."

I didn't want to delve too far. Benjamin Alvarez
deserved as much privacy as anyone. But I needed to
figure out the best way to motivate him toward my goal,
which I suspected he'd have had as a goal of his own if he'd
been given reason to think it might be possible.

I'd just have to give him that reason.

Impressions flitted through my senses. Insight wasn't a
direct ask-and-answer situation even when you asked a

specific question. You caught a glimpse of this and that inside the person's head and had to construct the meaning out of that.

Benjamin enjoyed the warmth of the sun and the soft cushion of grass beneath him. Pride rippled through his evaluation of the sketch he'd been working on—it was a building he was hoping he'd get to renovate someday back in his home town, wherever that was. I pushed a little deeper, sharpening my mind with thoughts of this school, of the potential hostilities of the other students.

Ah, there it was.

I caught a whiff of frustration in a memory of some guys jostling past him, skewing the line of his pencil. A general sense of always being watched. Unnerving pranks like all the writing instruments abruptly disappearing from his room. He rose above the tensions of the university pretty well, but the need for constant vigilance wore at him. I could relate to that feeling.

He wasn't going to need much persuading at all. He just needed to believe in the possibility enough to pursue it.

"*Look around*," I whispered, aiming a waft of magic tinged with compulsion toward him. "*Look at all that space. There'd be room for a small building right here. The professor would be impressed if you proposed a project that hands-on. A clubhouse for the scholarship students. Why shouldn't you have your own space, especially if you can build it yourself?*"

Benjamin's head had come up. He gazed around him, and inspiration brightened his face. I had to smile.

Beautiful. Of course, he'd be more likely to move forward if he had some concrete support.

"*Tell the others about it. They'll see what an awesome idea it is.*"

He turned and started talking to his friends with an animated gesture toward the field. A look of doubt came over one of the girls' faces, and I aimed another wisp of persuasion her way. "*You can make this happen if you campaign for it together. Just stand firm and draw your proposal up well.*"

Within a few minutes, the group was chattering away with excitement I could hear from where I was standing even if I couldn't make out their voices. I leaned back with a wash of relief and satisfaction.

The funny thing was, as large-scale as my plan was, it might be easier to pull off than what many of my peers would be attempting. They all wanted to push the Naries against their natural inclinations, to show how they could mess with them and lead them astray. I was giving them a task that appealed to them. I could nudge them along rather than drag them.

The hard part was going to be keeping them on track once my competitors figured out what path I'd set them on.

Footsteps rasped across the pavement, and I glanced around. Connar stopped a few feet away from me, glancing past me to the cluster of Naries and then meeting my eyes. He offered me a small but warm smile. "Getting a quick start on your summer project?"

My hackles came up instinctively, even though there

hadn't been anything threatening in his tone. I tried to exhale my nerves, but I stayed wary as I answered lightly. "If I was, I wouldn't be supposed to tell you, would I?"

He chuckled. "No, I guess not. I'll be interested to see what you do come up with, though."

I gave him a more intent look with a hitch of my pulse. "What are *you* planning to do to your Nary?"

"That's my secret too, isn't it?" he said, but his smile faded as he took in my expression. "I'm not aiming for anything big. Just enough that I can say I tried. The skills this assignment is going to take aren't really my forte." He paused. "And it's a little cruel, isn't it—setting out to push them around when they've got no way of defending themselves?"

"Yeah." I relaxed a little at those words and checked the time on my phone. "I've got to get to a seminar."

"I'll walk with you to the Tower? I have a Desensitization session." He made a slight grimace. What fears did that chamber throw in the Stormhurst scion's face?

I couldn't see how it would hurt to just walk with him. "Okay," I said. But we'd only taken a few steps across the green when I tensed up all over again—not because of Connar, but because of the lanky figure who'd emerged from Nightwood Tower to stride toward us.

Jude's gaze took the two of us in with a flick of his dark green eyes. I expected some kind of flirty comment or ribbing remark, but instead his expression soured in a way I'd never seen before. My body instinctively braced even more.

A response which mustn't have been lost on him. "You don't need to worry about me," he said to me in an unusually flat voice as he reached us. "I'm not going to make any demands on your precious time today."

Where had that bitterness come from all of a sudden? I opened my mouth, searching for an appropriate reply, but Jude's attention had already shifted to Connar. "Enjoy it while it lasts. It's not as if it's likely to for very long."

He marched on past us with such a grim smolder that I couldn't help staring over my shoulder at him as he disappeared into the hall behind us.

"What's going on with him?" I said.

Connar was peering after Jude too, his brow knit. "I don't know," he said. "Usually even when he's pissed off, he manages to sound a lot more energetic while he's ripping into you. I don't know if I've ever seen him quite that... deflated." He shook his head. "Whatever bad moods he gets into, he usually snaps out of them pretty fast, though."

I hoped that was the case with this one, rather than it being some kind of omen of worse to come.

CHAPTER NINE

Malcolm

My dad had a way of expressing disapproval with nothing more than the way he drew in his breath, like he did right now when the nachos I'd ordered while I was waiting for him arrived at our booth in the back of the bar. The nachos were as posh as the gleaming modern space itself—they had fresh crab meat on them, for fuck's sake—and they were the best food the place made, but no doubt Dad could only think "feeb food" when he looked at them.

"You're welcome to some," I said as I grabbed a cheese-and-crab laden chip. There was no way he'd touch the stuff, but he'd probably be even more irritated if I didn't offer than he was by my order in the first place.

"I've already lunched, thank you," he said in his usual cool tone, and took a measured sip from his Old Fashioned.

I wasn't sure what this meeting was about. He'd been working on some sort of business not far from the university and texted me to suggest an early afternoon drink in town. It couldn't be simply that he wanted to pass on instructions or criticism. The former he'd have handled by phone, and the latter he'd never have done in public.

Whatever was on his mind, it was important enough that he wanted to judge my response in person. That probably didn't bode well.

A Nightwood never let discomfort show. Or impatience. I took another chip, this one with ample salty avocado, and pretended I wasn't concerned about anything other than the crunch and the flavors mingling in my mouth.

They always had the air conditioning turned a little too high in this place. I'd worn a thin shirt today in consideration of the summer heat, and now I was fucking cold, but I couldn't let that show either.

Dad said a word and raised his hand, and I knew he'd cast a shell of privacy around our booth. The staff and other patrons wouldn't hear our conversation.

"You've made far less progress with the Bloodstone scion than you promised us," he said.

My back tensed automatically. I finished chewing and swallowed, but the mouthful sank like a lump of stone into my stomach.

"I've landed plenty of blows," I said. "She just keeps bouncing back from them. Growing up with joymancers and feebs obviously didn't dull the Bloodstone spirit all that much. The pressure will still be adding up. She'll crack eventually." I paused, glad I could observe *his* response to this comment face-to-face. "Especially now that her original mentor situation imploded in epic fashion."

If Dad had anything to do with or knew anything suspicious about Professor Banefield's violent demise, he didn't show it. His face stayed in that mildly bored expression that was at least better than his chillingly angry expression or his delightedly vindictive expression. Declan *could* be wrong about there being anything to the death other than a natural if potent illness.

But, as irritating as this fact could be, if Declan was confident enough in a theory to put it forward, he was generally right. The guy was nothing if not conscientious. And Dad could bluff with the best of them. So I really didn't know anything more about the professor's death now than I had before.

I'd have liked to think my parents were above murdering bystanders to get their way, especially when they'd supposedly been allowing me to make a go at their goals. Their methods might have been harsh, but there'd always been a clear if cold logic to the lessons they'd taught me. A Nightwood should have more honor than to slaughter respected members of the community because a foe proved a little difficult to tackle head-to-head.

Did Mom and Dad uphold those values to the letter, though? I couldn't say I believed that with total certainty. Rory was a pain in my ass and a threat to the balance of power at school, sure. To Dad, she was the final piece in a full pentacle, the one sticking point before the barons could do… whatever exactly they were so keen to get done. He didn't discuss policy with me.

He'd let me know when he felt I'd earned that right.

"I think you've had plenty of opportunity to make use of your own resources," he said now. "In some ways, you may have inadvertently encouraged her resilience. From here on, I think it's better if you don't associate with her at all, at least until she's had the necessary attitude adjustment."

I couldn't stop myself from staring at him for a second as he took another sip from his glass. "You want me to completely back off? To let her do whatever the hell she wants?"

Dad's eyes narrowed a smidge. "I trust you can handle the change in a way that doesn't diminish your standing."

You'd better handle it that way, his tone said, *or there'll be hell to pay when you're next home.*

"Whatever you've got planned, I can at least assist," I said. "I'm right there on campus—it doesn't make sense for me to—"

"We'll decide what's most sensible. And right now we have our next steps well in hand with no additional involvement necessary. Your observations may still be valuable, but that's all I want from you. Understood?"

Anger flared in my chest, sharp and searing. *I'd* been the one dealing with Rory's stubborn defiance from the moment she stepped onto campus. I'd nearly had her on her knees at least once. He'd talked to her all of once for five minutes and he thought he could judge how to tackle her better than I could? He thought he could accuse me of making things *worse*? What the hell would he have done differently?

"If that's what you think is best." I bit back that frustration and dug into my nachos instead. I'd done every goddamn thing he could have asked of me, and he—

With reflexes honed from two decades of vicious little tests, I registered the weirdly brittle texture between my teeth just as the first faint prick of pain echoed through my tongue. All my attention narrowed down to the sensations inside my mouth. Yep. Right there. Without my even noticing the spell, he'd conjured a sliver of glass into my lunch.

I kept my face impassive as I shifted the food carefully and raised my napkin to my lips. I didn't even look at the shard as I spat it into the cloth. A metallic hint of blood flavored the rest of my mouthful.

Dad didn't say anything, so he must have been satisfied with how unfazed I'd appeared. He threw back the last of his drink and stood up. "I know I can count on you. There'll be plenty more responsibilities ahead if all goes well."

I allowed myself a brief glower at his retreating back. He counted on me to do shit-all, as far as I could tell.

The plate in front of me no longer looked particularly appealing. That sliver of glass might be a one-off—or he might have laced the whole heap of nachos with them to express his displeasure with my meal choice. I debated for a second and then gestured for the bill.

The walk back to campus didn't do anything to burn off the prickling energy churning inside me as if I'd swallowed a whole plateful of glass shards. I kept going, past the main buildings to the kennel where my familiar was cooped up during class hours, as usual.

Shadow perked up at my entrance, his feet pattering against the floor as he bounded to the stall door. I stepped inside and sat down with my back against the wall, and he pushed right against me. With a pleased huff of breath, he nuzzled my shoulder.

I scratched his favorite spot behind his ears and breathed in his warm wolfy smell. It wasn't quite as comforting as it'd been when I was only twelve and I'd had a whole lot less weighing on my shoulders, but it still took the edge off.

I knew who I was. I knew what I was capable of, even if Dad didn't. Fuck him and the rest of the barons.

Not that even Shadow completely had my back when it came to Rory. He'd turned traitor thanks to her softening-up routine too. If she'd outright attacked me, he'd have defended me, but a wolf didn't understand the more subtle ways a person could pick away at your defenses.

I'd told her to stay the hell away from him, but she obviously hadn't listened. A ball lay in the corner that I hadn't brought for Shadow to play with. I glared at it, trying to summon more fury, but it was hard to be really angry about *that* with my familiar fawning over me showing just how hungry for attention he got in here. Maybe she was only visiting him to mess with me, but he did get something good out of it.

That was becoming a common theme. As Shadow

flopped down on the floor next to me, his head resting on my knee at the perfect angle for more ear scratches, my mind skipped back to that moment in the hall a few days ago. To the perfect sweet press of Rory's lips against mine. My heart thumped faster just remembering it.

I didn't think she'd been trying to soften me up with that. No, she'd been using it as one more ploy in our escalating feud. But damn, it *had* been good. To feel all the fierceness in her body radiating into me, to absorb some of that fire…

She'd made a show of dismissing the kiss, but I'd been with enough girls to get a read on when someone was into the moment and when it was time to ease back. For just a second before Rory had yanked herself away, she'd leaned into me. It'd been good for her too, even if she didn't like that she'd liked it.

I wet my lips, and a slow smile crept across my face. Dad didn't know what the fuck he was getting into, trying to break Rory down. I could step back from my other tactics, but she'd just opened up a whole new avenue of competition. There were so many ways I could throw her off without doing anything you could call harm, and I'd enjoy it a hell of a lot more than any skirmish we'd gotten into before.

I still ruled here at Blood U, and no one—not my dad, not Rory, not my traitor friends—was going to stop me from living that role to the fullest.

CHAPTER TEN

Rory

In some ways, the reduced student population during the summer was nice. There were fewer random seniors around to either try to take a jab at me or try to hit on me, both attempts to boost their own standing. More chance I'd get a little welcome solitude in my dorm room. Only half as many witnesses to any noise I made in the grips of the nightmares that still haunted me—not magically induced now, but still painful, with Professor Banefield's death taking a spot amid the reruns of my parents' murders.

On the other hand, fewer students meant I saw more of the same people in our sporadic classes. My current Physicality workshop included not just Connar but Victory and Cressida as well.

I'd chosen a spot in the front corner, and now I was regretting that. My two dormmates' murmurs and giggles from a couple rows behind me made my nerves jitter on high alert, but I couldn't see what they might be up to. With Professor Viceport gliding back and forth at the front of the room, eyeing my work with particular critical attention, I couldn't afford to let myself be distracted anyway.

All our classes during the summer session revolved around our project, and today Viceport had us focusing on conjuring scents. "Smell is a powerful but often overlooked sense," she'd said at the start of class. "It can provoke powerful emotions in an instant, draw a person in or repel them away. When you're directing your target, you may find it an incredibly useful tool."

We were actually working two different skills, though. So that we—and she—could evaluate our own conjured scents accurately, we'd first needed to construct a bubble of magic around us that would hold our work in and prevent mingling. Thankfully I had plenty of experience generating walls and other barriers at this point. Not that I'd ever thank Malcolm for that.

At the moment, we were supposed to be pulling together a scent that we felt would calm our target and make them more open to suggestion. The idea turned my stomach, but as long as no one was going to force me to use this skill on my Nary, I could go along with the assignment here.

I'd tried merging lavender, which was supposed to be relaxing, with a sort of fresh-baked cookies smell that brought an ache into my chest remembering that scent in my parents' kitchen. When I'd been a kid, I'd have found it comforting.

Viceport was making her way toward me now, stopping at the desk two over from mine to lean into that student's bubble. I drew in a breath and urged a little more buttery doughy scent into the mix.

A tingling sensation shot past my ear, and all at once the smell I'd conjured turned sour and rancid, as if the cookies had gone moldy. My stomach lurched, and I diffused the odor as well as I could. I didn't want to send it flying out into the rest of the air for the professor to notice. Not that I had much time to come up with something different to offer her now. She was just moving to my neighbor's desk.

A faint snicker behind me told me exactly who I could thank for the disruption, if I couldn't have already guessed. I gritted my teeth as I worked more of the stench out of the air.

I'd had enough of taking the high road. I wasn't going to stoop to Victory's level and launch unprovoked attacks, but she could damn well find out that if she took a shot at me, it'd rebound right back at her.

I condensed what remained of the smell into a compact spear of air. With a quick glance over my shoulder, I confirmed exactly where Victory was sitting. "Pierce," I murmured, and whipped the stench toward its creator with a flick of my hand.

I didn't have a whole lot of experience trying to sabotage people, so maybe I tossed it Victory's way a little more forcefully than was necessary. I knew it'd hit the

mark, at least, from her startled but furious gasp. Her
clothes rustled as if she were wiping at them—had I sent
the smell right onto *her* instead of just into her bubble?

The corner of my mouth twitched with a smile I
couldn't restrain. That should make her think again if she
felt like screwing with my magic, anyway.

I scrambled to recreate my original scent as Professor
Viceport nodded to my neighbor and offered a couple of
suggestions. The lavender prickled my nose a little more
pungently than I'd have preferred, and the sweetness of the
cookie scent overwhelmed the doughy aspect that I liked
best, but at least I had an approximation of what I'd been
going for when Viceport stopped in front of me.

"Ready, Miss Bloodstone?" she said in the icy voice
that only I seemed to receive. Her pale eyes, equally cold,
peered at me from behind the rectangular panes of her
glasses. Between that, her wispy ash-blond pixie cut, and
her skinny but elegant frame, she fit the "Ice Queen"
nickname a whole lot better than I ever had.

"It still needs some refining," I said, "but you'll get the
general idea."

I started to speak to adjust the bubble so she could
take a sniff inside—and another tingle raced past me, this
one ten times as violent as before. I didn't have a chance to
so much as flinch before my shell of magic burst apart
with a force that smacked my face. And Viceport's too,
from her wince. The scent I'd conjured dissipated in an
instant.

"Miss Bloodstone," Professor Viceport said sharply,
raising her chin and peering down her nose at me. "I

expect a mage of your supposed caliber to maintain far better control over your conjurings. Have you learned *nothing* in the last three months?"

My hand clenched on the desktop. I forced my voice to stay even. "There wasn't a flaw in my conjuring. Someone else shattered it."

She sniffed. "Come now, you should at least be above blaming others for your own failings. Although perhaps I shouldn't be surprised."

What was *that* supposed to mean? I held my frustration in by a fraying thread of self-control. "I'm simply telling you the truth. It isn't as if sabotaging other students is an uncommon occurrence around here, is it?" It wasn't that she couldn't believe someone would have done it, only that she'd rather blame me.

"I'm sure all of your classmates are currently fully occupied with their own work. You must admit you've had plenty of struggles in the past. Now—"

A low voice interrupted from the other side of the room. "Rory's telling the truth. I saw Victory cast something at her."

My head jerked around at the same time Viceport's did. We both stared at Connar. He looked back at us, his expression tense even though his tone had been matter-of-fact.

Victory had turned to look at him too, although *her* eyes were narrowed into a glare. Beside her, Cressida's face had turned pink with a nervous flush. They obviously hadn't expected to be taking on two scions today.

"Professor Viceport," my nemesis said quickly in her

most honeyed voice, "I think Connar must have misinterpreted what he saw of my casting—"

Connar shifted his already impressive form taller in his seat. "I'm the most skilled Physicality mage out of all the students at Blood U," he said firmly. "I know how to tell what I'm looking at."

Viceport's mouth twisted as if she resented having to address this new development at all. She sighed.

"Well," she said, "I can't give credit to anyone, since it appears you all bungled what you meant to do." Her gaze slid back to me. "Even if your fellow students decide to interfere, it's up to you to keep your castings solid. I'll evaluate your performance in this exercise based on past demonstrations."

A whole lot of which I'd struggled with for reasons I didn't totally understand. But I didn't see how else I could argue with her. At least Victory wasn't getting any praise for getting caught in her trick.

I thought that would be the end of it, but Connar spoke up again, his voice quieter but still grave enough to command attention. "There's actually something else I need to talk to you about, Professor. After class lets out."

Victory and Cressida shot wary glances Connar's way as they gathered their things to go at the end of the workshop, but he didn't acknowledge them in the slightest. Whatever he had to talk to Professor Viceport about, they were obviously worried it might have to do with them… but they couldn't defend themselves without admitting they'd done something that needed defending. After a moment, they filed out of the room with the rest of the class.

I grabbed my purse, planning to follow—very carefully, in case of potential ambush on the stairs—but Connar motioned to me as he went to the professor's desk. His expression wasn't just grim but a little green now. Whatever he was going to talk about, he didn't feel good about it.

"You should hear this too," he said.

Viceport folded her hands together where she was standing behind her desk, her lips pursing. "What is this about, Mr. Stormhurst? I don't think there's anything more to be discussed regarding today's performances."

"It's not about today." Connar inhaled sharply. "You've gotten a skewed impression of Rory's abilities in Physicality not just today but for the last two months. I've been intermittently… interfering with her conjurings. Weakening them, making them disperse. I know protecting our castings is an important skill too, but I think you can agree that expecting a student just learning how to control her abilities to protect herself from the top student in that area is above and beyond."

My whole body had chilled. It took me a second before I could force out the words. "You were throwing off my spells, all that time…?" He'd done it so subtly I'd never even suspected someone else's magic had meddled with mine.

Now he looked even more sick. "I stopped a couple of

weeks before the end of term. I shouldn't have—it's complicated." He fixed his gaze on Professor Viceport. "The successful castings that Rory has managed are reflective of her true abilities, not the others. I regret interfering, and I think she should be judged based on her actual talent. That's why I'm telling you."

Viceport had gone a bit paler even than usual. She pinched her nose just below the bridge of her glasses as if she had a headache. "All right," she said. "Thank you for your candor, Mr. Stormhurst. Credit to Physicality for carrying out your intentions in a way neither I nor Miss Bloodstone clearly caught on to. I'll keep this information in mind as we proceed."

I wasn't even surprised anymore that she didn't offer any punishment or even a chiding word. Blood U encouraged its students to be cutthroat. Any of the professors, even Banefield, would have said it was my job to learn how to defend myself. But Connar's admission still left me numb, as if I hadn't already known he'd made himself my enemy.

Viceport appeared to be done with us, so I hurried on out of the room. Connar didn't have any trouble catching up, though.

"Rory," he said, following me down the stairs, "I'm sorry. That's *why* I told her—why I wanted you to hear it too. I know I can't make up for everything unless you know everything I've done."

I walked on without looking back at him. "If you expect kudos just for owning up to doing something shitty—"

"I don't." He swallowed audibly. "I'm trying to do the right thing—that's all I've ever been doing. I honestly thought I was doing the right thing before. All I can tell you is how sorry I am and how stupid I feel for not listening to my gut sooner. And that's it. There's nothing else I did to trip you up that you don't know about it. I felt like shit the whole time I was doing even that much."

"So why the fuck did you do it?" I spun on him at the next landing. "I still don't understand that. Did Malcolm ask you to attack my work?"

The guilty tightening of his mouth told me enough.

"Oh," I said. "And of course you had to go along with it because he's such a good friend."

"He is," Connar said. "When he isn't being a jackass, anyway, which is actually most of the time, as hard as that might be for you to believe. But he's wrong about this— he's wrong about you—and I've told him that, more times than just the other day. I'll keep telling him until he sees it." He paused. "I can make up for screwing up your castings directly—if you want any extra tutoring—I can teach you the best tricks I've learned over the years…"

The hope that crept across his face with the offer made my insides ache all over again. "Let me see," I said abruptly.

He blinked at me. "See what?"

"That you're telling the truth. That this isn't another way to mess with me. Let me use insight on you."

I'd done it once before, skimming the surface of his mind, without him even knowing it. But I wanted full access right now—and I also wanted to see how he'd react to the request.

He hesitated, as I guessed anyone would when asked to open up the contents of their head for someone else to rummage through. Then he nodded. "Go ahead. Look as much as you want. I owe you that."

He came down the last step to stand on the landing next to me. I fixed my gaze on his forehead, tamping down on my awareness of his presence, his body, so close to mine.

"Franco," I murmured.

Connar had taken down any walls he normally kept up. I tumbled straight into the whirl of impressions. A pang of guilt raced through my awareness, followed by a burn of shame, a flicker of Malcolm's furious face in the scions' lounge, a wave of loss as I'd crumbled the dragon figurine I'd made for Connar in his hand. Over it all was the stark sear of desperation and longing as he looked at me right now, wanting so badly for me to recognize his repentance.

The force of all those emotions squeezed the breath from my lungs. I pulled myself back out with a gulp of air. Connar watched me, waiting, his hand closed tight around the railing.

He *was* sorry. I believed that now without a doubt. But he'd also honestly thought that tearing me down was a reasonable expression of loyalty not that long ago. The regret he felt today wasn't necessarily permanent.

"Okay," I said. "Apology accepted. Forgiveness might

take a little longer. So will deciding whether to trust you with that extra help."

"Of course," Connar said with obvious relief. "Take all the time you need."

He dipped his head to me and continued on down the stairs, giving me space as well. I watched him disappear around the bend, somehow feeling even more uncertain than I had before.

CHAPTER ELEVEN

Rory

I might not be looking to continue my romance with Jude, but he had taught me some useful things during our brief friendship-and-more. One of those was not to worry about breaking the rules so much as ensuring I didn't get caught. So I watched the hall that held the teaching staff's quarters carefully as I magically sprung the lock on Professor Banefield's office door, but I didn't hesitate before stepping inside.

It'd been nearly a month since his death, but the maintenance staff had left the room pretty much as it'd always been. I'd heard that Ms. Grimsworth was having trouble tracking down his next of kin. The new junior Insight professor she'd brought on had taken a different, vacant office.

As my gaze traveled over the familiar bookshelves and the desk where I'd so often sat across from my mentor, my heart squeezed. The air smelt a little stale and the space was dim with the curtain mostly pulled over the small window, but something of Banefield's upbeat demeanor still lingered.

He'd been the only authority figure at the school who'd been anything like warm with me. Maybe I hadn't agreed with his attitudes about Naries—the same ones so many other fearmancers shared—but he'd been willing to listen to my arguments. He'd seemed to really consider them. He'd talked me through so many of my worries and my struggles with my magic.

And when push came to shove, he'd put his whole life on the line to save me.

I dragged in a breath past the heaviness in my chest and began my circuit of the room. Every book, every container on the shelves, I needed to check for some spot, obvious or hidden, where the key he'd placed in my hand might fit. It didn't seem likely that he'd been keeping whatever he wanted me to find right here, or he'd have handed it straight to me, but I didn't have much else to go on.

The office didn't turn up anything. There were a couple of drawers with keyholes on the desk, but one of them was already unlocked and the other one didn't accept my key. I walked over to the far door that led into the professor's private quarters, the weight inside me getting heavier.

The last time I'd been in those rooms, I'd cured Professor Banefield of his cursed illness—and then he'd tried to destroy my magic. Instead he'd ended up gouging his own heart.

I braced myself as I murmured the unlocking spell and eased the door open. The hall on the other side was equally dim. But the maintenance staff had clearly come through here to do some basic clean-up. Only a hint of the sickly sweat smell from his long sickness remained in the air. The tiled floor in the kitchen shone pale beige, no trace of his blood remaining. Even in his bedroom, where he'd lain in a stupor for weeks, the bed had been made with clean sheets tucked neatly around the mattress.

I wouldn't have wanted to see the mess, but this sanitized space left my skin creeping. It was as if Banefield's final days and selfless sacrifice had been completely erased. You wouldn't have known anyone had existed in this space at all recently.

Walking into the kitchen made my wrist twinge where Banefield had gripped it so hard he'd bruised me. I shoved the memories aside and forced myself to focus on my search. I needed to find *something* to give me a direction. Otherwise that sacrifice of his wouldn't have accomplished half of what he'd wanted it to.

I didn't discover any secret safes or secured cupboards. My spirits had sunk by the time I reached the last focus of my search, the living room. No unexpected objects lay behind the sofa or the armchairs. The side tables had no compartments, and the drawer on the oak coffee table opened at my tug. All it held were a few papers.

With a looming sense of hopelessness, I sifted through them. My hand paused over an envelope. I drew it out.

The envelope and the papers inside didn't offer any specific clues. They appeared to be a letter from a friend or colleague about some area of magical study Banefield had been researching—nothing to do with me, as the date at the top was from before I'd even arrived here. But they gave me something else that might be even better.

The letter hadn't been sent to Professor Banefield here at the university. The writing on the envelope was an address in a town I didn't recognize somewhere else in New York state.

Of course Banefield had his own home apart from here. A place he might have felt was more secure from the people who'd wished me and him harm?

I took a picture of the address with my phone. As soon as I had the chance to take a road trip out there, I'd have to find out whether that place held the answers I needed.

As I took my seat for my morning Persuasion seminar a couple days later, I found myself eyeing Professor Crowford's lightly lined face more warily than in the past. I couldn't have said I'd been especially fond of him before, even though he'd intervened a couple of times to save me from potential embarrassment when Malcolm and I had faced off. The professor always kept a suavely detached air as if he saw our squabbles and other classroom activities as a mild amusement rather than anything serious.

The summer project he'd chosen made me rethink my neutral opinion of him. He wasn't just dismissive of the

Naries like every fearmancer I'd talked to other than Declan was—he'd thought it'd be a good idea to encourage the entire student body to manipulate them way beyond what normally happened here. There was a particularly cruel, callous side hiding under those fading good looks.

I was distracted from my analysis by Malcolm's arrival. The Nightwood scion didn't look at me as he sauntered across the room to claim the seat at the other end of the row, but my whole body sprang into extra alertness. Persuasion was his specialty, and he did enjoy using it on me.

And he still hadn't done anything to get back at me for that kiss I'd intended in mockery the other day.

A couple more students filed in, leaving one empty desk at the back. Professor Crowford considered it and then the doorway, and seemed to decide whoever hadn't yet arrived shouldn't hold up class. He stepped around his desk and clapped his hands authoritatively.

"All right, let's get down to business. Since I set you off on your project this summer, I suppose I'd better supply you with some innovative strategies for accomplishing your goals. One thing I want you to keep in mind is that while we most often focus on using persuasive spells to direct the *actions* of others, they can be equally powerful in directing thoughts and emotions. For a more subtle change in behavior, that's where you'll want to at least start."

He went on to describe a trick for provoking a mild emotion in your target using your own memories as a sort of fuel. I found myself listening intently despite my qualms about the project, because hell, I still needed to do some persuading, even if it was with good intentions.

Benjamin had seemed pretty excited about the clubhouse idea the few times I'd encouraged his discussions with the others along as they'd worked out their design proposal, but you never knew when doubts might set in. Especially since there were at least a couple other mages who'd be pushing him in different directions.

A faint warmth brushed over my left knee. I glanced down automatically, my leg stiffening, but... nothing was there. My pant leg looked perfectly normal.

But as I watched, the sensation returned. If I hadn't been looking right at my knee, I'd have sworn someone had teased their fingers across it and then, slowly, softly, settled their hand just above it. It wasn't an especially intimate touch, and the carefulness of it stopped me from leaping out of my chair in response. It held there, a spot of gentle warmth in a gesture that could have been comforting if it hadn't been so bizarre and unexpected.

My gaze jerked up with a sudden suspicion. Past the student sitting between us, Malcolm was watching Professor Crowford with apparently rapt attention. But his right hand was resting on his desk with the fingers slightly curved as if cupped around something about the size of a knee.

A person's hand could have fallen into that position by coincidence, but as I watched, he glided his thumb a few inches through the air. A teasing pressure traced over the outside of my leg.

Fuck. He must have cast some sort of illusion spell to

make me feel the movements of his hand as if he were touching me. To pay me back for the kiss? To try to distract me from the lesson? To make some other point about how I'd react?

Probably all three of those at once.

I just had to ignore it. A slight warmth on my knee— no big deal. If I *didn't* react, then I'd have won.

I focused my attention back on the professor's lecture. It should have been easy to tune out Malcolm's current gambit. The sensation wasn't that intrusive.

But his fingers moved again, a breath of a caress that grazed my skin through the fabric of my pants, and a quiver of heat shot up my leg. Just for a second, the kiss came back to me—the searing determination with which he'd kissed me back, the jolt of pleasure he'd managed to summon with one skillful shift of his mouth.

I didn't want him touching me, not even through an illusion. He was the last person in the world I wanted anywhere near me. So why did any part of me recognize that the stroke of his fingertips felt good?

Why the hell was I sitting here and taking this? I'd thrown Victory's spell back in her face a couple days ago, and I could do the same to Malcolm. It didn't matter how much he could affect me when I already knew I could affect him more.

I sorted through my thoughts for the right phrase, the right way of shaping my intention from my hand into an illusionary touch only he would notice. "Like a ghost, feel my touch," I whispered, so quietly the words were barely more than a warble of my breath. I drew my fingertips across the top of my desk, watching Malcolm from the corner of my eye. Imagining those lines traced across his back from shoulder blade to shoulder blade.

His stance twitched. I pretended not to see him glance toward me, but I let a smile curl my lips. He'd figured he was going to be the master of this game, did he? Let's see how well *he* could follow Professor Crowford's lecture now.

I eased my hand toward me as if down his spine. Malcolm was sitting perfectly still now. Fingers stroked over my knee once more, a little more insistently—and then that presence disappeared.

I stilled my hand. If he was giving up, I'd end this now.

But I should have known he wasn't done. A moment later, those ghostly fingers grazed my cheek. They reached my ear and then glided down along my jawline with such a tender caress my heart thumped.

Fuck, no. I closed my eyes to steady myself, trying to tune back into what Professor Crowford was saying, and skimmed my own hand upward. All the way up Malcolm's neck to splay over the sensitive scalp at the back of his head.

Malcolm covered the start of a sound with a forced cough. His posture drew straighter. I'd hit a provocative spot, clearly, because his touch faded away again. Before he could resume his attentions, I eased my fingers around in a slow circle, trailing sensation over his skin. I honestly had no idea what Crowford was talking about now, but if

I could convince Malcolm there was no way this tactic was playing out in his favor—

"Hello, good people of Persuasion!" a forcefully flat voice said from the doorway. Jude ambled into the classroom, his face flushed and his eyes a little glassy. He took his next step with a wobble. "Sorry I'm late. I hope you all managed that short while without me."

Professor Crowford stared at the Killbrook scion, and his nose wrinkled slightly. "Mr. Killbrook," he said, "have you been drinking?"

"Maybe a little. Just a little. I think I'm owed that much." Jude swung around, swayed, and fixated on the empty seat at the back. "There we go. I've found my place."

Crowford caught the scion's arm before he could really set off. He leaned close to say something I couldn't hear, but Jude shoved away from him with a scoffing sound. "Excuse me! I have a right to an education. *Every* fearmancer has a right to that. Don't you damn well tell me what classes I can go to."

The professor's mouth tightened. "You can come to all the classes you like if you're in fit condition to participate," he said. "We can try again next week."

"Next week?" Jude sputtered. "What the hell kind of—"

"*Go back to your dorm room and drink plenty of water,*" Crowford said in a slightly singsong tone I recognized as a casting.

Clearly Jude didn't have much in the way of mental defenses while alcohol was addling his brain. He spat out a few curses, but he also spun toward the door and sashayed back out.

Malcolm sprang to his feet. "Maybe I should make sure he gets to his room okay?"

Crowford shook his head. "Don't let Mr. Killbrook's foibles disrupt your own learning, as admirable as your concern for your friend is. I don't think he's in any real danger."

Malcolm lowered himself back into his seat slowly. When I looked at him, I saw the same confusion and worry on his face as were whirling inside me. He didn't know what to make of this performance any more than Connar had been prepared for Jude's dark comments on the green the other day.

If even the guys who knew Jude best had no idea what was wrong with him... it had to be pretty fucking wrong, didn't it?

CHAPTER TWELVE

Rory

I had to give my Nary credit for initiative. Benjamin had done his own research into school policies and figured out almost everything he needed to know to convince the headmistress to let his group go ahead with their construction proposal. I'd contrived for one last bit of obscure school procedure to land in his lap yesterday. Now I just had to make sure he didn't lose his confidence.

Right now he was standing with a couple of his friends in the main fore-room of Killbrook Hall, five minutes shy of their scheduled meeting with Ms. Grimsworth. Benjamin had already paced across the middle of the room several times, his shoulders up and his eyes a little wide. The scrape of his anxious footsteps echoed against the high ceiling.

None of these students had gotten the best reception from the fearmancer staff in the past. While the teachers might not outright bully them like so many of the mage students did, their disdain couldn't be hard to pick up on.

"Maybe we should reschedule until we've reworked the drawings again," he said, his voice carrying to me faintly where I was sitting on one of the hard, elaborately carved mahogany benches near the front door. "If they're going to go for this, everything has to be *perfect*."

I flipped a page in the book I was theoretically studying and thought back to my own moments of assurance in the face of uncertainty over the last few months. I'd managed to pick up some strategies from that Persuasion seminar a couple days ago, despite Malcolm's efforts at distraction. With an exhalation, I cast a stream of bolstering energy his way. "*You can do this. You're ready. Show the headmistress that.*"

"If you really think so…" the girl beside Benjamin said with a frown, looking down at the portfolio she was carrying.

Benjamin paused, and his chin came up a smidge. "No. We've done a ton of work. It should be enough, right? And if Ms. Grimsworth tells us it's not, then we'll have a better idea where the plan isn't strong enough."

The other two brightened, and they set off toward the staff wing. I sank back on the bench in relief, hoping my encouragement had been enough to get them through their meeting.

I wasn't only in the hall to keep an eye on my Nary. Yesterday I'd heard from the assistant of that blacksuit friend of my mother's, Lillian Ravenguard, asking if there was a good time for her to drop by. Apparently Lillian had found a few things she'd wanted to pass on to me, and she'd prefer the delivery happened in person. Since I'd known I'd be here to see Benjamin off anyway, I'd asked the assistant to meet me here a little after his meeting time.

The young woman who slipped into the hall a few minutes later had a presence about as far from her employer's as you could get. If Lillian was a tough lioness, then her assistant was a cuddly kitten. Silky waves of chocolate-brown hair framed her rounded face, and a pink summer dress floated around her petite frame. She caught sight of me and headed over with an energy so upbeat I half expected her to start skipping.

"You must be Rory," she said in an equally sunny voice. "Magnolia Duskland—but everyone calls me Maggie. It's great to meet you. Lillian would have come herself, but her work keeps her awfully busy."

"That's okay," I said, getting up to receive an enthusiastic shake of my hand. I didn't meet many fearmancers who were quite this… cheerful. As I sat back down on the bench and she joined me, I found I had no idea what else to say.

Thankfully Maggie had no problem diving right into the matter at hand. She dug a cloth bag out of her expansive purse and handed it to me. "Lillian said you mentioned you were feeling a little disconnected from your parents. She found some old letters and videos and that sort of thing that she thought might help you get to know your mom better. The digital media is all pre-loaded onto a phone in there to make everything easy."

I hadn't been expecting anything like this. Cautiously, I peered inside the bag. There was a phone, all right, and sheaf of pages filled with handwriting, and a couple of folders I couldn't make out the contents of yet. A strange shiver ran through my gut, one that might have been excitement or apprehension or both.

"Thank you," I said. "And please thank Lillian for me too. I really—I don't remember anything from the first couple years of my life—it'll be good to have some more context."

If Maggie had been waiting for a more effusive response, she didn't show it. "She wants to help you adjust however she can," she said. "She also asked me to remind you that you can reach out to her—and me, of course— any time. Oh, there's a letter from her in there too, explaining why she picked all the different materials, what she thinks is important about them."

"Perfect." Did Maggie expect me to start going through this stuff right here in front of her?

Before I had to decide whether I should politely end the visit somehow or try to act like more of a host, the assistant was springing up again. "I'm sure you're looking forward to checking all of that out. I won't keep you from that! I hope you find what you're looking for in there."

She gave me a quick look up and down as if evaluating me somehow, but her smile never dropped. Then she was vanishing out the front door as quickly as she'd arrived.

When I shuffled the contents of the bag around, I could squeeze it into my own purse. I definitely didn't want to delve into my family history here where any student or teacher could walk by. Hugging my purse close to my side, my pulse thumping away, I set off for the dorms.

As I crossed the green, my gaze caught on a broad figure beyond Ashgrave Hall. Connar was crossing the field toward the surrounding forest with a purposeful air that seemed odd for someone just planning on taking a stroll through the woods. I hesitated, watching him, my lingering doubts stirring.

It wasn't so strange that I'd want to know where he was going, was it? He'd messed with me in more ways than I'd even guessed, and breaking from Malcolm's orders obviously hadn't been easy for him. I was just making sure his loyalties weren't leading him in unfriendly directions again.

I came around the building, waited until Connar had stepped between the trees, and then hurried after him. By the time I reached the edge of the forest, I couldn't make out his brawny form, but here and there the crackle of someone moving through the underbrush reached me. I set off after that sound, placing my feet carefully so I didn't make much noise of my own.

I'd walked maybe twenty feet into the woods when an overwhelming rush of emotion hit me. What was I doing out here? I had things to take care of back on campus. If I didn't get on with that—

My feet had already carried me back in sight of the field before my thoughts cleared enough for me to realize what had happened. I didn't actually have any urgent business to get on with. There must have been a ward in the forest, a spell that had compelled me away. Why the hell would anyone do *that* unless they were trying to hide questionable activity?

I crept back through the forest even more warily this time. The sounds of Connar's passage had faded away completely. If I stayed alert for the first jab of the ward's effect, maybe I could—

Another jolt of emotion hit me, this one more fearful. My legs scrambled back from the unknown threat of their own accord.

I clamped down on the panic racing through me and tried to force myself to walk on through it, but my mind went blank. The next thing I knew, I was standing at the edge of the field again.

Shit. That must be quite the ward. I didn't think even one of the scions could have cast something like that in the short head start Connar had gotten on me. What was out there? I didn't remember getting redirected during any ramble through the woods before, but I wasn't sure I'd ever explored that particular section.

I wavered for a minute, but I hadn't been prepared to tackle a deflection that strong, and at this point Connar could have gone anywhere in the deeper forest. Even if I managed to break the ward—and that didn't set off some sort of magical backlash—I'd probably never figure out where he'd been headed. With a grimace, I turned back toward Ashgrave Hall instead.

My dorm's common room was empty. Some of the tension I carried around in me whenever I was out around campus released, but my hackles rose again at the scrabble of claws on the other side of my bedroom door. A scrabble much heavier than anything Deborah would have produced.

I mumbled a few hasty words to disable my deterrent spells and shoved the door open. A cream-and-chocolate-brown shape was just disappearing around the side of my bed. I dashed around the frame to find a slender, glossy-furred Siamese cat prowling alongside my desk.

Thank goodness, Deborah's voice reached me, reedy across the distance from wherever she was hiding. *That beast got in here ages ago, and it's been looking to pounce on me ever since.*

The door to my wardrobe stood ajar, as if the cat had tugged it open in its search. My teeth gritted. Wary of its claws, I grabbed the spare blanket off the top of the wardrobe and stalked after the cat. It spun on me with a hiss, and I pounced on *it* with the blanket at the ready.

The cat wriggled and spat as I lugged it out of my bedroom, but it couldn't fight through the blanket. I'd stopped in the middle of the common room, not sure what to do with the creature next, and Imogen came in. She took in me and the churning blanket I had clutched in my arms, her eyebrows rising.

"I don't suppose you know who a Siamese cat would belong to?" I said.

She winced. "That would be Victory. He's her familiar."

Of course it'd been Victory. Frustration bubbled up inside me. "Well, *somehow* he ended up in my room hunting *my* familiar. Unless he's learned to cast magic on his own, I'm pretty sure that wasn't an accident."

I marched over to Victory's bedroom door and squeezed one arm tighter around the cat while I tested her security spells. Oh, she figured that combination was enough to keep people out, did she? One of the two impressions with its cold sear through my stomach reminded me of a structure in the Bloodstone puzzle garden that I'd worked part of my way through with Jude weeks ago. I had experience my nemesis hadn't been prepared for.

I drew back a step so the repulsive effects didn't dig into my mind so deeply and started to talk my way through a counteractive casting under my breath. Imogen watched in silence. The cat kept squirming, but my anger sharpened my concentration. I spoke a little more forcefully with a jerk of my free hand, and the spells on the door fell away.

Ha. I strode inside, taking in the fluffy lilac-purple duvet and the matching lace curtains over Victory's much smaller window, the computer and library books positioned neatly on her desk, the tart perfume scent that lingered in the air. That last observation sparked an idea. Victory had wanted to inflict the downsides of a cat on me? I could remind her of another of those.

With a murmur and another twitch of my fingers, I summoned traces of water, ammonia, and other chemicals from my surroundings. Then I propelled the mix onto Victory's lovely bedspread. The purple darkened with a splotch that spread across most of the bed, and the stench of cat urine choked every other scent in the room. I dropped her familiar out of the blanket and quickly shut the door.

Imogen stared at me. "She's going to be *furious*."

"If she doesn't want cat piss in her room, maybe she shouldn't keep a familiar so poorly trained it goes roaming around in other people's private spaces," I said. "You don't have to mention that I did it."

"I wouldn't," Imogen said quickly. "But you know she's going to figure it out."

I shrugged. I was so done with caring how Victory felt about anything. She hated me no matter what I did, so why the hell not make it cost her? "I'll survive. And maybe eventually she'll figure out she's better off leaving me alone."

I went back into my bedroom, shut the door, and flopped down on the bed. It was only mid-afternoon, but I was already ready for this day to be done.

The covers quivered as Deborah scrambled up to join me. She nestled herself next to my hand. *Thank you. That horrible thing took me by surprise. It's a good thing I was close enough to one of my nooks in the wall to escape.*

"Be extra careful from now on if I'm not here," I said. "Who knows what she's going to try next."

Already planning on it. She nuzzled my fingers. *What did that blacksuit assistant have to say?*

After everything, I'd almost forgotten why I'd come back to my room in the first place. I sat up, setting Deborah on my knee as I crossed my legs, and tugged open my purse. "Some stuff to do with my mother—my birth mother. I made a random remark about not knowing much about my Bloodstone parents, and I guess she figured it'd be helpful."

Even though it was hard to think of anyone except the parents I remembered, the joymancers who'd raised me nearly my entire life, as family, I had to admit I was kind of curious. I'd gotten a brief glimpse into my birth parents' lives from a photo album I'd found at their country property nearby, but it hadn't come with much context.

The phone was loaded not just with videos but also photos and music, what Lillian said in her note had been some of my mother's favorite artists. I went to the videos first. They were grainy, the low quality you must have gotten with casual cameras a couple decades ago, but I could make out the action well enough. I held the screen where Deborah could see it too.

The first one was from a birthday celebration—someone's twenty-first. My birth mother, her dark brown hair just a little longer than mine was right now and her make-up done with professional polish, clinked glasses with a man I recognized as my father from the photos I'd seen, a younger version of Lillian, and another guy sitting with them. "Let's see who's not afraid to do another round of shots," she called out to laughter around the room.

That one reminded me uncomfortably of the fearmancer parties I'd navigated here, but the next video showed my mother in a garden I recognized as that country property, her dress still tailored but more casual, her smile bright as she motioned to whoever was holding the camera. "Just watch this!"

She spread her hands a few feet above a bare patch of ground. The soil trembled, and a sprout poked its way through. She urged the conjured plant up until it stood at her knee height, a vibrant blue flower opening at the peak of its stem.

"I wonder if Physicality was her focus," I said. Watching her brought a tingle of recognition into my chest—the joy that came with creation. She'd felt it too.

Deborah made a humphing sound inside my head. *Of course this friend would send all the happy videos. I'm sure plenty of death and destruction was edited out.*

"We don't actually know that my birth parents ever hurt anyone," I said. "Badly, anyway." Being a fearmancer meant you pretty much had to cause some distress on a regular basis to fuel your magic. We *did* know that some joymancers had been horribly violent toward my birth parents, so it wasn't as if the capacity for violence didn't exist on the other side. I'd seen the report on their deaths, photos and all—I was never going to get the images of those burnt bodies out of my head.

Violence wasn't what I wanted for this place when I brought it down. All the sick practices and the sadistic behavior the fearmancers encouraged needed to stop, but I didn't want anyone slaughtered.

The next video made my chest clench up. It was my mother in bed with an infant clasped tightly to her chest. An infant who must have been me. My mother's hair was mussed and her face weary, but that didn't diminish the happiness that shone through her expression.

"Say hi to Auntie Lillian," she said in a teasing voice,

turning me toward the camera. Then she pulled me back to her to kiss the top of my head.

An unexpected burn formed behind my eyes. For the very first time, looking at the woman I couldn't remember, some part of me responded with a pang that said, *Mom.*

Lorelei? Deborah said. *Are you sure you want to watch this—that it isn't just going to upset you?*

"It's fine," I said with a rasp. "I want to know." Maybe this was only the good-parts version of my mother's life, but… it meant something that there had been good parts.

It meant something that I'd lost the love I could see so clearly on the phone's screen.

CHAPTER THIRTEEN

Connar

I was so focused on the event to come that I think Rory must have called my name at least twice before I heard her. I stopped where I'd just stepped into the woods around campus and turned with a mix of delight and concern. Delight that she was seeking me out at all, and concern about what might have made her feel she needed to.

She came to a stop by the first trees, her deep blue gaze serious as she studied me. She might have been even more wary now than the first time she'd stumbled on my clearing on the cliff over the lake. The thought made my stomach twist.

It was my fault. I'd betrayed her, not just once but over and over. That kind of wound could take a long time to heal.

"Where are you going?" she said abruptly. The warm

breeze tickled past me and ruffled the dark waves of her hair. The leaves hissed together overhead.

For some reason it hadn't occurred to me that she'd come to ask about my plans rather than to tell me something. My tongue stumbled. "I—what?"

She folded her arms over her chest. "Where are you *going*? I saw you head off this way a few days ago, and when I went after you, some super powerful ward shoved me back. What's out here?"

Ah. Maybe I should have been amused that she hadn't picked up on my trips into the forest sooner. A small part of me balked, but at the same time, my spirits lifted. This could be one more way for me to show her how open I'd be with her now—how much of my life I was willing to trust her with. And that might help her trust me more in turn.

If I didn't terrify her, that was.

I beckoned for her to join me. "It's nothing illicit. The wards are to make sure no Naries stumble on the spot— and some of us like to be sure of privacy in general."

"Privacy for what?" she said, but she eased after me without hesitation. I had to remember that Rory didn't terrify easily.

"Shifting." My gaze veered away from her as I said the word. I was proud of my talent, make no mistake there, but it wasn't something I generally talked about. Not many students had enough control over their powers to perform a full shift, and those who couldn't sometimes got a little weird about those who could. "There's a clearing set up out here for those of us who are capable of performing that magic, so that we can practice without being disturbed. Easier to keep the transformations hidden when we have a spot off in the woods."

"Oh," Rory said, sounding a little startled. "That makes sense. I didn't even realize." She paused and glanced over at me. "If you'd rather I wasn't there, I don't have to tag along. I'm sorry about the questions. There are just so many secret agendas at this place, I can't help wondering when I see something odd."

And that right there was what had made me fall for this girl. She had every reason to be suspicious of me, but the second she'd recognized that I wasn't doing anything shady at this specific moment, she'd apologized and offered me whatever space *I* needed. She cared that much even after what I'd done to her. It just came naturally to her.

My throat tightened. I had to be able to pay her back for all the kindness she'd shown me, so much of which I'd thrown in her face before.

I stopped by the main ward. "Do you want to see me shift? I don't really show off the skill very much, but… I don't mind you watching. You might even appreciate my second form more than most do."

Curiosity lit in her eyes. "What do you shift into?"

I couldn't help grinning at her. "Come along, and you'll find out."

She made a face at me, but she came. When she'd passed the ward, I spoke a few words to activate it. It'd set off a chain reaction effect through other wards placed around the shifting grounds to create a ring of protection.

The clearing was only a few minutes' walk farther. Sunlight streamed down into the open circle amid the trees, nearly a hundred metres in diameter. I soaked in its heat, letting the sensation loosen my muscles and melt away any worries I had. To perform the shifting magic, I couldn't be at all distracted—one of the other reasons we took so much care to make sure we weren't disturbed.

Rory sat down with her back against a tree trunk at the edge of the clearing. Under her thoughtful gaze, another potential problem occurred to me. A sharper heat crept up my neck.

"I, ah, normally would get undressed for the transformation. I *can* shift clothes too, but it's harder and not entirely pleasant…"

Rory blinked at me, and her cheeks pinked slightly. "Er. Well. I guess I have already seen all you've got to offer." One eyebrow quirked up.

Sure, I'd been naked with her that once before, but we'd been naked *together*, not her watching me in a sort of performance. I debated with myself and then said, "I think I'll maintain a *little* modesty."

She laughed, and that reassured me enough that I started unbuttoning my shirt. I pulled it off, folded it, then made short work of my shoes, socks, and pants. The boxers could stay on. I didn't need to put everything on display, and one piece of fabric wouldn't be too hard to work with.

With the fresh air teasing over my chest and legs, I was abruptly aware of the picture I presented. Of how most other people reacted to my strength. Rory had trusted me to be gentle before. Did she still see that capacity in me, or only the brutality this body could inflict?

A fresh jolt of uncertainty shot through me, but I'd committed now. It'd be worse if I asked her to leave after inviting her here. I had to believe… that she'd see what this form really meant to me, the way she'd seen something good in me before.

It was strength, yes, but not the brutal kind. The power to protect, the power to rise above.

I dragged in a breath and lowered my head. When I spoke my casting word, the magic in my chest flared. I focused on its spread through my limbs and over my back, the burn of it up over my face.

With each wave of searing sensation, my muscles and bones stretched and expanded. The sinews ached with the now-familiar process. My jaw extended; my eyes moved farther apart. More heat burst in my back as new limbs sprouted, wings rising and unfurling with the breeze tingling over their surface.

My body shuddered and settled into its new shape. I peered down at Rory from twice my previous height, my clawed feet braced against the ground and my wings spread on either side of me. She stared up at me, her jaw gone slack.

I knew what she was seeing because I'd had to picture this form inch by inch for months before I'd been able to complete the shift. I knew it as well as my human reflection in the mirror.

A dragon stood before her, far more alive than the little sculpture she'd conjured, ruddy scales dappled with orange running along my throat and belly, purple across my wings. I didn't dare move, my dragon heart thudding as I waited for the rest of her reaction.

Her mouth snapped shut. Her eyes were still wide, but a small smile crept across her lips, growing more with each passing second. "And you asked me if I liked dragons," she said, her voice awed and amused and not terrified at all. Her hand rose to the neckline of her blouse, where the chain that held her glass dragon charm disappeared behind the fabric.

A dragon couldn't really smile—and if I tried, it'd look more like I was baring my many impressive teeth. I could put on more of a show for her, though. I came out here not just to keep up my shifting practice but to work out my body in ways I couldn't in human form.

I took a few broad steps backward and to the side, and then sprang toward the other end of the clearing. My wings caught on the breeze with a massive flap. I glided up to the level of the treetops and circled around, pulling off a roll I probably wouldn't have bothered with if I hadn't had an audience. Rory whooped in encouragement.

Bringing her here had been right. I should have known that for sure from the start. Even after she'd been angry with me, it'd only been for what I'd actually done, not for any vicious potential she imagined in me like even Declan and Jude clearly did sometimes.

I flew several circuits of the clearing until the first prickling started to spread over my skin. I could have fought against it and held the shift for several minutes longer, but the warning sensation would only escalate from discomfort to actual pain. Rory had gotten a good show already.

I came back to earth and rolled my joints a few times before I released the magic. That first moment, when my body collapsed in on itself, always sparked a flicker of panic before I caught my balance and control. I contracted the rest of the way into my natural form as easily as breathing.

Rory's face was still lit with wonder. "My mentor told me people could shift a lot larger than their human bodies, but it never occurred to me—I didn't think—" She laughed again. "That was amazing."

"Not horrifying?" I said in what I meant to be a teasing tone, but maybe some other emotion leaked into it.

Her expression turned more serious as she watched me pull my clothes back on. "Not at all. Anyone who thinks you're horrifying like that needs to have their eyes checked." She glanced around the clearing. "This isn't much space for you. Do you ever get to really fly?"

"Back at the main Stormhurst home, there's a hilly area where I can cruise around without worrying about being seen."

"I'm glad you have somewhere." Her voice softened. "Thank you for letting me see."

"Now you know all my secrets," I said with a crooked smile. I sat down a few feet away from her, my feet still bare in the soft grass. After a shift, it was nice to take a little while to linger here until the dragon impressions completely faded away.

At the tensing of her mouth, I regretted that flippant comment instantly.

"Not all of them," she said in the same quiet tone. "Connar… Will you tell me what happened with your brother? I want to hear it from you, not go by rumors."

Of course she did. And asking this couldn't have been more fair of her. Still, I closed my eyes against the rush of guilt that rose up even at the mention of Holden.

I'd told myself I wanted to show her how open I could be. How could she ever trust me completely if I wouldn't own up to the past horrors I'd inflicted? If the truth meant she never trusted me at all, then that was my own damn fault.

She'd seen the beauty in my dragon, but there wasn't anything pretty in this story.

"What do you already know?" I asked. My voice came out raw.

"What I *heard* is that you have a twin brother, and the two of you had some kind of… fight, and he never ended up coming to the university."

"That's all true." I forced myself to look at her. I deserved to see her reaction as it played out in the moment. "I have a twin brother named Holden. Non-identical, not that you'd ever need to worry about confusing us these days." I exhaled shakily. "It was always going to be a complicated situation. The inheritance of the barony is usually decided by seniority, but when you're only a couple of minutes apart, that's not considered enough of a deciding factor."

Rory knit her brow. "So you were expected to fight it out?"

"Not exactly. Even with siblings who are farther apart in age, occasionally the older one abdicates because they don't really want to rule, or they feel their younger sibling will do a better job… We should have had lots of time to decide. I don't think either of us was really in any position to hash it out before we'd even come into our magic, and it's going to be more than fifteen years still before my mother ages out and anyone needs to take over."

My fingers twisted into a patch of grass. The violence had been so stupid, stupid and pointless.

Rory watched me quietly until I was ready to continue.

"My parents… are very competitive," I said. "If you've heard about my brother, you've probably also heard that my mother wasn't the original heir to the Stormhurst barony either. She grabbed it from my uncle."

Rory inclined her head. "That part did get mentioned too."

"I guess it must have really gnawed at them, the two of us having equal claim—not knowing who the real heir was. They wanted to know who was stronger as soon as possible. Or maybe they just enjoyed jerking us around… Anyway, pretty much from the moment my mother took over the barony, she and my father started pushing Holden and me into conflicts. Setting up little competitions where only one of us could get a reward. Punishing both of us if one of us made a mistake. Showering one of us with attention while completely ignoring the other one day, and switching it up the next. Having a brother started to feel like a punishment in itself."

"That's awful," Rory said. Her eyes had widened again, but not with any kind of awe this time.

"There are worse parents. I'm not sure I'd have been better off with Malcolm's, for example." I grimaced. "But, even with all that, my brother and I didn't really want to fight with each other. We knew our parents were the real ones at fault. And they hated that we didn't hate each other. So as it got closer to our fifteenth birthdays when our magic would show up soon, they kept ramping up their efforts."

I had to pause for a second to brace myself against the memories. "In the end, they shut us in the attic together. It's like a greenhouse up there in the summer, and they didn't turn on the air conditioning. They barely gave us any food or water, and what they did give us always tasted funny…" My impressions of that time were hazy, a mass of sweat and dizziness and a hollow stomach, powdery sensation on my tongue, buzzing in my brain. "They told us neither of us could come down until the other *couldn't* come down."

I'd thought Rory would recoil as I told the story. Instead, she eased across the grass to clasp my hand. The compassion in that contact wrenched at me.

"I think we'd been up there maybe a week when it happened," I said, willing my voice not to falter. "They'd been messing with our sleep too, conjured noises at random intervals to startle us awake. And that night—or maybe it was day, my mind was pretty jumbled by then—I heard Holden's voice shouting me awake every time I started to drift off. I was so fucking tired and starving and dizzy with the heat… I snapped. I don't remember what I was thinking; I just remember hitting him, so hard, as hard as I could so that he would just stop. So that it would all stop."

My throat closed up. The hand Rory wasn't holding had clenched against the grass.

"I broke his back," I forced myself to say. "And fractured his skull. He's paralyzed from the waist down, and the brain injury—he's still in there, but he can hardly communicate, can't get his words out well enough to do much in the way of casting. Which is why there wasn't any point in him coming here. But I can't say that I feel like I won."

"Of course you don't," Rory burst out. "Your parents —Christ—they tortured you until you broke, like anyone would if they were beaten up enough."

I swallowed hard. "Yeah, but I broke first. He never came at *me*."

"Connar…" She squeezed my hand so tightly the bones ached. "I still don't think you're a horrible person. *They're* the horrible ones. I can't even—to put your own kids through that—" She let out a wordless sound of fury. As if I were worthy of defending.

It occurred to me that I did owe someone else one more thing. "You should know," I said, "even after that, Malcolm never treated me any differently. Declan and Jude—well, they'd been wary from the moment my mom stole the position, and that just made it worse. And everyone at school, when I got here, just knew that I'd beaten my brother to a pulp to claim scionhood, so they kept their distance. Malcolm was the only person who made being here bearable. Who made me think maybe I could move past that. The last thing I ever wanted to do was turn on him too."

Rory got what I was saying. "When you put it that way, I can see why you'd have picked him over me. Not that you had to go that *far*—"

"I know. I panicked and I overcompensated and— there's no excuse. I was awful to you. I just wanted you to know it wasn't blind loyalty. Malcolm really has been there for me when no one else was. I just hope he can snap out of this furor he's gotten into now, because it's not good for any of us."

"No." Rory looked down at our joined hands. Her jaw worked, and she raised her eyes to meet mine again. "But I want you to know that I'll never be like that. I'll *never* expect you to hurt anyone else, to betray anyone, on my behalf. You decide what you do on your own. I just ask that you don't hurt *me*."

For the first time since she'd brought up my brother, I felt capable of a smile, if only a small one. "Yeah," I said, gazing back at her with a hum around my heart like nothing I'd ever felt before. "I think I can manage that."

CHAPTER FOURTEEN

Rory

"Well, now, I suppose we can order anything on this menu without it being a hardship to your accounts," my grandmother said with a twitter and a fluff of her silver-white curls. The laugh was supposed to tell me she was only teasing, I thought, but the ravenous gleam in her pale little eyes told a different story.

How had Jude described my paternal grandparents? "Grasping" was the word that came to mind first, maybe because I'd seen plenty of evidence of that just in the first five minutes of this lunch I'd reluctantly arranged. My grandmother had immediately vetoed the nice but casual restaurant I'd picked because I liked the food in favor of one of the town's few posh offerings. While my grandfather was more subtle, he'd already made an inquiry about the Bloodstone collection of vehicles hinting that I couldn't possibly need all of them and should gift one to him.

I'd have been happy to hand over a car or three if it meant the senior Evergrists would have gone away and never hassled me or Declan again, but I had the feeling they'd be like a toddler handed a cookie to soothe a tantrum. As soon as you gave in once, they'd come back kicking and screaming for another even more insistently than before.

Thankfully, the Bloodstone accounts *could* handle the entire menu with no trouble at all, so I pretended I'd only heard the comment as a joke. "Order whatever you like," I said, and picked out a Cobb salad for myself. I could get through that and therefore this lunch pretty fast.

It was hard to imagine what kind of son these people might have raised. If he'd been anything like them, it was even harder to imagine what my mother, as the heir of Bloodstone, would have seen in him beyond the grasping for power. But then, people didn't always follow in their parents' footsteps. Connar was clearly nowhere near the monster his parents had tried to bully him into being.

The memory of that recent conversation brought a fresh ache of sympathy into my chest. God, to be raised by people like that—to be brutalized and battered into brutalizing in turn... I restrained a shudder.

I wanted to think that my birth parents hadn't been anything like that. That if I *had* been raised by them, my life wouldn't have been horrific. But... I really didn't know, did I? How a mother responded to a newborn might be very different from how she'd act as that kid grew up, as the expectations grew. From the pictures in their photo album, my Bloodstone mother had been friendly with Malcolm's dad, who was his own brand of asshole.

And she'd also connected herself to the two people sitting across from me, who turned on the viciousness in their falsely sweet way the second after our meals arrived.

"So," my grandmother said with a sharp smile as she speared a piece of her pasta, "you've become quite fond of that Ashgrave boy, have you?"

My fingers tightened around my fork instinctively. I kept my expression and my tone as blasé as I could manage. "Well, you know, he's a fellow scion. It's good for us to get along."

My grandfather cleared his throat. "It looked as though you were more than 'getting along'."

Declan had stonewalled them, so they were looking to get some telling admission from me. Fuck that. I smiled back at them, my mind leaping to a possible diversion. "Oh, at the country property? That was more like a study break. I've had a lot of catching up on my magical practice to do, as I'm sure you can imagine, and sometimes it's hard to concentrate on campus. I've actually found I'm enjoying the company of the other scions more when I'm not studying."

That wasn't the direction they'd wanted to steer me in, but my grandmother's gaze lit up eagerly anyway. She just loved gossip, no matter what information she was getting. "Oh, really," she said in a cajoling tone. "I suppose they are all a fine lot of gentlemen."

Gentlemen was probably not the word I'd have used for all the scions, but I could go with that.

I set my face in a dreamy expression. "They are. Jude can be so charming—and Connar... There's something about a guy that physically powerful..." I shook my head as if in bemusement, although my mind had slipped back to the awe-inspiring form he'd shifted into the other day. That dragon—I couldn't have drawn or sculpted anything so vibrantly spectacular. "The hard part is deciding who I want to focus on. But I guess there's nothing wrong with playing the field, right?"

"Of course not," my grandmother said, but she looked a tad disgruntled. Me dallying with those two scions didn't give her any blackmail material. She obviously hadn't let go of her main goal, though, because a few bites later, she remarked, "The Ashgrave boy should be more careful about appearances. I don't think it'd do for him to seem to be getting too close to a student he's supposed to be helping teach, scion or not."

"I'm sure he's well aware of that concern," I said, resisting the urge to grit my teeth.

My grandparents prattled on about this thing and that —what I should do with the Bloodstone properties, how much they'd like visiting access to one of them, various possessions of my father's they wondered pointedly about —until our plates were cleared. I couldn't summon the bill fast enough. I'd thought I'd make my escape then, but as we stepped out of the restaurant, my grandmother grabbed my elbow and tugged me in the opposite direction from the road to campus.

"It's been so long since we had you with us, we must extend the visit a little longer. We can have a stroll and window-shop."

Somehow I suspected "window-shopping" was going to turn into "make noises about how lovely it'd be if Rory bought one thing or another for us." And even if it didn't, I had zero desire to spend one minute longer in the company of these people, family or not.

"I actually have to get back to school for class," I said. The class in question wasn't for another hour and a half, but they didn't know that.

"Oh, what are they going to say if you miss one? You're the Bloodstone scion! You deserve to enjoy some freedom."

Walking around with her clutching my arm wasn't exactly what I'd consider freedom. I suppressed a wince as her fingers dug in tighter, groping for a way to refuse more firmly without totally pissing her off—because Lord only knew how she'd retaliate against me or Declan then—and of all people, Professor Viceport came ambling down the street toward us.

I tensed automatically, expecting my difficulties to multiply, but my new mentor glanced over the three of us, and something shifted in her reserved expression. She strode right up to us.

"Miss Bloodstone," she said. "I believe you're wanted on campus, as soon as you can get there. A concern about your project."

She put a slight emphasis on that last word and gave me a meaningful look. I stared back at her, only fully comprehending when she turned her gaze on my grandparents with a tight slant of her lips.

I'd finally found someone the Physicality professor liked even less than she liked me. She must have recognized my discomfort, and she was offering me an escape route.

"I'd better get on that right away," I said gratefully, extricating my arm from my grandmother. "So sorry to run, but my summer project has a tricky balance to maintain. The whole thing could end up ruined."

"But—" my grandmother started.

Professor Viceport interrupted her with a curt little cough. "Miss Bloodstone's education must be a high priority to her family, I'm sure, considering the time she's lost from it."

My grandmother snapped her mouth shut. My grandfather, at least, looked chagrinned. "Of course," he said to me. "You do us proud now."

Gladly. "I'm sure we'll talk again," I said. I couldn't quite bear to add a "soon" to the end of that sentence. With a brisk wave, I hurried away.

The afternoon class I actually needed to attend had been labeled as Illusion, but when I looked at my schedule again as I got ready to leave, I noticed the location wasn't a classroom but someplace called "Casting Grounds." Where the hell was that?

To my relief, when I set off to figure that out, I ran

into Imogen on the green. "Hey," I said. "Can you tell me where the Casting Grounds are?"

"I can show you," Imogen said with a quick smile. "I'm heading there too. Looks like we're learning by example today if they're calling everyone out there. It's a clearing in the west woods not too far from the lake for larger scale practice in conjuring and illusions."

She led me past Nightwood Tower and across the west field to the woods. When we reached the clearing after about a ten-minute walk through the forest, it turned out to look pretty much the same as the Shifting Grounds where Connar had shown me his mythic transformation: a wide circle of trimmed grass framed by trees on all sides. I guessed there had to be wards up here too, preventing Naries from wandering out this way when we were working magic.

As Imogen had suggested, it looked like all the fearmancer students currently on campus had been called to this lesson. A few dozen students already stood along the edge of the clearing. Professor Burnbuck, who'd taught my Illusion seminars so far, was poised in the middle of the grassy space with a woman whose name I didn't know but who was probably the junior Illusion instructor.

"Come around, spread out," the woman said with a sweeping gesture. "No need to cluster together. We want you all to have a good view."

"What's happening?" one of the other students asked.

"Some of our most advanced students will be giving a demonstration in the full capabilities of illusionary magic,"

Professor Burnbuck said with a tip of his head toward a few figures gathered at the far end of the clearing.

I drifted away from Imogen, studying that bunch. Jude wasn't with the group or anywhere else around the clearing that I could make out. Surely he should be part of this demonstration? I might not have appreciated his prank with the illusionary bears last term, but there was no mistaking he had plenty of skill in that area. As scion, he was probably the best in the school, just like Connar was in Physicality.

Was he off somewhere getting drunk again? Or getting into some other kind of trouble? My stomach clenched at the thought.

The rest of the students must have arrived. As Professor Burnbuck began his introductions, I spotted Victory and her crew across the clearing from me, Victory shooting me a narrow look before turning her attention to the professor.

The first advanced student stepped forward to show off his skills. I stepped closer to the trees as he sent a streak of light singing around the clearing—and nearly bumped into someone I hadn't heard coming up behind me.

"Careful there." Malcolm's voice came out smooth and quiet. He set his hand on my waist as if to steady me as I caught my balance, but it lingered there. His thumb traced a line up over my side like he'd caressed my leg through his magic the other day, and a flicker of warmth I didn't like at all raced over my skin.

"Sorry," I said flatly. "You can let go of me now."

"Are you sure that's what you want? I think you like

this." He teased all of his fingers over my side with a slow stroke, pulling them together and then splaying them.

So we were ramping up the game, were we? For a second I was torn between pulling away from him and pushing back, but the second impulse won. Walking away was backing down, wasn't it?

Even if I liked the sensation a little, he wanted this more than I did. That gave me the power.

I eased backward half a step so my body came to rest against his. The faint hitch of his chest at the contact brought a smile to my lips. "Are you sure *you* don't like it too much? I'm not the one getting hot and bothered." Just... warm and slightly distracted.

There was a moment when I thought Malcolm might be the one to back down. Then his hand clasped my waist a little more firmly. "Usually it's the people who play with fire who get burned."

"Hmm. So your mistake is assuming that you're the fire in this equation when it's actually me."

I adjusted my stance just a smidge, just enough to create a bit of friction between us as I moved. Malcolm's hand slid to my hip, his voice rough when he spoke next.

"Not so good anymore, are you, Glinda?"

"I guess that depends on your definition of 'good'."

The glide of his thumb over my hipbone sent a deeper flare of heat to my core. I concentrated all my attention on the display the first advanced student was just wrapping up, willing my body's reactions to fade into the background.

It was kind of ridiculous, wasn't it? My grandparents

had been all caught up in the idea of me with Declan, and I'd fed them that story about bouncing between Jude and Connar, but I'd been more physically intimate with the guy behind me than any of those three in the last couple weeks.

That thought might have given me more pause, except as the student giving the first demonstration stepped back, Victory made an odd gesture with her hand. My back stiffened in recognition that she was casting before I even saw what she'd produced. Then my entire body froze.

She was playing with illusions too. A white mouse shimmered into being in the middle of the clearing between us, floating in mid-air—larger than Deborah was so people could see it from the fringes, but I had no doubt it was my familiar she intended to represent.

In that moment, I forgot Malcolm completely. I sucked in a breath, and the mouse's body began to tear apart limb by limb. It shuddered and spasmed as one leg wrenched off its abdomen, then another, then the chest flayed open with a spurt of blood—

My stomach heaved. I had to clamp my mouth shut to avoid spewing half-digested Cobb salad all over the grass. Across the clearing, a triumphant grin had curved Victory's lips.

She still hadn't learned her lesson.

I balled up all my horror at her display and whipped a surge of energy toward the illusionary mouse with a tautly whispered word. My magic flung the image straight at her, so abruptly she had no time to dodge.

The white ball of fur exploded in a burst of far more

blood than any mouse's body could really contain, splattering Victory's face and blouse.

It wasn't real gore of course, any more than the mouse had really been Deborah. But I'd thrown a metallic stink and the tacky feel of congealing blood into my casting, and she'd be experiencing all of that as if it were real. With a yelp of dismay, she swiped at her face and arms—but she couldn't dislodge an illusion like that.

She caught my gaze from across the clearing, looking twice as fierce with red streaked across her forehead and cheeks. I didn't have to find out what she'd have tried to do to me next, though, because Professor Burnbuck lifted his voice right then.

"Thank you for the additional demonstration, but I'd appreciate it if we could get back to the ones planned now."

He shot a firm glance Victory's way. I wasn't sure he'd even realized who she'd been sparring with. She took a step back and then faded farther out of sight between the trees, presumably to dispel my illusion.

Malcolm leaned close enough that his breath spilled warm over my hair, bringing me back into tingling awareness of his presence. "Not so nice at all, Bloodstone. You do have that fearmancer viciousness in you somewhere, don't you?"

His voice held a smolder hotter than before, as if watching me lash out had turned him on. The heat of it sank right into me. "Maybe you should keep that in mind when you're trying to mess with me," I shot back.

"Mmm. I don't mind if you pay me back for this kind

of messing around." His mouth grazed the back of my head. His fingers caressed my hip again, and the heat he'd provoked in me pooled between my thighs.

"Oh, yeah?" I made myself turn to look up at him. I'd known how I meant to end this, but the hunger in his gaze stopped me for a second, radiating into me.

I remembered that one kiss. I remembered how good it had felt. An echo of the sensation tingled over my lips.

Malcolm was obviously thinking along similar lines. His head dipped down, and I snapped out of that momentary daze. He'd just given me the perfect opening.

"What if I pay you back by leaving you hanging?" I said, and slipped out of his grasp just before his mouth could catch mine. I walked off along the edge of the clearing behind the other gathered students, not gratifying him with so much as a backward glance. As if nothing we'd just done had any impact on me at all.

It had, though, in ways I hadn't even expected. Simply walking away from him sent a weird thrill through me even hotter than what his touch had stirred. My nerves were humming with it.

It turned *me* on, knowing I could provoke that hunger in him and leave him wanting.

I came to a stop several feet away from him to focus on the demonstration again, but that sudden piece of understanding settled inside me with an uncomfortable jab. What did it say about me if I could enjoy jerking someone around like that, even someone who'd jerked me around as much as Malcolm had before? How much of the predatory fearmancer instinct was innate, something waking up inside me rather than something I'd escaped when the joymancers had taken me?

Had my birth mother even liked my dad… or had he simply been useful to her in some way I couldn't comprehend yet? Maybe I was following *her* footsteps in ways that never would have occurred to me.

A sour flavor filled my mouth. I made myself raise my chin as I listened to the next planned illusion with its swell of music.

I didn't have to be as cruel as most of the fearmancers I'd met could be. I didn't have to be as calculating. But if I had the instincts to fend for myself in a community full of predators… was it really so wrong to use them?

CHAPTER FIFTEEN

Rory

I wasn't so naïve as to think that my take on the summer project would go undisturbed. After some research in the library, I'd constructed a spell that I'd attached to the soil around Benjamin's chosen building site that should send a jolt of magic my way if anyone expended much of their own magical energy there. I'd had to bolster the spell's power a couple times a day to make sure it stayed effective, but the time and effort I'd put in proved to be worth it when the first jolt hit me just as I was rinsing my dinner dishes.

The signal shivered up my spine, and I nearly dropped the plate I was holding. I set it down on the other, unrinsed dishes that my dormmates had left behind—I still couldn't quite bear to leave all the work to the maintenance staff—and headed straight out the door, wiping my wet hands on my pants.

I took the stairs at a swift pace, my shoes clattering against the hard surface, but I could tell something had already gone wrong as I came around the outside of the building. Someone was talking in a raised, anxious voice.

Benjamin and his three friends from the architecture program were standing by the site. Earlier today, the maintenance staff they'd been allowed to rope into their plans had prepped that spot for the foundation of their scholarship clubhouse. The smell of freshly dug earth reached my nose on the breeze.

One of the girls was flinging her arm toward the cleared and flattened ground. "It's going to look awful," she was saying. "This whole idea was stupid."

"Come on," Benjamin said. "We've gotten so much done—we got the whole ball rolling. We can't stop now. I still think it's going to be great. You did awesome work on it, Cassie."

She shook her head before he'd even finished speaking. "It's taking up so much time too. I have—I have other things to get done."

Other things like whatever her various assigned fearmancers had planned? I set my jaw, staying where I was. In the fading evening light, no one was likely to notice me there beside the building. If I walked closer, onto the field, they might get nervous and scatter. None of them knew I was on their side.

Benjamin was my official "target," but I hadn't heard anyone say we couldn't cast magic on other Naries too. I trained my eyes on Cassie and gathered the energy thrumming at the base of my throat.

"You remember how great it would be to have a place where the regular students can't hassle you. Think about all the work you've put in. You're just feeling a little overwhelmed. You really do want to see this through."

As I watched, she hesitated. Then she swiped her hand across her mouth. My persuasion might have swayed her thinking, but she wasn't expressing those new thoughts to her friends.

"The staff don't really want to help us either," she said after a moment. "We're architects—and not even real ones yet—not builders. If they're going to take forever…"

Had my classmates been messing with the maintenance workers too? I made a mental note to stop by while the three guys I'd seen handling this project were out here tomorrow. But in the meantime…

My gaze slid over to where a few other students, also with the gold leaf pins that marked them as Naries, had wandered onto the field nearby. The more support my bunch had, the harder it'd be for anyone else to shake them from their goals.

"Ask what they're doing," I murmured, training my attention on the nearest guy, and then shifted my focus to Benjamin. *"Tell them the truth."*

As the one guy asked and the other explained their plan for the clubhouse where they could relax without worrying about harassment from the rest of the student body, satisfaction unfurled in my chest. I shouldn't get complacent, though. While the other Naries exclaimed over what a great idea the building was, I whispered a few more lines to shape my warding spell across that distance.

I thought I could get it to not just warn me about magic being cast, but deflect at least some of that energy. It wouldn't protect the Naries all over campus, but it'd shelter them a bit while they were joining the work out here.

Cassie had brightened with the other students' enthusiasm. It looked as though I'd kept them on track. I drew back around the building, meaning to head back up, but as I reached the green I caught a flash of copper hair as a lanky form stalked into Nightwood Tower.

Where was Jude going? There weren't any classes this late.

He must be heading up to the piano room. That was the place I'd seen him retreat to after Malcolm had torn him a new one for expressing his interest in me last term. I didn't think he turned to his music when he was in a cheerful mood.

I wavered for all of half a second, and then I hurried after him. Whatever had gotten into Jude, it clearly wasn't getting out again easily. I'd taken a chance confronting Connar the other day, and that had worked out just fine. Maybe I could figure out what Jude's problem was just as quickly.

At the very least, I wanted to try. Maybe I was angry about the way he'd treated the Naries and his lack of remorse, maybe I couldn't see us being anything more than colleagues, but I was allowed to worry about a colleague who was going off the rails. I didn't wish misery on Jude. He might have messed up priorities, but I didn't think he was an awful human being. If there was something making him miserable that I could help with... I'd do what I could.

This time, I was far enough behind that I didn't need to use any magic to disguise my approach. I knew where I'd find him without trailing close behind.

After more than three months of tramping up and down the tower's stairs, I managed to make it to the piano room on its high floor without getting winded. I stopped outside, leaning close, and a clang of aggressively played keys reached my ears. Yeah, he didn't sound happy at all.

I nudged open the door. Jude's hands jerked to a halt where they'd been moving over the keys. He stared at me for a second, his expression tight with an emotion I couldn't read. Then he said, flat and dark, "Get out."

"No." I shut the door behind me. "Whatever's going on, I think you should talk to someone about it. Drinking, skipping classes, and being a jerk to everyone around you clearly isn't fixing anything."

"And you think you can fix it?" He let out a hollow chuckle. "Let it go, Rory. You didn't want me anyway."

"So I'm only allowed to care what happens to you if I'm also willing to date you?" I came over to the side of the piano. Jude studiously kept his gaze on the instrument. A chill tickled through me with a sudden thought—what if he'd found out something to do with *me*? That was, something to do with whatever malicious plots were still going on around me. Something that disturbed him but that he didn't believe he could fight against, so he was shutting me out.

His father was a baron, after all. Jude might not have

known much when Declan had talked to him, but that could have changed.

"Look," I said, "you're going to tell me, or I'm going to pick it out of your brain. I'd rather it didn't come to that. You know I wouldn't ask so I could hurt you, Jude. Please."

He shifted his gaze back to me then, his dark green eyes steely. "You can try to take a peek in there, but I don't think you'll get very far. I've got plenty of strength in Insight."

I had actually thought I'd turn to my chosen area of magic. But in the face of his defiance, the memory swam up of how Malcolm had turned the tables on me my first day back. While I'd been shielding myself against insight magic, I'd left chinks where a persuasive spell could slip through.

Jude wouldn't expect persuasion from me. I'd been getting a lot of practice with the summer project, though. "We'll see about that," I said, and focused on his head, willing a surge of magic up my throat and onto my tongue. I shot out the spell with all the power I had in me. "*Tell me what's been bothering you.*"

I felt the spell pierce through and saw its success in the flicker of Jude's eyes. The color drained from his face even as his mouth opened by my compulsion. "Rory, don't— I found out my parents are expecting."

"Expecting…"

"A baby."

"Your mom's pregnant?" I said, puzzled. "What's so horrible about that?" He'd never seemed close enough to his parents to be devastated over the arrival of a sibling who'd take up some of their attention.

My spell was still wriggling around in his mind. He knew he hadn't given the full explanation. His jaw clenched for a second before the words wrenched out. "They don't need me anymore."

"What are you talking about? You'll still be the senior heir." Connar's explanation of the barons' system of inheritance was fresh in my mind. "You don't even know what this kid will turn out like. Will they even be old enough that your dad could make them baron when he's got to step down?"

"It doesn't matter." Jude's shoulders sagged. All at once he looked utterly hopeless, as if he couldn't see any point in even fighting this conversation anymore. He turned to the piano and gazed blankly at it. "They have a real Killbrook heir now. Out goes the fake one with the trash."

"The fake one," I repeated, staring at him. None of this made sense. Was he speaking metaphorically? "How could you be—I don't understand."

"Are you really going to make me spell it out?"

My throat tightened thinking of how I'd forced this confession out of him. I'd had no idea it'd be something this fraught, something that clearly had nothing to do with me and my security at all.

"No," I said quietly. "I'm sorry. I'll go if you want me to. But do you really think you'll feel better if you send me off with nothing to do but speculate?"

He considered that for a long moment. Then he

tugged out the keyboard guard to cover the keys and set his elbows on it, tipping his head into his hands.

"I'm not my father's son," he said in a rough voice. "I'm not a Killbrook."

My jaw went slack. "*What?* How... Why...?" My mind couldn't wrap around that idea to figure out the question I most wanted to ask.

Jude sort of answered all of them. "It was some stupid plan... They tried to have a kid for years and nothing worked, and Dad must have gotten scared about his younger brother getting ambitions if he wasn't continuing the family line, so he and my mother arranged—I don't think she even *wanted* to; it was all for him—that she would get pregnant with some other man, and they'd say the kid was theirs. It worked. That's me."

Holy fuck. My legs wobbled. I sat down on the edge of the bench, leaving as much space as I could between Jude and me. "How did you find out?" I ventured.

He sighed. "I overheard them arguing about it when they thought I was someplace else. My dad... has basically regretted it from the start. For twelve years, I had no idea why he acted like he couldn't stand me, and then—and then I find out it's all his fault in the first place—" He ran a hand over his face. "They don't know I know. I've wanted to scream it in his face so many times... but I have no idea what he'd do with me if he realized the secret's out."

"And this new baby...?"

"Means they don't need me, like I said. It was always going to come out eventually. There's a ceremony when you take the barony. But I had years and years to go yet. Now, as soon as that kid is born… He's going to want to cover up his lie. It's basically plotting treason."

Something clicked in my head through the swell of horror I was feeling on his behalf. I paused, but it gnawed at me too insistently for me to set it aside.

"Is that why you started wooing me? You figured you could ditch the barony that wasn't really yours, but stay part of the circle by marrying me?"

"I don't give a flying fuck about the barony," Jude said. "I just… Like I said, the truth was going to come out, one way or another. And you're the only mage I'd ever met who I didn't think would care. You think it's all bullshit too. And you've got the balls to say so. Why the hell wouldn't I like you? The ridiculous thing is it took me so long to realize how fantastic you are."

The flattery wasn't enough to dissuade me. "If you didn't think I'd care, why didn't you just tell me to begin with?"

"I was going to. When things got serious, I'd have told you. But then… shit went down. You got kind of judgy." He glanced at me sideways, his forehead still propped on his hands. "I wasn't going to start spilling secrets when you'd hardly talk to me."

"Jude…" With the distress he was obviously in, I couldn't bring myself to be annoyed by the way he'd described the situation. "I had no idea you had something like this weighing on you."

"Would you have been less pissed off at me if you had?" He shrugged. "I didn't know about the baby factor until a couple weeks ago. The rest is old news. You didn't want us to be anything other than colleagues—well, I'm not even that. I'm a lie. A con. I'm fucking *treason*."

"No," I said with a rush of vehemence. I scooted over on the bench to clasp Jude's shoulder. "Your father lied. Your father conned people. You had no say in it. I—I might get 'judgy', but it's never going to be about who your parents are or what *they* did or what position you're supposed to inherit."

"No? It doesn't even matter that I'm a weaker mage than everyone thinks? My father arranged to be on campus to skew the assessment results. I've only got two strengths, not three."

I let out a sputter of a laugh. "Who the fuck cares? Jude, you could be a *Nary* and that'd still have shit-all to do with whether I want to be your friend or—or whatever else. All that matters to me is what you do and what you believe."

He raised his head, his gaze holding mine, a furrow creasing his forehead. "You really mean that, don't you?" he said after a moment.

"Of course I do. It's part of how fantastic I am." I pushed my mouth into a smile to go with the weak joke.

Jude just blinked at me. His eyes had widened, his pupils dilating. Then he gave a breathless laugh and wrapped his arms around me in a tight embrace.

"Yes, it is," he mumbled into my hair. "You *are* fucking fantastic. Apparently I still hadn't really realized it."

I hugged him back, abruptly choked up. "You know

this doesn't mean—I still don't think us being a couple is a good idea—"

"I know," he said. "I promise I'm not angling for that. Can I just... hold onto you for a little while?"

"Yeah," I said, bowing my head next to his. "I can give you that." And I sure as hell wasn't letting his father or anyone else get rid of him. Maybe if I could figure out how to take this place down before it came to that—there could be some sort of asylum for people like him who needed it—

But that was a long ways away still. Right now all I knew for sure was my heart was aching for the guy in my arms and all the pain he'd been enduring behind the jokes and the smirks. Even if I couldn't see any solid future with him, I didn't really want to let him go.

CHAPTER SIXTEEN

Rory

Imogen let out a huff as we left the tower after a class, the hot July air smacking us in the face. She swiped at the sweat that had instantly started beading on her forehead.

"You know what we need?" she announced. "A swim. Let's go down to the lake."

Even thinking about the water gave me a rush of relief. "Sounds perfect."

We grabbed our swimsuits and towels and went down to the shore. We hadn't been the only ones with this bright idea. A few senior girls I didn't know particularly well were drifting around just past the boathouse. I set my towel down at the end of the dock, eyed the rippling water, and decided to take it in one jump.

The flood of cool rushing over my skin was delicious. I

surfaced with a laugh and floated on my back while Imogen entered more tentatively by climbing down the ladder. She took the last short distance with a little leap and a gasp that turned into a grin.

The water warbled around me, and the sun beamed over my skin wherever my modest bikini didn't cover it. I glided along with a light kick, soaking all the sensations in. A few parts of Villain Academy were awfully nice, I had to admit.

Imogen cruised past me, and I turned to swim after her farther across the lake. As far as I could see, dense forest stretched along the rise and fall of the rocky shoreline. I couldn't make out any cottages or other buildings. The lake was huge, but apparently we had it all to ourselves.

As we headed back toward the shallower water, a pleasant burn forming in my arms and legs with the exercise, another group came ambling down to the shoreline. A couple of guys I'd seen playing football with Connar before... and Malcolm, unmistakeable from the golden gleam of his hair. My pulse stuttered.

I had the impulse to make straight for the dock and get the hell out of there, but I summoned my resolve instead. I was just as much a scion as he was—and *any* student had a right to enjoy the lake. Why should I let his presence chase me off? I'd even kept the upper hand the last few times we'd sparred in the interesting new form of combat we'd found ourselves engaged in.

And if it was hard not to notice his impressively

muscled chest as he pulled off his T-shirt and strode into the water, this was the perfect opportunity to work on that.

Imogen had noticed the new arrivals too. She glanced over at me as we came to a stop a few feet from the dock. I made a face to her as if to say, *Not happy about it, but what can you do?* and started treading water.

"How's your summer project going?" I asked. I wasn't sure which Nary student Imogen had been assigned to or what her plans for the kid were, and to some extent I hadn't really wanted to know. She was the only even sort-of friend I had here at the moment. But it was probably better to know just how malicious she could be toward the Naries than to bury my head in the sand.

"Oh, I don't know," she said with a bit of a groan. "I didn't know what to pick as a goal, and what I went with is so low key I don't think anyone will be impressed." She dropped her voice, mindful of the fact that one of her competitors might be among our fellow swimmers. "I got one of the music program girls. I'm just encouraging her to listen to and then learn how to play songs by one of my favorite bands. It seemed like something I could pull off."

And not particularly harmful. The tension that had gripped my gut as I'd asked released. "You're expanding her musical horizons," I said with a smile.

"Yeah. I know I'm not going to win—there's never really any chance of that. I only come because my dad's got to be on the grounds during the summer anyway, and maybe the extra work will help improve my skills."

The lake's currents had been shifting around me the whole time, but right then one seemed to condense, teasing around my bare torso like a tracing of soft fingers. My skin tingled, and I caught myself just before my gaze jerked toward Malcolm.

Who else could it be? I didn't have to give him the satisfaction of showing I'd noticed his efforts.

He and his friends had stayed where they could stand on the lake bottom, the water up to their shoulders, with shouts and laughter as they tossed what looked like a frisbee conjured out of water between them. Malcolm had his back to me at the moment, but I guessed he'd gotten a clear enough sense of where I was before he'd taken his current position.

I paddled a little farther out, where I could also more easily keep an eye on him without being obvious about it. With a casting word I hid in an exhalation, I swiveled my hand by my side under the water. We'd see how well *he* could concentrate with currents caressing across his chest.

"How about you?" Imogen asked as she drifted after me. "Are you happy with your progress? We're already almost halfway through."

I thought of the foundation I'd seen laid out this morning, ready for the rest of the building to commence. The staff on the job might be working slowly, but the clubhouse was coming together piece by piece. "I think it's going well. I'll tell you the details when it's done."

She arched her eyebrows, and I wondered if she could already guess that I might be responsible for the activity on the field.

Malcolm hadn't shown any sign of reacting, although his spell was still licking across my belly. I drew my fingers down through the water to send my spell stroking over the planes of his own abdomen, just as the conjured disc soared toward him.

Malcolm's arms twitched, and the watery frisbee flew past his reaching hands. I suppressed a triumphant smile.

He must have redirected his own spell in retaliation, because a few seconds later, it flowed up my front, over the fabric of my bikini. The caressing sensation swept across the curves of my breasts and kissed my nipples with a jolt of pleasure that made me gasp.

Imogen knit her brow. "Are you okay?"

Fuck. I hoped he hadn't heard that sound. "Yeah," I said, fighting to keep my voice steady as the current stroked over my breasts again. "I think a fish brushed my foot. Silly thing to get startled by."

Despite the cool of the water, a flush was rising in my cheeks. Nope, if Malcolm thought he was winning this battle, he could forget about it. Without letting myself second-guess the idea, I raked my fingers even farther down.

Even from some twenty feet away, I heard Malcolm's breath catch as the current would have flowed over his groin. The throw he'd been about to make went wide and crashed into the water.

His friend shook his head with a chuckle and conjured a new disc. "You're off your game today, Nightwood."

I'd braced myself, but I still wasn't quite prepared for the rush of heat as the current shifted against me again. It slid over me until it reached my thighs and trailed over then just below the spot where they joined. An ache formed there, begging to be satisfied, even as I kicked my legs to try to disrupt the spell or at least distract myself from its effects.

I curled my fingers into a cupped shape, and Malcolm let out a sudden cough that might have been disguising a groan. The water flicked right up over my clit, and I closed my eyes with a clench of my jaw to hold back a whimper.

"Rory?" Imogen said tentatively.

"A little dizzy," I managed to answer. "Must be an aftereffect of the heat."

"Do you want to get out?"

Before I had to answer, the purposeful current fell away, leaving only a faint echoing of sensation in its wake. When I opened my eyes, Malcolm was motioning the other guys out of the lake. "I'm cooled off now. Let's find something more interesting to do."

He was giving up. I'd won again. This victory didn't feel all that sweet, though. An unsettling heat was still coursing through my body.

He wrapped his towel around his waist awfully quickly, I noticed. As soon as the guys were well on their way, I pushed myself toward the dock. "I think that's enough for me."

Imogen climbed out after me. I tugged my towel around myself, but it didn't mute the tingling of my nerves. Malcolm and the guys had stopped halfway to the Stormhurst Building. My body balked at the idea of walking past him feeling this exposed.

Imogen started off, and I hesitated at the end of the dock. "You know, I left something in the boathouse the other day. You go on ahead."

"Okay." Her glance was curious, but even if she suspected there was more I wasn't saying, she wasn't going to push the boundaries of our tentative friendship by hassling me about it. She walked on, and I ducked into the dark interior of the boathouse.

By the far side, a motorboat bobbed in the water with a faint squeak of the cables that held it partly suspended. In the stall near me, a couple of kayaks floated. A canoe was propped on the wooden aisle that ran between the two stalls. Lifejackets hung from hooks along the wall over a rack of paddles.

I leaned against the rack, pulling my towel tighter around me. Humid air and the smell of damp pine wood enveloped me. I just needed a few minutes to gather my composure and shake off the effects of Malcolm's teasing.

My pulse had only just started to even out when the boathouse door swung open and Malcolm barrelled in.

"You," was all he said, his voice a rasp, and then he'd reached me, catching my chin to tip my mouth toward his.

I should have pushed him away. I shouldn't have liked it. But every inch of my body sang out in relief with the crash of the kiss.

My mind went blank with the rush of need. My fingers tangled in his cropped curls, digging in tight, my other hand sliding down his bare chest. He groaned against my lips. His hand caught my thigh. My towel dropped to the floor as he lifted me onto the paddle rack.

My legs splayed around his waist. His mouth trailed along my jaw and to the side of my neck with scorching heat. "We can fight more later," he muttered against my skin. "Right now—you've been driving me fucking crazy."

I couldn't find the wherewithal to disagree. The flames we'd been kindling between us blazed through me, and every press of his lips sent them flaring higher. It didn't mean anything other than getting a release.

"I've been driving *you* crazy?" I couldn't help shooting back. Other than that first kiss, he'd been the one lighting the first sparks. I'd have left him alone if he hadn't kept working magic on me.

But I couldn't point that out, because Malcolm was tugging down the strap of my top. His mouth closed over the peak of my breast with a shock of pleasure ten times as intense as anything I'd experienced in the water. I gasped and tipped my head back against the padding of a life jacket.

After a rough swipe of his tongue, the Nightwood scion leaned in to claim my lips again, his hand rising to continue his attentions on my breast. His body pressed against mine, still damp from the lake but even hotter than my own felt. His breath seared over my cheek. "God, I can't wait to be inside you."

Those words cut through my haze of pleasure like a butcher's knife. My back tensed, and my thoughts tumbled back into sharper clarity.

This was Malcolm Nightwood—my tormenter, my

enemy. I'd spent the last few months doing everything I could to keep him out of me. I didn't want him penetrating my body any more than I'd wanted him delving into my mind. The idea sent a chill through me that washed away all the heat of the moment.

I yanked myself away from Malcolm, stumbling as my feet hit the floor. Before I could make it more than a couple of steps, he caught my wrist with a chuckle.

"Where do you think you're going? I think we've had enough of a chase."

He tugged me around, and I pulled against him. My feet slipped on the wet boards. Malcolm's grasp slowed my fall, but my ass still hit the floor. He bent over me, kissing the crook of my jaw, one hand cradling the back of my head as the other ran down my body. The strength radiating from his well-built form as it loomed over me set off a flash of panic.

"Get off," I snapped.

He chuckled again. "We're nowhere near finished."

I smacked at him, and he snatched my wrist before the blow landed. A fresh wave of fear raced through me. It must have coursed into Malcolm, since he was the one who'd caused it, but he brought his mouth to the side of my neck without any sign of caring. My pulse stuttered.

"So you're going to *rape* me?" I said, and spat out a word full of magic. "*Off!*"

He was already recoiling when the wallop of energy slammed into him. It threw him not just off of me but staggering a few feet back. I scrambled up into a sitting position, pulling my knees up defensively and hauling my bikini top back into place.

Malcolm was staring at me, his chest heaving. "I—You *wanted* this."

He took a step back toward me, and I flinched. He must have been able to feel the shudder of my anxiety as well as seeing it. He froze, his stance going rigid.

"Not with you," I said, not quite able to smooth the quaver from my voice. "Not like that."

A waft of answering fear flowed into my chest. Fear of what I'd do next? Fear of what *he'd* almost done?

His expression had stiffened too. "I didn't mean—" he started in an uncertain tone, and then his jaw clenched. "*You're* the one who started this."

That was a fair point. I pulled myself onto my feet, groping for my towel. The feel of the thick fabric draped around my shoulders steadied me.

"I did," I said. "And I'm sorry I did. So now I'm stopping it. Don't touch me again, in any way, or I'll break every bone in your hands. Are we clear?"

He opened his mouth and closed it again. His face had paled and flushed at the same time, turning it blotchy. "I wouldn't have forced you," he said finally, his voice ragged. "Just so we're clear on *that*. I thought you were into it. I thought it was all more messing around."

My teeth gritted. "Then you weren't paying enough attention. I was fucking terrified." And he had no real excuse for not being perfectly aware of that other than he'd ignored the emotion because he'd been too caught up in his own desires.

Which he knew just as well as I did. He took another step, away from me this time, with an audible swallow. I couldn't see that there was anything else to say here. Hugging my towel around me, I hurried out of the building.

I made it most of the way to Ashgrave Hall without running into anyone. But when I reached the green, Declan was just crossing it, heading toward me. He stopped in his tracks at the sight of me, the worry that flashed across his face enough to tell me how out of sorts I must look.

"What happened?" he said, marching over. "Are you all right, Rory?"

There'd been a time, early on in my education here, when he'd asked a question like that and I'd thrown it back in his face because I'd known he wouldn't help me. Now, I could see the determination to defend me all through his posture, gleaming in his eyes. It made my throat close up.

He wasn't supposed to be defending me. He was supposed to be pretending he barely cared about me at all. I could ruin his life because of all the impulses I'd given into just as easily as I'd set Malcolm and me on that path toward near disaster.

There were a lot of problems here at Blood U, but I couldn't say I had no part in them.

I dragged in a breath. "I'll be okay. Really. Thank you. I'm sure you've got more important things to worry about."

Declan's jaw worked, but he schooled his expression to

be more detached at the same time. "If you change your mind—"

"I know." I managed a small smile that seemed to convince him. He hesitated for a second longer and then continued the way he'd been going. I dashed the rest of the way into the shelter of the dorm building with a lump of guilt expanding through my stomach.

CHAPTER SEVENTEEN

Rory

The cry rang out loud enough that it pierced my closed window and reached my ears through the hum of the air conditioning system. I jumped up from my bed where I'd been flipping through a magical text from the library and leaned close to the glass. From that angle, I couldn't make out the cause of the disturbance. A few students on the ground nearby had turned to look at something out of my view—something to the east. Where the clubhouse was being built.

My heart lurched. The spells I'd laid down hadn't given me any warning, but I knew better than to count on them to work perfectly. I dashed out the door and down the stairs, wishing for the thousandth time that the school administration had invested in elevators.

The second I came around the building, I knew my fears had been right. Several students were gathering around the construction area where the framework had just started to go up. I spotted Benjamin and a couple of his friends among them, his shoulders tight as he gestured toward the site with jerky motions. I hesitated and then let myself drift over for a closer look.

Lots of people had heard that cry. I wasn't the only one who'd come by to see what the fuss was. My presence wouldn't be too conspicuous.

As I approached, my spirits sank even lower. The boards that had gone up over the last few days lay splintered and ragged across the ground. A large stone, practically a boulder, lay in their midst, as if it had caused all that damage smashing through from who knew where.

That wasn't how it had happened at all, of course. Someone had destroyed the frame purposefully like magic, leaving that boulder to give the Naries a plausible if unexpected explanation.

Beneath the scattered boards, the concrete foundation was split with cracks, some as wide as my thumb. I winced inwardly at the sight of them. Shit. That whole slab would probably have to be dug up and laid all over again. Were the Naries supposed to believe the randomly falling rock had smashed the cement hard enough to cause all that damage too? A few damp spots gleamed on the cement in the mid-morning light—maybe they were supposed to think a sudden swelling of groundwater had contributed?

It didn't really matter what they believed. Either way, so much of the progress they'd made on the building was ruined.

One of the girls from the architecture program was

sputtering angrily, and the other boy offered her a hug, looking like he needed one too. Benjamin picked his way around the site, shaking his head, his expression stormy. From where I stood several feet away, I murmured a few words to test the wards I'd put up. They didn't respond to my magic at all. Whoever had done this had picked them apart first, so carefully the spells hadn't triggered.

A couple of the other Naries who'd been helping the architecture students had joined the onlookers. "What the hell are we going to do now?" one of them moaned.

Watching them in their obvious distress, my stomach knotted. In some ways, this was my fault. I'd come up with this idea; I'd decided I could beat all the other fearmancers in the school, direct not one but several Naries, and create some sort of permanent haven for them. I'd only had a few months to get a handle on my magic. Maybe I'd taken on too much, gotten in over my head…

It wouldn't be the first time I'd gone careening way over a line I should never have crossed. The thought of Malcolm in the boathouse two days ago, the way I'd *welcomed* his passion when he'd first come in, made my stomach turn.

I'd pushed these people so far for my goals, and now they were devastated, and I couldn't even step in and tell them I had their backs. I couldn't even promise, openly or not, that I'd make sure they could see this endeavor through. It could be I'd pumped them up for nothing but a whole lot of failure.

The doubts stole my breath. I backed up a step. Should I just let it go now? I obviously couldn't protect this project the way I needed to in order to ensure they ever finished the building...

But as I grappled with the idea of retreating, Benjamin stepped toward the others. "We can't let them take this away from us," he said, his voice raw.

The other guy from his class stared at him. "You think it was—?"

"I think those assholes had something to do with it. They can't stand the thought that we'd have our own place. That's why we needed this so fucking much." He kicked at the grass in a futile gesture.

"So, what can we do about it?" the girl said, swiping at her eyes. Tear tracks glinted on her cheeks. "I don't want to give up. I wanted this to work so badly. But... look at it."

I swallowed hard, watching them. I could see how much this project had come to mean to them on every face, in every stance. Maybe it'd been my idea, maybe I'd nudged them into taking it on, but the pain they were feeling right now, I hadn't conjured. They were upset because having this safe place amid the hostility they faced here truly mattered that much to them.

I drew up my chin. I'd dangled that hope in front of them. I'd gotten them this far. It might have been crazily ambitious of me, but I was the goddamned heir of Bloodstone, powerful in all four domains of magic, and I would *make* this thing work. Because I owed them. Because it was the one really good thing I'd started to do here.

Just let the other fearmancers try to stop me.

I walked back to the central buildings, but once I reached them I found a spot on my own and turned to watch the Naries again. "*It's just a setback, that's all,*" I said under my breath, focusing on Benjamin. "*You know you've got enough time to start over. You can start clearing away the wrecked pieces right now. The workers will start over—they're committed.*"

Or at least, they would be after I'd worked some persuasive magic on them too.

First, though, I had to rebuild my protections—and build them better—so no one shattered the building efforts all over again. I nibbled at my lower lip, thinking over the various strategies I'd read about in my research over the last few weeks. The one I'd used had seemed like the best option. Was there something I could add to it?

Maybe I just had to re-power the spells more often? If it'd help keep this site secure, I'd set an alarm to get out there in the middle of the night as well as however many times it took during the day.

The Naries had started lugging the boards off of the cracked base, tossing them into a heap to the side of the site. Obviously Benjamin had passed on the inspiration I'd sent into his head. I eased closer again, giving the site a wide berth but studying the grassy landscape around it as I considered the possibilities.

Footsteps whispered through the grass toward me. I looked up to see Connar coming to join me, his hands slung in the pockets of his slacks, his face set in that cautiously hopeful expression it often had around me these days. After his openness with me out at the

Shifting Grounds, his presence didn't make me tense up anymore. Right now I needed to strategize, not talk, though.

As Connar had apparently already figured out. He stopped beside me, took in the clubhouse site and the field around it, and glanced my way. "So this is your take on the summer project, huh?"

"Is it that obvious?" I said, a little warmth creeping into my cheeks. I'd been *trying* to keep my involvement secret, but I couldn't say that subterfuge was necessarily one of my strong points.

He chuckled softly. "Knowing you, I could make an educated guess. I think a lot of other people are starting to catch on, though, because of the scale and the direction you're going in. There aren't many students here who'd come up with an idea this ambitious that'll make it *harder* for anyone to harass the Naries."

"Which is exactly why they need a place where no one can," I muttered, and let out a sigh. All right, so the cat was out of the bag. Connar didn't sound as if he was bothered by the direction I'd taken. He had offered to help me with my magic before. With Physicality, though—I wasn't sure that was the angle I needed to take here. My previous protective spells had been a mix of illusion and persuasion.

"I need to figure out how to stop the others from wrecking this all over again," I went on with a subtle tip of my head toward the demolished structure. "I had wards up to warn me about magic being cast and to try to drive people away, but they didn't work well enough, obviously."

Connar nodded and wet his lips. "Do you... want some help?"

His uncertainty about how I'd respond to his offer sent a twinge of affection through me. "Sure. If you've got ideas, I'm happy to hear them. And if you don't mind supporting someone else's bid for the win."

He gave me a crooked smile. "Somehow I don't think seeing this thing built is about winning the contest for you. And even if it was, I'd rather see you take it. How did you handle your original wards?"

He listened thoughtfully as I explained the pieces I'd brought together and my reasoning, with a hum here and a nod there. When I finished, he turned and motioned for me to follow him. "Come on."

"Where are we going?"

"Just to the forest. It'll be easier to find what we're looking for there." He walked a few paces past the first trees and then scanned the ground. After a moment, he bent by a jutting root and picked up a rock about the size of his palm. "That's got a good heft. Look for more like that or even a little bigger. If you want something to act as an anchor, it works better if it's got some literal weight to it."

"An anchor?" I repeated, brushing the dirt off the rock and dropping it into my purse.

"You've been fixing your spells to the ground in general," Connar said, moving on with his search. "That works, but the energy tends to disperse faster when it's not tied to a specific object. And you can concentrate the magic for a stronger effect when you have a concrete thing you're imbuing. We can even reshape them so they'll conduct the energy more effectively."

That fit with some of what I'd read. A powerful mage could imbue the right object with a spell that could last centuries, like my puzzle garden. But—

"I just figured it'd be a lot easier for someone to displace them, if they can spot the object I've tied the spell to. Having the magic spread across the ground makes it harder to target a counterspell." I crouched to pick up a rock.

"True. But I think you can get around that. Embed a few of them in the dirt right before they pour the concrete again, for example. No one will be able to dig them out easily then, but you'll know where they are if you need to boost the spells."

"Right. I should have thought of that." They'd just been nowhere near the concrete pouring stage when I'd first set up my wards.

"You're new at this," Connar said calmly. "You'll get a better handle on what works best for any given situation as you gain more experience."

"As people keep telling me. I guess it's pretty obvious how far behind I still am."

Connar stopped abruptly and swiveled to face me. "You've been doing amazing, Rory. Don't let anyone tell you differently. Who else would even have tried to take on a project like that?" He waved toward the field.

Warmth bloomed in my chest at the compliment, but I found it hard to fully accept. "I think it matters more whether I actually pull it off. Ambition isn't much good without follow-through."

"Without ambition, there's nothing to follow through *on*, is there?" He picked up another rock and brought it over to me. His fingers brushed mine as I took it from him, with flickers of a different sort of warmth that were fanned by the appreciation in his eyes. "You've already gotten pretty damn far. And I'll help you make the rest of it happen. There's no harm in calling on allies." He grinned.

I'd always loved the way that bright smile could transform his chiseled face from something handsome but grim to absolutely stunning. Its effect on him and on me hadn't changed. My pulse fluttered as I smiled back at him. "You really don't have to do this," I said.

"Haven't I made it clear enough that I want to?"

It would have been the perfect moment for him to lean in and kiss me. If all the awfulness between us had never happened, he probably would have. As it was, he motioned for me to sit down next to him. "Shaping conducting pieces definitely falls into my domain. I'll show you the elements you need for a good ward anchor."

He took one of the stones back from me and cupped it in his hands. "We want this part more rounded and hollowed for the right resonance of containment," he said, the enthusiasm of sharing his knowledge animating his voice. "And a point protruding at the bottom to steady it."

I leaned close as he talked me through the process step by step, transforming that one stone carefully before my eyes and then watching while I worked with one myself.

His hand brushed mine again when he made a small suggestion. In the midst of my concentration, my shoulder came to rest against his. He nodded, his head bowed close to mine.

"That's perfect," he said softly when I'd finished.

I looked up at him, and an eager quiver ran through me at his nearness, his light blue eyes fixed on mine. The memory of how it felt to be held by him rose up with a rush of eager warmth. I couldn't say I had any doubts left about whether this change of heart was genuine. He'd thrown his lot in with me completely.

But, damn, it'd been bad enough a couple months ago when I'd been grappling with my attraction to both Declan and Jude. Those feelings hadn't faded, not really, even if I was reining them in with both guys, and something in me had sparked with Malcolm, as much as I hated that it had. Now, to feel drawn back to Connar on top of all that... What the hell was wrong with me? How could I be caught up in four different guys all at the same time?

I ducked my head, shame prickling over my skin. "Maybe you shouldn't be here. I'm a mess, Connar. You have no idea... *I* have no idea what I want. Or maybe it's that I want too many different things." I exhaled with exasperation. "It doesn't really seem fair to pull you into that."

"Rory." He touched my cheek, just lightly, but that gentle touch sent tingles through my whole body. "Look at who you're talking to. You want to talk about messes? You can't get much messier than me. The way we're raised, the kind of people we're supposed to grow up to be—I'd be surprised if there's anyone on campus who isn't some kind of mess. I don't mind. I'm not here because I expect anything from you. However much *you* want me is all I care about—and I'll take that as it is."

The tender warmth that had spread through me before stretched even further, filling my throat, wrapping around my lungs. I rested my hand on his chest tentatively.

Accepting everything he was offering wouldn't hurt him. It shouldn't hurt me either. That was more than I could say for any of the other guys right now. Connar had been the first one to really understand me.

And God, I was getting so tired of having to pull back, to walk away, to tell myself no. I didn't want to go rushing in right back to where we'd left off... but I could allow myself a little indulgence, couldn't I?

"I do want you," I said quietly, raising my eyes. When he dipped his head, I lifted mine to meet him. And his kiss was every bit as sweet as I remembered.

Once we'd started, I didn't want to stop. One kiss slid into another, each deeper and more tender than the last. I hadn't really remembered what it was like to kiss a guy I was *allowed* to want, who I couldn't ruin and who wasn't out to ruin me. The joy of it took my breath away.

I couldn't let it overwhelm me, though. Getting lost in the heat of the moment had gotten me into too much trouble already. I let myself lean into one more kiss, reveling in the press of Connar's mouth, and then I drew back, tipping my head against his shoulder instead. He clasped my hand. For a few minutes, we just sat there in companionable silence.

A thread of tension ran through my sense of peace. I shouldn't be getting comfortable at all. The conflicts of life here on campus had distracted me from my bigger concerns for too long. Professor Banefield's key was still tucked in my purse, unused.

Thanks to Connar, soon my project site would be much better protected. Protected enough that I could risk leaving campus for long enough to do some more investigating.

CHAPTER EIGHTEEN

Jude

As I stood in the entranceway of the New York City brownstone, waiting for the upper apartment to answer my buzz, my heart thumped away at an erratic rhythm. My attempts to will it into evening out had little effect.

My mission here really was a silly thing to get nervous about. Sure, I didn't have the slightest idea whether I really would be able to convince the man living in that apartment to go along with my plan, and if he did and we were found out, we could both be punished harshly under fearmancer law. I might be expelled from Blood U on top of that. And then there was the whole matter of my relationship with Rory possibly riding on this act.

But really, when you cut it down to the core of the matter, I was a Killbrook calling on a close family friend for a favor well within his expertise, and that sort of thing was standard practice. I'd never really liked claiming benefits through the Killbrook name, not since I'd found out it wasn't really mine, but if I was going to lose it soon enough, I might as well take advantage of it while I could.

Since I'd called Dr. Wolfton to arrange this appointment, he was expecting me. The door to the stairway unlocked with a click, no inquiring voice crackling through the intercom. I started up at a brisk pace. If he agreed, we might even see this mission through today.

I'd never visited the doctor at his home before. He was a regular guest at the Killbrook Manor, a close friend of Dad's from college whose placid demeanor always set Mom at ease too. No doubt he'd been dropping in on them even more than usual the last few months while I'd been at school, overseeing the early stages of Mom's pregnancy.

In the years since I'd made my world-upending discovery, I'd sometimes wondered how involved Dr. Wolfton might have been in my parents' initial attempts at producing a child. Did he know just how much they'd struggled, just how clear it'd become that they were unlikely to ever conceive? Had he ever suspected that my arrival, therefore, might have involved some trickery?

I'd studied him closely during many visits since then, and I'd never seen any sign in his attitude toward me that he saw me as a sort of interloper. The cautious insight spells I'd tried on him hadn't revealed any wariness. Actually, he was much more likely to laugh at my more cutting jokes and ask me with genuine interest how my studies were going than many of my parents' friends.

If he'd known the full extent of their difficulties, he must have thought my mother's first pregnancy was as much a bit of unexpected luck as her current one.

Dr. Wolfton opened the door as I reached his floor, smiling his usual calm smile. His whole aura was so soothing I found it hard to imagine how he ever generated enough fear to fuel his magic, but maybe he could turn on the menace as needed. Or he might make extensive use of his familiar. Unlike most fearmancers, he'd opted for a non-predator animal, but in a city mostly inhabited by Naries, a rat could generate plenty of panic just by making an appearance in a nearby apartment.

"Jude," he said in his equally calm voice. "Come on in. I'm curious to hear this mysterious request of yours."

When I'd called him, he'd offered to come by the school so we could talk, but I'd told him I'd thought it'd be better somewhere there was less chance of us being overheard—that the topic was somewhat "sensitive." Now I just had to find the right way to pitch it to him. Thankfully I should be able to count on my magic for that. Insight was my one other true strength, and one from past experience I knew Dr. Wolfton either couldn't or didn't bother shielding against very carefully.

"Thanks for letting me come over," I said, figuring it couldn't hurt to lead with politeness.

He ushered me into an apartment with a weird contrast of grand moldings, fine architectural stylings, and totally modest furnishings. "Can I get you anything to drink?" he asked.

I sank down on his linen sofa. "I think I'm all right. Might as well cut to the chase, right?"

He sat across from me in an armchair, his gaze intent. To him, I wasn't just the son of his best friend but a scion and one of his future barons, I reminded myself. He'd *want* to make me happy if he could.

"What's this about?" he said.

I clasped my hands on my lap. "I have a favor to ask. A medical favor. Someone I'd like you to perform a magical treatment on… but it would have to be done without them realizing any magic was used."

Dr. Wolfton's eyebrows rose. The hesitation that crossed his face made my gut twist.

"It would be for their benefit," I added quickly. "It's only that—the person in question is a Nary. That's why the secrecy."

His eyebrows stayed up. "And how did you become so invested in a Nary that you're going out of your way to handle their medical treatment?" he asked with a hint of bemusement.

"It's a fellow student from the university."

The doctor waited, obviously not considering that enough of an answer. I restrained a grimace. "Seeing this matter taken care of is important to me. I hardly have the skill to do it myself. That's why I hoped you could help."

Dr. Wolfton ran his fingers through his fine gray hair. "I'm assuming if the university medical staff felt they could reasonably intervene, they would have."

"They don't have half the skill you do," I said. "And you know how over-cautious they can be. I wouldn't be here asking if I wasn't sure you could pull it off."

He looked as if he was about to shake his head. Before he could express any more doubts, I leaned on my last gambit. "Actually, I am kind of thirsty. If I could just get a glass of water…"

"Of course." He got up, maybe relieved to have a respite from the awkward conversation, and walked past me through the kitchen's wide arched doorway.

I turned on the sofa to watch him. As he reached for a glass in the cupboard over the sink, I fixed my gaze on the back of his head and murmured an insight spell by way of a question. "*What do you want?*"

It was a nicely broad avenue of inquiry. I slipped into the flow of his thoughts and emotions with only the faintest hitch of a breach. Images washed over me.

Well, I couldn't offer *that*. That was too simple for a situation like this. Ah, there we were.

A smile curved my lips. I'd have him. It was only a matter of putting the offer to him in the right terms.

"Look," I said when he came back with the glass, "I realize this is a big ask. I wouldn't expect you to do it just out of the goodness of your heart. I'll repay you."

The doctor adjusted his glasses as he sat back down. "I couldn't take a fee for something like this."

"Oh, no, that's not what I meant at all." I gave him my most winning grin. "I gather there are some people you're looking to impress. I can cast some very impressive illusions."

Dr. Wolfton paused, but he couldn't hide the flash of hope that lit his eyes. My grin widened. Jackpot.

"What exactly did you have in mind?" he said slowly, leaning forward in his chair, and I knew it was only a matter of negotiation now.

Honestly, it was hard to look at the little town we'd driven into and not think it was awfully drab. Dr. Wolfton didn't look concerned as he parked down the street from the address I'd looked up, but this place was a far cry from both New York City and the elegance of the Killbrook properties.

"She has to think you're a regular doctor," I said, as if we hadn't already been over this, as if he didn't know the consequences of a mistake as well as I did. My nerves were twitching away. "It's better if she thinks the other doctors made a mistake, not that you fixed something they couldn't."

"I know," the doctor said in his usual mild tone, and patted my shoulder. "From what you described, I don't imagine it'll be much trouble. Take a walk around if you'd like to. I expect I'll be a half hour or so."

I didn't think I'd want to wander around this place, but after a few impatient minutes twiddling my thumbs in the car, I couldn't bear to just sit anymore.

My feet carried me off without much sense of direction. I ended up at a park a few blocks away. The sun beamed brightly over the whole place, warming my skin.

A woman was walking her dog in the broad grassy area. Children clambered over the playground equipment while their parents or other caretakers watched. I meandered around the fringes, feeling utterly out of place.

This was the right move, wasn't it? Suddenly my entire plan seemed ridiculous.

And yet Rory's voice rose up in the back of my head, repeating the words that had echoed through my mind over and over since the moment she'd said them. *All that matters to me is what you do and what you believe.*

I sucked in a breath, and with it my resolve steadied.

I knew her. I thought maybe I was starting to really understand her. And this—this was *doing* something. Trying to woo her all over again had never been the right tactic. She already knew how I could be with her. My charms had never been the problem.

It might be too late to fix the actual problem, but at least I could give it my best shot. And… even if this didn't change her mind about me, it wouldn't be for nothing. I'd done damage that I hadn't meant to, that the recipient hadn't deserved. Some part of me felt a little relief just knowing I might be able to reverse that. Which wasn't an emotion I'd ever have anticipated experiencing in these circumstances, but…

In the playground, one mother and father clasped their toddler's hands as they eased him down the slide. The child burst into excited laughter when he reached the bottom. I propped myself against a tree to watch, and a hollow sensation opened in my stomach.

Look at these people—these people without magic.

Was there really anything all that different about them other than that fact? Could I really say that mother and father were worse than my own? That their child deserved less than I did? God, could *anyone* deserve less than the lot my father had inflicted on me?

The thought still jarred uneasily inside me, but it was starting to sink in. The look on Rory's face when she'd said it wouldn't matter if I were a Nary, that my magic didn't even factor into what she thought of me... In that moment, it'd hit me just how much she meant that.

I had less magical skill than everyone around me believed. Did I really believe that made me less of a person than Malcolm or Connar or Declan? And if it didn't... then why would these people in front of me be anything less than some half-assed mage who could barely cast a coherent spell?

Because it let us feel powerful. Because we enjoyed having someone to lord it over. Because we were all full of fucking bullshit.

That was the way my father thought—about appearances, about clinging to status. I'd thought I was nothing like him, but I'd bought into an awful lot of the same ideals, hadn't I?

I watched the Naries go about their lives for several minutes longer, and then I headed back to the car. None of the thoughts that had been whirling around inside my head felt easy. But I'd opened my eyes to something I'd missed before, and that could only mean I was heading someplace better.

I just hoped I hadn't taken too long getting there.

CHAPTER NINETEEN

Rory

I t appeared I'd made it to Professor Banefield's home off-campus just in time. Or maybe not quite on time, considering that the truck for some storage company was parked out front and the workers were already prepping it to be loaded. Whoever Banefield's inheritors were, they'd obviously heard about his death by now, and they'd decided to pack up the contents of his house.

I watched from my car down the street, suddenly wishing I'd rented something inconspicuous rather than driving the Bloodstone Lexus from the university garage. None of the workers had glanced my way yet, but the Lexus didn't exactly fit in on this suburban street. My mentor might have been an expert at his craft, but he mustn't have been much for extravagance—or maybe he'd just downsized a lot after his wife's death. The pastel-trimmed bungalow didn't look like anything a fearmancer would want to be caught in, dead or alive.

I needed to look through the contents of that house before these people shipped them off. Something in there might fit the key he'd given me or at least lead me to the place I needed to go. Which meant I had to find some way of diverting the company for at least an hour or two to give me time for a thorough search.

My back tensed as two of the men walked up to the front door. What would make them leave—and stay away for a while? They were here to move furniture and box up the other possessions… They wouldn't be prepared to deal with anything more fraught than that.

An idea unfurled in my head as one of the workers fit a house key into the lock. As many issues as I'd had with Victory, she'd demonstrated plenty of repulsive spells I could use for inspiration. I didn't have the chance to give the brainstorm a lot of thought. As the guy pushed open the door, I muttered the word "rancid" under my breath with a flick of my hand.

My magic coursed through the air and condensed into a sensory illusion that flooded the front hall. The worker coughed and backed up a step, waving his hand in front of his face.

"What the hell?" he said. "Something's gone *very* bad in there. We can't work in a place like that."

The guy next to him caught a whiff and turned a bit green. "Call it in to the office. They've got to let the owners know to put a cleaning crew through there before we can get on with the job."

They tramped back to the truck and closed the ramp. I exhaled in relief. I couldn't imagine the inheritors would be able to find a cleaning crew in an instant, even if the storage company reached them right away. The gambit should buy me enough of a window.

I waited until the truck had pulled out of sight around a corner farther down the road and then gave it another ten minutes just to be sure. In an ideal scenario, I'd have made myself invisible so no one even saw me walking over to Professor Banefield's house, but from what I'd gathered, hiding one's self from all angles across a significant distance wasn't the sort of thing you should first attempt in potential view of dozens of Naries. Rendering myself invisible on an open street was several orders of magnitude above cloaking my descent ten feet down a solid wall.

Instead, I relied on the illusion of looking like I belonged here. I ambled down the street as if I wasn't in any particular hurry and headed down the driveway to the back of the house like I lived there.

The high picket fence around the backyard meant I didn't have to worry as much about witnesses there. I popped the lock with a quick casting and slipped inside.

My stink illusion had remained at the front of the house. I dispelled it with a word and a wave so I wouldn't have to inhale it and started my search.

The house's interior definitely gave the impression that Professor Banefield hadn't invested much energy in the space since he'd moved here. The pots hanging in the kitchen were coated with a layer of dust; a few pieces of framed art leaned against the walls in the living and dining room, but nothing had been hung. Here and there, moving boxes sat open, some with just a few objects lying in the bottom, some still mostly full.

In the second bedroom, where the mattress was bare, I came across a stack of closed boxes labeled "Delia." His wife's name, I guessed. Looking at them, a lump rose in my throat. She'd died in a car accident several years ago— while pregnant with their first kid. I couldn't imagine how awful that'd been for Banefield. Her absence must have still haunted him.

I didn't come across any safes or lockboxes. The house didn't even have furniture with locked drawers here like he'd had in his office.

After I'd riffled through every room, I came to a stop in the hallway with a sigh. If I didn't find anything here, I had no idea where to look next. This was my last lead.

If the key didn't fit anything here or in his office, then he must have another property, or a storage unit, or a safety deposit box. That would cost money. Money left a paper trail.

There'd been a file box full of receipts and banking statements in Banefield's bedroom closet. I crouched down next to it and pulled out the first few papers. Those were from three years ago. Would he have had whatever the key opened that long? I dug farther, but he seemed to have tossed records in haphazardly. Here was one from this past winter, here one from five years ago.

The growl of an engine right outside made my skin turn cold. I got up and eased over to the window. My pulse hiccupped.

Another van had pulled up outside. The inheritors had gotten their act together faster than I'd anticipated. Shit.

I wavered and then grabbed the box of financial records. These distant family members had been out of the picture so long they were only just taking care of Banefield's belongings. It wasn't likely they'd realize this box was missing... and if they did, they'd have no idea who'd taken it. Hefting it in my arms, I dashed for the back door.

The picket fence created a problem now. There was no easy escape route other than back up the driveway where the van was parked. I braced myself by the back of the building and peeked around the corner.

Four figures were getting out of the van. Two of them retrieved baskets of cleaning supplies from the back. Then they all trooped over to the house.

The door squeaked open and thumped shut behind them. I hustled along the driveway, past the van, and down the street, slowing when I'd gotten a few house-lengths away. As soon as I reached my car, I tossed the box in the trunk.

I wasn't sure I could bring that into my dorm room without raising all kinds of questions... but at least I had it now.

In the end, I opted to leave Professor Banefield's records stashed in the trunk of the Lexus. No one had messed with my car yet. It had an actual lock, unlike my bedroom door, and I enhanced that with an extra casting that should punish anyone who tried to open it by magical means with a sharp electric zap.

I headed up to the dorm intent on grabbing something to eat and then checking on the clubhouse site. When I opened the door, I stopped in my tracks, my jaw going slack.

"Shelby?"

The Nary girl turned with a swish of her mousy brown ponytail. It *was* her, with her usual shy smile as if she couldn't quite believe I'd be happy to see her.

A much wider smile sprang across my face. I grabbed her in a hug and then eased away, joy and disbelief mingling inside me. "Are you really back? Like, back in the program and everything? What happened?"

My reaction had left Shelby beaming. She raised her hand where her wrist had been broken and waggled her fingers. No cast, no sign she'd ever been injured other than a slight pallor to her skin around the joint.

"It was amazing," she said. "Two days ago, this doctor just showed up at my house. He said he looked over the records of my treatment and thought the other doctors made a big mistake in interpreting the X-rays—something about shadow fragments or I don't know what. Anyway, it was about time for the cast to come off anyway, so he took it off and led me through these exercises, gave me a cream to rub into it, and by the next day, my wrist already felt as strong as before. I can play no problem!"

I blinked. A doctor showing up out of nowhere? And her wrist *had* been broken.

The guy must have used magic to make her recover that quickly. But who would have—Ms. Grimsworth had said there was no way the school could interfere—

"The headmistress called me yesterday afternoon," Shelby went on. "She said a 'concerned party' had been following my case—I guess one of the people on the scholarship panel?—and they'd heard I might be able to continue with the courses here after all. I told her I was sure I could, and…" She gestured to herself and her room. "I just got here half an hour ago. I guess it's pretty quiet during the summer, huh?"

"Yeah," I said, still reeling. "Only some people come for the summer session." A suspicion started to form in my head. There were very few mages who knew about Shelby's situation and would have gone out on a limb like this. Declan might have wished he could, but he wouldn't have compromised his position over a girl he hadn't even known. I didn't think I'd ever talked about Shelby with Connar. So…

"It's so great to be back," Shelby said. She snatched up her cello case and hugged the neck of it. "I've got to get going—there's a class about to start and I don't want to fall any more behind—but maybe we can go get dinner tonight? Imogen too, if she's around and wants to?"

"Yeah, that'd be great. You go show them you haven't missed a beat."

I gave her a minute's head start, and then I went out too—down to the fourth floor to the dorm room across from Declan's. When I knocked, a burly guy with a scraggly moustache opened, with a little jolt of nerves that echoed into me when he saw who'd come calling.

"Hi," I said. "Ah, is Jude around?"

The guy looked as if he was afraid of what I'd do to him if he didn't produce Jude instantaneously. "Killbrook," he called over his shoulder. "It's one of your colleagues."

He stepped back to let me in, and I stopped just past the threshold. Jude emerged from his bedroom in the corner looking vaguely irritated until his gaze found me. He brightened so quickly a pang shot through my chest.

I hadn't thought he was capable of caring enough about the damage he'd done to make real amends. I hadn't been sure he could even understand that harm done to a Nary was actual damage.

He strode over, his gaze never leaving my face. "She's back at school?" he said, erasing any lingering doubts I might have had about who Shelby's mysterious benefactor had been. "It all worked out?"

The lengths he must have gone to—my God. And he looked not just pleased with himself but *relieved*, like he'd really been worried about whether his efforts would succeed.

"It worked," I confirmed. "You…"

No words felt adequate. A couple of his dormmates were watching us, and the urge rose up inside me to show both him and them how much I adored him in this moment. I clasped the front of his shirt and tugged him into a kiss.

I'd meant it to be a quick one, not much more than a peck. But Jude made a tight sound and kissed me back hard, and it took me a few seconds to think of anything other than the intensity of his mouth against mine. I managed to swallow a gasp as I drew back.

"How did you—" I started, lowering my voice, and hesitated with the awareness of our small but avid audience. "Is there somewhere we can talk?"

Jude's head twitched toward his bedroom, but he must have had the same awareness of the thin walls as I did.

"Come on," he said, setting a tentative hand on the small of my back to guide me. "There's the scion lounge."

His hand dropped away as we went down the stairs, but he sidled a little closer. "So, that kiss," he said in his teasing tone. "Was that just a one-time, 'thank you so much' kiss, or was that a 'you're the love of my life, Jude, and I never want to stop kissing you again' kiss?"

I elbowed him, but I couldn't help smiling. "Maybe give me a little more time to decide?"

"I suppose that's fair." His cavalier attitude faded for a second, his expression turning serious. "I didn't help her only because I knew you'd appreciate it. It wasn't just some kind of ploy to win you back. I—I wanted to do the right thing. I don't want to be responsible for screwing up people's lives. Maybe that's a little hard to believe—I'm not sure I'd have believed it a few months ago—but, if you want to poke around inside my head to see I mean it, or—"

"It's okay." I touched his arm, the earlier pang coming back at his fumbling earnestness. "I believe you." Something had changed in his perspective, something that hadn't quite clicked all those weeks before. It would've been easier to pull off a scheme like this when Shelby had first been injured, and I'd have been just as happy about it then, but he'd needed time to find his way there.

And after our conversation in the piano room the other evening, we were way past lying and pretense. Maybe it'd been something about the vulnerability of his confession that had opened him up in other ways too.

I hadn't given much thought to the location he'd suggested until I was descending the basement stairs and my chest clenched up. It squeezed tighter as I stepped into the lounge room with its cluster of seating, the pool table, the bar cabinet.

The last time I'd been in this room, the guy standing next to me had made me believe he was feeding Deborah to his familiar. He'd smirked at my panic.

Jude noticed my reaction and stiffened with a wince. "Maybe this isn't the best place after all. We could go outside somewhere…"

I shook my head, letting the emotions well up inside me. "No. What happened here really happened. If we can't face that, then we haven't gotten anywhere."

He turned to me, his head bowed. "I'm so fucking sorry," he said hoarsely. "If I'd known—if I'd seen—" He let out a frustrated sound. "I should have been the one bowing down to you."

He dropped to his knees as he said it, in a motion every particle in my body rejected, especially after what he'd told me about his parentage. I grasped his shoulder with the urgent need to bring him back onto his feet. "No. You're not less than I am. You're never *less*."

I wasn't sure he believed me, but as he got up, his gaze searching mine, it struck me how it must have felt to him back then. What it must have been like for a guy who'd spent the last seven years knowing he was wearing a false crown, that at any moment the rug could be pulled out from under him and he'd lose everything, faced with a girl who'd had all the same handed to her in an instant only for her to try to throw it away.

Of course some part of him had hated me. He hadn't known any of the other things I was going through.

I leaned in again, seeking out his lips, wanting to confirm the connection we had now. Jude cupped my face as he met me. This kiss, I let linger on, soft and tender. The two of us, together. Understanding each other. There was something miraculous about how far we'd come to unite in this moment.

Jude's hand lingered against my cheek as our mouths parted. "Well," he said, "I'm glad to know it was at least a two-time thing."

A laugh tumbled out of me, but I didn't think his question before had been totally in jest. "I'm not making any declarations about the 'love of my life' anytime soon, just so we're clear." I thought of Connar in the forest, the comfort I'd taken from his embrace. "I can't even say you're the only one I'm going to be kissing. You should know that."

"You're a woman who wants to keep her options open," Jude said with a nonchalance I could tell took some effort. "I can respect that. I'll simply endeavor to continue to be the most appealing option." He paused, and his eyes narrowed slightly. "You and Connar…?"

And Declan. And Malcolm. Although I supposed the former didn't matter since he'd rejected any possibility of a real relationship, and the latter didn't because no way in hell was that happening again. So, Connar. I decided it couldn't hurt anything to admit this much. "To be fair, he was there first, before anything ever happened between us."

"He—*what?*" Jude looked so flabbergasted by this announcement it was almost funny. "When—*how*—you're joking."

"Nope. While you were busy figuring out ways to make me miserable, he and I ended up talking and getting to know each other, and one thing led to another…" I spread my hands.

"But—I saw him lay into you."

My expression tensed. "That was after. I'm not saying there weren't any hitches along the way. But you've had plenty to sort through too, haven't you?"

"Still. Connar."

I socked him in the arm. "I don't think the rest of you give him enough credit. He's more than just a musclehead, you know." How much did the other scions even know about what had really gone down with Connar's parents, with his brother? That part wasn't my story to tell, though.

"Okay, okay. He's a great guy. I just need to be greater." Jude winked at me, having recovered his composure, and I relaxed again.

I nudged him toward the couch. "We'll see how that

goes. Are you going to tell me about your grand plan to restore Shelby to Blood U or not?"

He grinned. "Well, I can start by telling you that I'd better not need any *other* favors from Ms. Grimsworth in, oh, the next few centuries or so…"

CHAPTER TWENTY

Rory

I wasn't sure I trusted Lillian Ravenguard and her assistant all that much more than I did my grandparents, but at least brunch with them was a hell of a lot more pleasant than that earlier lunch. Lillian had encouraged me to pick the place and ordered off the menu without any hinting commentary, and she was paying for her and Maggie's meals anyway. Why Maggie had come along when her employer could be present no one had explained, but the younger woman was enthusiastic enough company that I didn't mind.

"So what's your summer project this year?" Maggie asked not long after we'd sat down in the café. "I remember having some pretty intense assignments during my school days." Which, from the look of her, couldn't have ended more than a few years ago.

When I explained the gist of our task, Lillian leaned

her elbows onto the table with an intent expression. "And how are you approaching that mission?"

"Oh," I said, feeling abruptly awkward. "My Nary is in the architecture program, and I've got him designing and arranging for the construction of a small building on campus." I hesitated to say anything about the intended purpose of that building or how I was attempting to protect as many other Naries as I could from the other students' influence. From the calm way the blacksuit and her assistant had reacted to the general idea of the summer project, they obviously didn't see Naries as worthy of protection.

"Make use of his strengths." Lillian nodded. "That's a solid approach. I look forward to hearing the final outcome. Your mother won the summer prize at least once during her school days."

"Did *you* ever win?" Maggie asked with a little smile.

Lillian laughed. "No, I don't think I was quite creative enough." She waved a finger at me. "The professors like to be surprised, in a good way. Keep that in mind."

Well, I was pretty sure they'd be surprised by the angle I'd taken when the whole thing was finished, although whether it'd be in a good way by their standards was debatable. If the clubhouse actually *got* finished, that was.

"If there's any aspect you're finding particularly challenging, I'd be happy to talk it through with you," Lillian added as our food arrived with a buttery whiff of fresh-baked breakfast rolls. "You can be sure all the other students are drawing on their parents' and other experienced mages' expertise."

There were probably all sorts of facets of my project that a blacksuit could advise on, but that would mean admitting my intentions. Between my strengths and Connar's, we seemed to have the situation under control.

"Thanks," I said with a smile. "I think everything's going to plan right now, but I'll keep that in mind if I run into any problems."

Besides, I hadn't accepted Lillian's brunch invitation to talk about my summer project. I had another, unofficial project to tackle that was both much more important and much more secret. I'd spent a good part of the night figuring out the best questions to ask that might help me find what I was looking for in those papers I'd stolen from Professor Banefield's house.

"I was wondering," I said carefully, digging my fork into my slice of feta and spinach quiche, "I found a couple of notes in the Bloodstone house that my mother wrote that suggested she'd sent a few valuables to be stored off the property, but I haven't been able to figure out where. Is there sort of a standard company or bank or whatever that fearmancers would normally work with for something like that?"

Lillian considered me with evident curiosity, and I kept my expression as innocent as I could. I hadn't found any notes like that at all, and as far as I knew all of the Bloodstone valuables had stayed on Bloodstone ground, but I didn't think even a best friend would assume she knew every little thing a person had done with her possessions. And I couldn't exactly ask where Professor Banefield might have stashed important materials without raising a whole lot of other questions I wasn't ready to answer.

"What sort of valuables?" Lillian asked.

"There weren't any details—it was all pretty vague." I offered a sheepish shrug. "Maybe she never ended up doing that. I just wondered so I'd have the right context if I stumble on any more information."

Maggie tapped her lips. "Most of us have our accounts with Yewsley," she said. "They've got a few fearmancers in the upper management, so there's that extra level of security. Most of their branches would offer safety deposit boxes."

"You'd have to know which branch to narrow it down," Lillian said. "Do you want me to look into that for you?"

"Oh, it's really not urgent," I said quickly. "I'm sure you've got a ton of much more important things to take care of. I'll see what I can find the next time I'm home and if I'm still stumped then maybe I'll call in that favor."

Yewsley. I did remember seeing that name on some of Banefield's records. I'd have to scrutinize those more closely.

The other question required even more care. My heartbeat sped up as I braced myself, pushing through a moment's doubt. "There was also—do you have any idea what she'd have meant if she mentioned a 'reaper'?"

Maggie frowned with what looked like genuine puzzlement. Lillian... If I'd had any hope of breaking through a top blacksuit's mental shields, I'd have given all the magic in me to use an insight spell on her right then.

Her face went blank, but so perfectly it was hard to tell whether she was completely confused or making very, very sure she didn't give anything away.

"A 'reaper'," she repeated, with a quizzical tip of her head. "Where did you see that?"

"It was just—she liked to write thoughts in the margins of her books sometimes, you know?" That much was true, to make this story plausible. "I was looking through the library and one of them said something like 'tell reapers'... I don't remember exactly. It didn't make much sense to me. There aren't actually, like, mages who go around like the grim reaper deciding on deaths or something, I assume?"

I added a giggle to show how absurd that idea supposedly was to me, even though it actually sounded reasonably plausible given how many deaths this community seemed to orchestrate.

"Odd," Lillian said, in a voice as carefully even as the blankness on her face. A prickling sense crept over me that she *did* know something. The blacksuits should know more than just about anyone when it came to the inner workings of fearmancer society, right? But I couldn't even tell whether reapers were a good thing or a bad thing from her response. Damn it.

She swirled her fork in the yolk of her eggs benedict. "You'll have to show me that book some time. Maybe with the proper context there, I'd be able to connect the dots. Your mother had a poetic side—it might have been some kind of metaphor."

"I'll see if I can find it again," I said. There were a few

thousand books in the Bloodstone library, so it wasn't likely Lillian would be able to determine I'd been lying about the note in the first place. I didn't think Banefield would have answered my question about who'd wanted him to attack me with metaphors, though. *Some* group literally called themselves reapers. And that group had wanted to destroy me.

I'd have felt a lot better if I'd known whether Lillian was trying to protect me from that fact or protect them from threat of discovery.

The tension that had balled in my stomach while I'd maneuvered through that conversation didn't leave much room for hunger. I forced myself to gulp down the rest of my brunch and switched to talking about some of the videos Lillian had sent, with honest appreciation of the gift. By the time she and Maggie dropped me off back on campus, though, my whole abdomen felt like one giant knot.

I had an hour or so before class, so I figured I'd wind down in my room for a bit. The common room was empty —always a relief. Victory hadn't lashed out at me since our bloody tiff during the illusion demonstration, but I wasn't naïve enough to assume I'd cowed her.

I started toward my bedroom, scanning the door for signs of intrusion, and my gaze slid along the rest of the wall. It stopped at Shelby's room. A ragged bit of red fabric protruded from under the door by about an inch. Just far enough to be easily spotted if you happened to be looking, but not so obvious it looked deliberate. I had the sinking suspicion that was a pretense, though. Someone had wanted me to notice.

If Victory or her friends had gone after Shelby, it wouldn't be because they hated her returning so much. It'd be to strike a blow at me, because they knew she was my friend. Not much different from Victory setting her cat after Deborah.

I knocked on the door tentatively. "Shelby?"

When she didn't answer, I nudged the door open, since of course she didn't have any lock on it at all. The whole school was set up to make the Naries as easy targets as possible even before you considered this year's summer project.

My jaw clenched as I stepped inside. Torn fabric in all sorts of colors and of all kinds of textures scattered Shelby's bed, desk, and floor. And not just random swaths. There was a chunk of sleeve. There a shred with a beltloop from a pair of jeans. And the doors of her wardrobe hung open. Nothing remained inside.

Nausea swelled inside me. This was cruel in so many ways. They'd destroyed every piece of clothing Shelby wasn't wearing. Some of those pieces she'd probably loved. Some might have had special significance, like my charm bracelet had. And even if none of her clothing had meant all that much to her, she was here on scholarship. A fearmancer could have ordered a bunch of replacement outfits without batting an eye. Shelby's family wouldn't have that kind of money.

All the more reason for Victory and the others to hit her like this instead of me.

I closed my eyes for a second as my queasiness rose to the bottom of my throat. Professor Banefield had warned me about this once—that being friends with someone "weaker" than me would make me vulnerable too. But I didn't regret being Shelby's friend because of how it hurt me, seeing this. I just hated that it was my fault she'd been attacked. *She* might have been better off if I'd never given her the time of day.

No. I couldn't let myself believe that. The other girls had been tormenting her long before I'd arrived at Blood U—and if I hadn't finally gotten through to Jude, she'd have lost her spot in the music program forever.

Still, I had to make this mess as right as I could.

I picked up a few scraps that looked like they went together, and hopelessness washed over me. Victory and her crew had shredded the clothing so thoroughly that I wasn't sure I had the skill to put even one item back together, let alone all of them.

Okay. First priority then: reducing how traumatic this would be for Shelby. I could at least clean up the mess so she wouldn't have to walk into this horror show of fashion carnage.

Partly with my hands and partly with gusts of magic, I gathered all the bits into a heap. I nearly threw it all in the garbage, but then it occurred to me that if there was a particularly special item in the mix, Shelby might want the pieces of that. Instead, I stuffed it all into a few bags and shoved those under my bed in my own room.

Now, how was I going to arrange for her to get new

clothes? I worried at my lower lip as I came back to her room.

Maybe it didn't have to be all that complicated. There were plenty of assholes at Blood U, but Shelby knew she had at least one benefactor. It might seem totally reasonable that someone could be both at the same time.

I scrawled a quick note on an envelope, tensing my hand to disguise my handwriting. *Your clothes needed an upgrade. Take this and refill your wardrobe.* Then I stuffed it with a bunch of the cash I'd started hiding away in my room in case I decided I needed to make a quick run from the university and didn't want to risk accessing the Bloodstone accounts. I'd accumulated about ten thousand dollars over several withdrawals—I gave Shelby half of that. She should be able to get more than enough clothes to replace what she'd had here with that amount, and it wasn't even a dent in my family's holdings.

She was still going to be at least a little horrified, but I couldn't think of any better way to mitigate the damage. Hopefully I'd be around when she came back to the dorm so I could offer moral support too.

It was a good thing her cello pretty much always left the dorm when she did. Lord only knew what the other girls would have done to *that* if they could have gotten their hands on it.

I wasn't quite done, though. I'd made a promise to myself that I wasn't just going to take anything Victory threw at me… and attacking Shelby was an attack on me, no doubt about it. My queasiness came back as I moved to my nemesis's bedroom door.

How much retaliation would it take before she decided she was better off leaving me and the people I cared about alone? How far was *I* going to have to go, lashing back at her?

Always an equal effect. I wasn't going to hit her with anything she hadn't already hit me with. These were just… natural consequences.

She'd sealed her room more securely than when I'd done the trick with the cat urine, but within fifteen minutes, I was inside. I opened the doors to her wardrobe, looking at the row of hanging silk and linen, and folded my arms over my chest.

"All right," I said to myself, shoving aside my revulsion at the ravaging ahead. "Let's do this."

CHAPTER TWENTY-ONE

Declan

The library in the Fortress of the Pentacle was open to all scions once we reached a certain age, but I was pretty sure I was the only one of the current generation who'd set foot in here. I hadn't encountered even the other barons all that often in the dim room that smelled of stale ink and dust, although some spell kept any particles from accumulating.

To tell the truth, I winced a little to think of how much time *I'd* spent in the dreary space. More than once, though, the historical precedent of some past ruling had given me the authority I needed to overturn one of my aunt Ambrosia's schemes for retaining or regaining power, so that time had been worth it.

The library contained the official documents on fearmancer law, records of every case handled by the blacksuits from inception to outcome, and the minutes from every meeting of the pentacle. Those minutes were somewhat edited—I'd find no proof of the treason the other barons had hinted at toward Rory during recent meetings—but there was still a chance I'd come across something useful.

These "reapers" her mentor had mentioned had apparently been working alongside the barons. They might have been a more legitimate presence in the past, a group that was openly talked about. If there was any mention of them that would help me figure out who they were—and Rory figure out how to protect herself from them—I meant to find it. It was one of the few things I *could* do for her without jeopardizing my family.

I leaned back against the shelves where I'd hunkered down on the floor and flipped another page in the thick volume open on my lap. The stuffy air always made me sleepy, but I kept my focus on the task at hand. It really was too bad we still insisted on keeping all our records physically instead of digitizing them. Imagine if I could simply do a search for "reapers" and have the results in seconds. But no, for this we were stuck in the dark ages, maybe specifically so that anyone searching for inside info on the barons would have to work to dig it up.

I didn't remember coming across the term "reapers" in my previous readings. I hadn't found any mention of it so far today. With a sigh, I turned the page and kept skimming. At least I'd gotten good at scanning for the material I was looking for quickly.

The door squeaked open. I looked up from the book, and my back stiffened against the shelves.

Baron Nightwood stepped into the room with an air of subtle disdain, as if he couldn't see why anyone would bother with the records in here. He came to a stop a couple of feet in front of me and peered down. I debated between standing up so I could look him straight in the eye and staying put as if I didn't feel the need.

Doing this research wouldn't jeopardize my family, no... as long as none of the other barons realized exactly what I was searching for in here and on whose behalf.

"Ashgrave," Nightwood said smoothly, his voice just a touch deeper and more acerbic than Malcolm's. "Hard at work as always, I see. What problem has you holed up in here for hours on end now?"

I opted to stay sitting. Easier than trying to pull off a nonchalant leap to my feet. "I wanted to double-check some of the past rulings regarding young barons without regents," I said, keeping my tone relaxed. "Considering we are going to have to start integrating the Bloodstone scion into the pentacle before too long."

Nightwood hummed with faint approval. "If you find anything interesting, do share it. Although I think we're on our way to having her well in hand."

Were they? Not through any strategies they'd discussed while I was around. I dropped my gaze to the book as if I wasn't all that invested in his answer. "I'm glad to hear that. I didn't realize we had any current plans in the works."

The other baron's hum was more on the dismissive side this time. "Not every action needs to be a group activity. You haven't missed out on any official policy-making, I promise. This summer session should give us a final measure of her, I think. We'll just have to see whether the outcome shakes her or steadies her, and there are ways we can handle either eventuality."

That sounded ominously vague. "If there are any other ways you'd like me to be involved at the university…"

"No, I think at the moment we're best off giving her plenty of free rein with which to hang herself." The corner of his lips twitched upward.

I could only return the smile tightly. "I suppose I'll be waiting to see that outcome too, then."

"I wouldn't waste too much time on the fine details," Nightwood said. "You have your own studies to worry about if you're going to take your full spot at the table."

As if I needed the reminder—which might have also been a veiled threat. "Oh, I'm staying on top of those," I assured him.

He examined a couple of the volumes on the shelf nearest him, possibly waiting to see if I'd reveal anything else in the awkwardness of the silence. When I turned all my attention back to my book, he sauntered out of the room.

He was probably using the Fortress for some sort of business meeting, which was one of the perks of the barony. Even if you weren't acting in your capacity as ruler, meeting a prospective client or partner here cast a long shadow of authority over the proceedings.

I expected that'd be the last I heard from him today, but just as I'd reached the end of my current book and gotten up to pick out another, footsteps came rasping back over the stone floor beyond the door.

"Ashgrave," the baron said as he pushed the door open, "can you think of any particular reason the elder Evergrists might be paying a call here?"

My head jerked around. "Who?" I said, and then hoped feigned ignorance hadn't been a bad gambit.

Nightwood cocked his head. "Our Bloodstone scion's grandparents on the non-Bloodstone side. They've pulled up in the lot a couple of spots over from your car, but they haven't gotten out. Very peculiar."

It was. Very peculiar, and also highly annoying.

Nightwood obviously didn't want anything to do with them, which I supposed worked in my favor. I offered him a puzzled shrug and shoved the book I was holding back into its spot. "I was just finishing up here. I can go out and see what's going on."

"Please do. And let's not have them in the building, all right? They're liable to walk off with the table and half the decorations if they have the chance."

He stepped back for me to leave ahead of him rather than setting off himself. I thought his gaze followed me with a little more scrutiny than normal as I passed him. He hadn't spoken to the Evergrists, but them being here at all was odd enough that it had to be raising questions in his head. What the hell were they thinking?

Who was I kidding? This would be exactly what they were thinking—that showing up at the Fortress would make me uncomfortable and put me in a potentially difficult position. It was a power play, pure and simple.

The only real question was what they wanted at this exact moment.

Well, that and how they'd known I'd be here right now. I wasn't able to make the trip very often between classes I was taking and classes I was TA-ing for. Had they paid off someone on staff to let them know if I left the university? Did they have someone watching the likely places they thought I might go?

A chill crept up my back. Whatever the case, my denials and Rory's clearly hadn't shaken their certainty that they were holding something over me. And I didn't think they'd hesitate to call my bluff if I pushed back much harder.

Rory's grandparents had indeed parked their silver-blue Cadillac two spots away from my Honda. I strode over with as casual an air as I could summon.

The Evergrists didn't bother to get out. Stella, in the passenger seat, simply rolled down the window.

"Mr. Ashgrave," she said in a saccharine voice. "What a lovely surprise."

I managed not to snort at that remark. "What are you doing here? We didn't arrange any meeting." And there was no other reason for anyone besides the barons to visit the Fortress, as any fearmancer knew.

Rory's grandmother brushed her fingers over her pale curls. "That's true. Perhaps we should arrange one. We've been getting the impression that you've forgotten about our request. It really wasn't a very large one, was it?"

The business venture they'd wanted approved. I forced a smile. "It's got nothing to do with my memory, Mrs.

Evergrist. The pentacle has a backlog of proposals to consider. The one you were interested in hasn't even come up yet. I can't support a venture that isn't on the table, can I?"

"Maybe you can see about having it bumped up, then," Rory's grandfather said, leaning over in the driver's seat.

"We really have been quite patient," his wife added. "And it would be such a shame if a comment happened to slip out that put your conduct into question. If we get impatient, it may be harder for us to stay circumspect."

And there was a direct threat. I guessed it'd only been a matter of time. I crossed my arms over my chest and stared down at her with the baronic glower I'd had years and ample reason to perfect.

"If you have some complaint about my behavior, you're welcome to put it to whoever you'd like. Attempting to skew the proceedings of the pentacle could be considered treason. I'm sure you didn't intend to cross that line."

"It seems as though we'd both be best off if no complaints are made on either side." Mrs. Evergrist tipped her head coyly. "We've waited a long time for our granddaughter to be returned to us, Mr. Ashgrave. Naturally we have a stake in what happens to her. We nearly are Bloodstones ourselves by marriage. That should entitle us to a certain amount of respect."

I was tempted to recite a line of my father's about respect being earned rather than bought, but I didn't expect that would go over well. I just wanted them gone.

As they no doubt well knew, the longer we stayed here talking, the more suspicious the interaction would look to anyone taking note. Like Baron Nightwood, for example.

"I've told you I'll see what I can do about your business endeavors," I said. "The reminder wasn't necessary. I'd imagine that proposal isn't too far back in the queue."

As intended, they took that as acknowledgment that I'd move it forward, not that I had any plans of doing so. "I'm so glad we're on the same page," Rory's grandmother simpered. She rolled her window back up and gave me a little wave as her husband pulled out of the spot.

My stomach clenched as I watched them drive away. If I didn't follow through, how far would they go next time? In one escalation, they'd already jumped from calling my house to showing up at my workplace. If it'd been the day of a full meeting—if Aunt Ambrosia had been here, if she'd talked to them—fuck.

I couldn't see any way this stand-off was going to end well.

CHAPTER TWENTY-TWO

Rory

After a string of clear, sunny summer days, it was a little depressing stepping out of Ashgrave Hall into cool, humid air under a sky choked with gray clouds. As I went around the building to the field, I rubbed my arms, wishing I'd picked a warmer shirt than a tank top.

Connar was already waiting by the far corner where we had a good vantage of the clubhouse. He shot me a warm smile as I joined him, and I resisted the urge to sidle right up to his well-muscled body and soak up even more warmth that way. I wasn't here for snuggling.

Across the field, the workers who'd been assigned to the clubhouse were just finishing the new frame with the intermittent whir of their electric screwdrivers. Would they have been putting their magic to use constructing the thing too if they hadn't had Naries watching so eagerly?

Benjamin and a couple of his friends were supervising, pitching in by passing along tools or steadying beams where they could.

"Ready?" Connar asked. "I doubt you're going to need much help from me. You're usually a quick study."

"But you promised help, so you'd better deliver it," I said with a teasing waggle of my finger. "Can we check the wards from all the way over here? I don't want the Naries wondering why I'm lurking around the clubhouse."

"It's not a problem at all. Just requires some additional concentration. You remember where we buried them?"

I nodded. We'd planted one shaped stone at each corner of the foundation and a fifth in the center for good measure. They were buried under not just dirt but a thick slab of concrete now. The spells on them must be working, because work on the clubhouse had resumed without any further hitches, but Connar had recommended testing them every few days to make sure the magic was still holding strong.

He touched the back of my elbow as if to form a point of connection. "The easiest way to get at them is to let your magic move through the earth to them rather than trying to leap straight to the wards. I'll guide you to the first one, and if that goes well, you can probably do the others on your own."

"Okay." I trained my eyes on the grassy ground a few feet from one corner of the structure. "Feel," I murmured, because all I was doing, really, was feeling them out.

A spark of magic leapt up from my chest through my

mind, and my senses sharpened to take in the dew dampness still clinging to the grass, the grainy dirt flecked with pebbles. Connar said something quietly beside me, and a tingle of energy that must have been his coursed over my skin and wound through my awareness. It urged me on through the soil.

I pictured the stone we'd shaped for the ward, reaching for the curved hollow of it. An earthy but not exactly unpleasant flavor filled my mouth. The impression of darkness momentarily threw me, but Connar's magic nudged my awareness to the side, and the ward's magic flowed into me with a jolt.

The spell he'd helped me plan still thrummed through the stone with a crackling power. The shaping we'd done had worked—the magic was holding steady rather than fading the way it would have in most circumstances. I pulled back into my body with a sigh of relief.

"Still working perfectly," Connar said. "You did a great job with those. Even Viceport wouldn't find anything to criticize."

I let out a short laugh. "I don't know about that. She's very committed to her cause. Okay, let me see if I can find the next one on my own."

The ward at the other near corner wasn't difficult at all to locate now that I knew what sensations I was looking for. The far corners took a little more effort, but I confirmed those wards were functioning properly with a clenching of my jaw as I concentrated. I got a bit lost trying to find the central ward, which didn't have a clear physical marker on the building to guide me, but Connar eased alongside me after a few moments and together we hit on the right spot.

That stone's magic didn't feel as vibrant as the others. "It's fading," I said, half my awareness still trained under the ground. Damn it.

"Four out of five good conducting pieces is a great result for your first attempt," Connar said. "The other four might be more than enough on their own, but we can bolster the spell on the fifth. Consider it useful practice."

I grumbled something under my breath but focused even more tightly on the central ward. More magic fizzed at the base of my throat. I drew it into my words and refilled the stone's well with the effects I wanted to generate.

The tingle of Connar's magical presence stayed with me until I pulled back from the clubhouse completely. I'd never really cast *with* someone else before, and there was something compelling about the act. I could almost feel Connar's dragon form in that essence of him, powerful and fierce but not without a certain grace.

"I don't think anyone will be damaging that building any time soon," he said with a grin. "If you want me to pitch in any other way, just let me know."

"Thank you," I said. "You've done a lot already."

He shrugged, his gaze still holding mine. "I owe you a lot. And I'm looking forward to seeing you win." He paused, and his expression turned stern. "If anyone hassles *you* again, whether it's Malcolm or someone else, you can count on me then too."

I'd seen Connar's protective side come out in full force

before. The memory of those times threw me back to my last confrontation with Professor Banefield in his quarters, to the agony in his voice as he'd grappled with the magic controlling him to save me from himself. I swallowed hard.

Connar thought all he had to protect me from was the jabs of the other students. If he took too big a stand, he'd be making himself a target too.

I rested my hand on his arm, giving him a firm look. "I appreciate that, but I don't want you rushing in at the first sign of trouble, okay? I can look after myself pretty well, and anyone who comes at me should have the chance to figure that out. No need to put yourself in the line of fire if I can handle it."

"You shouldn't have to handle it."

No, I shouldn't, but this place and these people were what they were. "That's why you need to look after yourself too instead of just worrying about me," I said with a playful tap of his chest. "The pentacle needs some good barons when it's time for the next generation to take over."

He couldn't know how seriously I meant that sentiment—and how much I really did think I needed to worry about *his* safety if he threw in his lot with me—but the words made his chiseled features soften and his light blue eyes brighten with an emotion that sent a flutter through my chest. He leaned in, and his kiss drove away any lingering chill from the clouded morning. I let the heat and pleasure of it wash through me.

After the kiss, he tugged me into his arms. I leaned my

head against his solid chest, reveling in all the strength he wanted to offer me, and my gaze slid across the grounds beside us... to land on Declan, who'd just glanced our way where he was crossing the green.

The moment our eyes met, the other scion tensed. Then he jerked his gaze away and hurried on toward the Stormhurst Building as if it hadn't mattered anyway. There wasn't enough time for me to do anything about whatever he might have thought or felt—and what could I really have done anyway? He'd vetoed any idea of us being together more than once for multiple very good reasons.

Still, my stomach sank at his reaction. I must have tensed a little myself in Connar's arms, because he drew back to look down at me.

I sucked in a breath. There were things I definitely should say to Connar, even if I couldn't say everything.

"You should know," I said, "I—I'm kind of seeing Jude again. Which doesn't mean we can't..." I made an awkward gesture between the two of us to indicate the embrace. "He knows that I'm, er, dating around. But I didn't want to give the wrong impression. I guess... you and I couldn't really get all that serious in the long run anyway, could we? Since you're the only possible heir of Stormhurst."

"Yeah. I've been trying not to think about that." He bowed his head over me again, his chin coming to rest by my forehead. "I guess it's a weird situation all around, isn't it? I can't ask you to go all in on me, considering. If Jude is making you happy, then I can't complain about that."

"You make me happy too," I said softly.

I felt his jaw shift with a smile. "Good. I think… I just want to be with you as much as I can while I can. The barony's a long way off for most of us. It doesn't have to matter yet." He nuzzled my hair. "You make me feel like I don't have to be that guy everyone thought I was, Rory. The guy I didn't want to be anyway. The last few days… I'm starting to believe I can be someone I like better. And that'll mean something no matter what happens in the future."

My heart squeezed. I hugged him again. "It means something to me too. When I first really talked to you, I could tell you weren't that guy."

"I've still got plenty to make up for," he said. "Not just with you. But helping you with projects like this…" He nodded toward the clubhouse. "Maybe I can make up for some of the hurt I've done in the past by stopping other people from getting hurt."

It wasn't you who hurt your brother, I wanted to say. *It was your asshole parents.* But I didn't think he'd ever fully believe that. And maybe it'd be wrong of me to try to take any sense of responsibility away from him. He'd been there. I hadn't been. He needed to do what felt right to him.

I might not have needed to say it. Connar kissed me again, so full of passion and tenderness that I felt a little giddy when he eased back. No, I definitely wasn't looking forward to having to give this up somewhere down the road. Not thinking that far ahead seemed like a perfectly good plan for now.

"Unfortunately, I've got a class to get to now," he said. "You know how to find me if you need me."

I grasped his hand just for a second. "I'll see you soon."

After he left, I lingered beside Ashgrave Hall for a while longer, watching the progress of the construction, willing the clouds not to let loose any rain that would end today's work. A few of my fellow fearmancers wandered by the site, but if they attempted any magic on the structure or the people building it, the wards deflected those spells. Benjamin stepped back to take the whole building in with a satisfied grin that strengthened the resolve inside me.

Whatever else happened to me here at Blood U, at least I'd have made one change for the better.

"Hey, what're they up to over here?" Shelby meandered up beside me, staring at the half-finished clubhouse.

I'd forgotten my friend would have missed all of this. "The scholarship students are building a clubhouse just for their use," I said. "Ms. Grimsworth approved it. A little escape for you guys from the mean girls and the rest."

If Benjamin's grin had buoyed my mood, that was nothing compared to the effect of seeing Shelby's face light up. She beamed at me and then at the structure. If her expression had tightened a bit at the same time, no doubt it was because of her hostile supposed benefactor who'd stolen all her clothes.

"That's amazing," she said. "I guess I missed a lot. I wonder if there's any way I can pitch in."

I couldn't help beaming back, and not just because of

her obvious happiness. I also hadn't thought about how much easier my project might become with Shelby back on campus. Unlike any of the other mages, I had an ally among the Naries. I didn't need to use any magic on her to encourage her in the direction I was hoping for. I could be totally open with Shelby about how I felt.

"I'm sure you can," I said. "A bunch of the other scholarship students have been helping out here and there. You should go on over and ask."

She patted the cello case she'd set down beside her. "I have practice right now, but afterward, I'll definitely have to do that. I can't wait until it's done." She paused and gave me a slightly guilty look. "Not that I'm looking forward to excluding *you*…"

I laughed. "It's fine. I know what the people around here are like. You deserve a space where you don't have to worry about any of us. We've got plenty of other places where we can hang out."

"Yeah." Her smile came back, and she bounded off with her ponytail swinging.

Watching her go, my gut tightened. Shelby needed a shelter like that even more than most of the Naries *because* of her association with me. Would the other fearmancer students start targeting her even more if she started contributing to the clubhouse?

I had to make sure I protected her as much as I did the building.

A few possibilities flitted through my mind. I was about to turn away from my vigil to pursue them when a tall, grim man came striding across the field toward the clubhouse.

"We've gotten too many noise complaints from the staff and students," he said with a jerk of his hand. "You've got to stop construction, now."

CHAPTER TWENTY-THREE

Rory

One of the nice things about the town just off campus being so small was that many of the scattered stores carried multiple kinds of merchandise. So it was totally plausible that I could be deciding between sterling silver pendants in one corner, and Declan Ashgrave might just happen to pop in to check out the ties on the rack behind me.

When I heard him come to a stop, I turned partway around, holding a pendant in each hand as if studying them in different light. I hadn't been sure he'd appreciate me dropping in on him—literally—another night, and meeting like this had seemed like the next best option if we were going to talk.

"Thanks for coming," I said quietly. The other shopper currently in the store, a Nary who wasn't from the school, stood at the other end trying on scarfs, but it couldn't hurt to stay cautious.

"I feel like I've stumbled into a spy film," Declan said, but there was enough tension in his voice that the joke didn't quite land. "What's going on?"

His briskness told me I should get straight to the point. "I know you've done a lot of reading on fearmancer policies and so on—do you have any idea of the best way to fight a noise complaint at school?"

He was silent for a moment, no response other than the rustling of the ties as he sorted through them. A fan was whirring on the ceiling, but it barely stirred the summer heat enough to cool the sweat forming on my skin.

"I can't say that's something I've looked into specifically," he said. "But most of the university policies are designed to ensure safety and security within essential bounds, while leaving room for the students to learn. I'd suspect your best bet is going to be coming from the angle that the noise is actually productive to student learning somehow."

Given what I'd see of how Blood U worked, that sounded reasonable. "Okay. I'll see if I can work with that. Thank you. How have you been?" It felt weird that I could consider him one of the people at school I was closest to and yet I had no idea what his life had been like the last few weeks.

"Pretty much the usual. I don't think it's a good idea for us to just chat, Rory."

He moved as if to leave, his tone outright brusque now in a way I hadn't heard in a long time. My gut twisted.

"Wait," I said, as firmly as I could without raising my voice. "Did something happen? You seem more… worried than before." Another thought occurred to me. "Or, if this is about Connar—"

Declan stopped. "No," he said quickly. "It's not that. I told you before—I know I don't have any right to be jealous, no matter who you're with. I just…" He exhaled raggedly. "Your grandparents were nosing around the Fortress of the Pentacle, making threats. I'm lucky it wasn't an official meeting day and only one of the other barons saw them. I'm still working out if I can find any information on the barons' plans or these 'reapers' that would help you, but unless I do, I think it's better we don't take any chances of even seeming slightly friendly for now."

"They followed you all the way out there?" Abruptly I felt twice as sick. My father's parents clearly cared way more about any advantage they could gain from this situation than having a real relationship with me. "I'm sorry. I had no idea."

"It's not your fault. They're just… the way we are." He paused. "It's probably for the better in the long run if we interact as little as possible anyway. I can't keep indulging my feelings for you when it's impossible for us to have anything real—that's only going to make things harder."

"Yeah." It felt awfully hard right now, thinking I might not even talk to him again except as a distant coworker. I dragged in a breath. "I understand. If I can think of any way of getting them off your back, I'll do it."

"I don't want you making yourself a target either. Be careful—not that I need to tell you."

His voice gentled for that last remark. Then he strode over to the counter with a tie he'd picked out, not so much as glancing my way. I forced myself to keep my gaze on the pendants I was holding.

It wasn't as if I'd really lost a friend and ally—and whatever else we'd been—even if my stomach had balled into a knot. He'd be around. He'd said he was still trying to help me.

And I had other allies I could still talk to who needed *my* help. I looked over the pendants one more time, and my fingers closed around the best one. When Declan had left the store, I followed his footsteps to the counter.

Victory and her friends were lounging in the common room when I went over to Shelby's bedroom door. Their gazes followed me with an ominous sensation even though they didn't speak.

Their presence made me twice as glad that I'd decided to take this step. Maybe I couldn't protect every Nary in this school perfectly, but I could put all my power to looking after the one who'd been my friend since my first day here.

"Hey," I said when Shelby opened the door. "Can I come in? I, ah, got something for you."

The other girl looked surprised, but in a pleased way. "Sure! You really didn't have to. I mean, I got the whole clothing situation sorted out."

"Yeah, but I owed you one." I took the little cardboard box out of my purse. "I finally got myself my own chain for that charm bead, so I can give yours back to you. And as a thank you, I saw this pendant I thought you'd like…"

The brightening of her face when she opened the box told me I'd made the right choice. She held up the silver chain she'd lent me months ago to study the pendant: a violin with curves and grooves I'd managed to reshape slightly to contain the magic I'd cast on it. The structure wasn't perfect—I'd probably need to strengthen the ward every week or so—but if I'd worked the spell right, it should deflect any of the usual sorts of spells my fellow students might have cast at a Nary. If someone started up a brute force attack, the one small ward wouldn't be enough, but I couldn't exactly drape her in them. Hopefully it wouldn't come to that.

"It's beautiful," she said. "You *really* didn't have to."

"I'm just glad you like it. I know you play a cello, not a violin, but I figured it's pretty close…"

She laughed. "Close enough. I don't figure there are many cello necklaces out there." Undoing the clasp, she drew the chain around her neck. The charm settled just below her collarbone. "Thank you. I was just happy I could help you out."

"It looks great on you," I said, figuring the more enthusiasm I showed, the more likely she was to wear it as often as possible.

Apparently I'd missed Imogen's entrance—and some disagreement between her and Victory. I stepped back out into the common room to Victory sashaying out the main door with a toss of her hair, Cressida and Sinclair in tow. My nemesis tossed an acidic comment over her shoulder. "Maybe you could just go to your dad about that."

Imogen glared after them where she was standing by one of the sofas. Her shoulders came down with the click of the door shutting behind them. She turned to me. "Don't ask. Just Victory being Victory."

"No surprises there." The fact that Imogen's father ran the maintenance department at the university rather than holding some more prestigious position had apparently made a lot of the fearmancers turn their nose up at Imogen. Victory had already used her relationship with her dad to threaten her into betraying me once.

But... that connection could work the other way too, couldn't it? To my benefit?

I hesitated and then ventured, "Hey, I... actually need to speak to someone in Maintenance about something. Preferably the higher up the better. Do you think you could get me a few minutes with your dad?"

Imogen raised an eyebrow at me. "Is this about the stalled construction on that building in the east field?"

Yeah, my involvement with the clubhouse wasn't much of a secret anymore. I gave her a sheepish smile. "Cat's out of the bag, huh? If you don't want to help the competition, I totally get it."

She waved off my concern. "I told you, I don't have a hope in hell of winning anyway. Just tell me: if you get this done, is it going to make things more difficult for the assholes like Victory?"

I couldn't stop my smile from stretching into a grin. "Yeah, I'd say so."

"Then consider me in. Come on, we can go right now. Dad'll always make time for me if I say it's important."

We set off across the green and over the west field to the squat brown maintenance building. Imogen marched right in as if she worked there too. The hall inside smelled of lemony wood polish, although I didn't know what they'd been polishing since the floor was gray linoleum that squeaked under my shoes.

Halfway down the hall, Imogen popped a door open a crack. "Dad? Do you have a minute?"

"Sure, Genny," said a warm voice from within the room. "Come on in."

"I brought a friend," Imogen said, motioning for me to join her. "She needed to ask you about something."

I'd been a little nervous about approaching Mr. Wakeburn, but the sight of him put me at ease. He had the same dark blond hair as Imogen, a little shaggy as if he were one of those California surfers I'd see at the beach back home, and the corners of his eyes crinkled with his smile. If the other fearmancers thought Imogen was worse off having a dad like this instead of the kinds of parents they seemed to cope with, they obviously had no idea what a healthy family looked like.

"Sorry to interrupt you, Mr. Wakeburn," I said with a bob of my head.

"That's totally fine." He pushed back his chair from his

desk, sinking into a relaxed pose. His body tensed slightly once he'd had a chance to take me in. "You're Rory Bloodstone."

"Um, yeah." I hadn't really thought about how my position as scion and almost-baron might give me a certain authority here. But I didn't want to bully him into agreeing. I launched into my pitch. "Some of the Nary students have been working with the maintenance staff to build a clubhouse on the east field. The work was shut down yesterday with a noise complaint. I'd like to challenge that complaint and call for the work to be resumed."

Imogen's dad raised one eyebrow much the way his daughter had minutes ago. "On what grounds?"

"The whole philosophy behind everything we do at Bloodstone University is to prepare us to handle the challenges of the real world. We can hardly expect to never experience a little irritating noise in the background. This gives students the opportunity to practice honing their concentration. The construction work should be finished fairly soon anyway."

Declan's advice appeared to have been on the mark. Mr. Wakeburn nodded as if he could see my point. But he didn't agree right away. "We have gotten *several* complaints. I have to take that into consideration."

"Dad," Imogen said in a pleading voice. "You know that's got to have more to do with the summer project competition than them actually being bothered. Remember the berries two years ago?"

His lips twitched, and he chuckled. "Okay, point

taken. I suppose I could make a sort of jam out of this."
His gaze slid back to me. "I'll see the Naries get their
workers back."

"Thank you," I said with a rush of relief tempered by
confusion.

As Imogen and I headed out, I glanced at her.
"Berries?"

"It's sort of an inside joke. Long story. He got the
picture, and you're back in the game." She offered me a
high-five.

I returned it, but the gears in my head had started
spinning in a totally different direction.

People used sort-of codes like that all the time—
referencing shared experiences or understanding to get
their point across quickly... or if they didn't want other
people to know what they were talking about. My
searching through Banefield's records hadn't turned
anything up so far, but I'd been looking for the sorts of
clues *anyone* would have recognized as meaningful, like
bank names or something obviously labeled as a storage
facility.

He must have known there was a good chance he
wouldn't be able to tell me everything he had to in the
moment. He'd have hoped I'd come searching if I needed
to know more. Maybe the answer was in there somewhere
—but left for me in a way only he and I would
understand.

CHAPTER TWENTY-FOUR

Malcolm

All told, this was a pretty wretched party.

The summer parties often were. With only about a quarter of the usual student population, the crowd couldn't summon the same energy. The summer nights didn't get quite cool enough for the heat of the bonfire to be enjoyable, and the humidity kept the smoke lower to the ground, seeping into our lungs. Not to mention everyone was a little at odds because of the term's project, eyeing each other across the flames or over the beverage table as if trying to determine who their biggest competition was.

Tonight, though, I had to admit that some of the wretchedness was happening inside me.

I circulated through the revelers nursing my beer and making sure everyone knew I was there and keeping an eye on things. I had Victory and a few of the other girls hanging off me at one point, and a bunch of the guys tagging along with their flattering remarks hoping to get in good with the king of the scions. That should have been all I needed.

But about a half hour in, I glanced up to see a couple ducking into the boathouse in mid-kiss, and my next gulp of beer seemed to burn right through the bottom of my stomach. I'd turned away, only to notice Rory standing farther down the shore with that dormmate of hers, the one whose father was in Maintenance.

The Bloodstone scion didn't so much as glance my way. She meandered along the edge of the crowd, slipped over to the tables briefly to grab a wine cooler, and retreated into the shadows beyond the firelight again.

She'd never acted all that enthusiastic about these parties, although maybe that was because of the treatment she'd received at her first ones. Was she being even more hesitant than usual to avoid me? Because she was afraid of what I might try to do in the dark once I had a beer or two in my system?

That question made my stomach churn harder. I ended up setting my beer down by the firepit and abandoning it.

Rory wasn't the only one giving me a wide berth. Declan had dropped in briefly, as was his usual party MO, and offered me a nod. Jude and Connar hadn't acknowledged me at all.

Neither of them were exactly sticking *with* Rory, but Connar always moved when she did, staying where he could keep an eye out for anyone else coming at her, I guessed. Jude wove through the crowd with his usual jokes and pranking illusions, always managing to be on the opposite side of the fire from me.

I could take a little comfort from the fact that he was behaving normally, other than the avoidance thing. Whatever dark mood had gripped him recently, it appeared to have lifted.

My gaze kept returning to Rory, seeking her out as if by a supernatural pull. I must have noted her travels through the party a couple dozen times before I caught a glimpse of her back as she headed up the path toward the campus buildings, leaving early.

Just not her thing, or too many uncomfortable memories?

Victory laughed at something Chandler had said and squeezed my arm as if it'd been my wry remark. Bradley made some comment about how the awesomeness of this party was obviously thanks to me. For just an instant, I wanted nothing more than for a black hole to open up in the ground beneath me and warp me away from here.

A Nightwood didn't run away from his problems, though. A Nightwood looked them in the face and tackled them head-on. Even if those problems were of his own making.

The thought of running into Rory alone in the night made me queasy all over again. I waited several minutes until I was sure she'd have reached her destination, and then I gave my fans some quick excuses and ducked away to tap a message into my phone.

Meet me in the lounge. We need to talk. Scions are meant to be family.

I set off without waiting for a response. That last line would bring them if the order didn't.

The fresh air farther up the field was a welcome change after the fire's smoky heat. I sucked it into my lungs and let it wash over my skin. I still couldn't say I felt particularly cleansed by the time I reached Ashgrave Hall and descended to our basement lounge.

I went over to the bar cabinet but decided halfway through reaching for a glass that having this conversation as sober as possible was probably the wisest move, if not the easiest. I wandered back to the seating around the TV and dropped into one of the armchairs.

Declan showed up a moment later, the most prompt of the others, of course. He gave me that nod again and sat down on the sofa. I guessed he realized there wasn't much point in asking what I wanted until they were all here to hear it.

Connar arrived next, with a wary glance toward me and then around the room. He stopped by the side of the sofa, not sitting down. Jude sauntered in a minute later with a cooler from the party still in one hand, but the steadiness of his steps told me he hadn't drunk much other than that.

"All right," I said, leaning forward. "We're all here. I—"

"We're not all here," Jude said tartly, dropping into the chair across from me. "Unless you've forgotten how to count. Last time I checked, there were five scions."

I glowered at him. "I wanted *us* to talk, just the four of us."

Connar pulled back from the sofa. "If you're still shutting Rory out, I don't really want to be part of this conversation. If this is about some new scheme to tear her down, you know I'm out, and if it's about something else to do with the pentacle, she has a right—"

"I know," I snapped. "Will you shut up for a second and let me explain?"

Connar went still, but the tendons in his square jaw flexed. I rubbed my hand over my face. "I'm sorry. We were here first, all right? We've known each other way longer than Rory's been in the picture. Whatever... Whatever I have to say to her, it's not the same thing I have to say to you. So I'm keeping them separate for now. That's all."

I didn't even want to think about Rory right now. There was nothing in this room that should remind me of that encounter last week when we—when I—

I closed my eyes for a second, but the images flashed through my mind anyway. Her hair, so fucking soft, and her lips somehow even softer but still fierce as they pressed back against mine, and nothing had existed in my body except fire and wanting until that cold shock of terror had torn through everything.

That wasn't really what had happened, though. The fear had been there before, flowing from her into me. I didn't know when exactly it had started, but it wouldn't have come out of nowhere. I'd been so caught up, so drunk on *her*, I'd tuned out all the rest of my senses until she'd said those words and shoved me back. The look in her eyes, afterward—the strain in her voice…

Shame and horror curdled inside me like they had then, like they had every time I'd remembered it since. Rory thought fearmancers were monsters. That's why she preferred the prissy joymancers on their high horses. But I'd acted just like a monster, hadn't I? I'd been enough of one in that moment for her to think that I'd—that I'd really—

I didn't want her broken, not like that. And sure as hell not by me. I laid down the law. I made sure people got in line. I taught lessons where they needed teaching, so the juniors smartened up, so the seniors remembered where they owed their respect. That was what a Nightwood did—that was what the leader of the scions was meant to do. He didn't *savage* people for his own personal gratification.

But maybe I'd broken a lot of things without really seeing what I was doing.

The other guys had stayed silent as I gathered myself. I raised my head and looked from one of them to the next.

"I *am* sorry," I said. "That's the main thing I wanted to say, to all of you. I let the whole feud escalate way too far, and I lashed out at you when I should have thanked you for trying to snap me out of it, and that's not… that's not how we're supposed to be. We're a family. And however much that's screwed up right now, I recognize it's at least mostly my fault. So let's make it right and move on. I don't want the pentacle to stay fractured like this."

Jude's eyes had widened, as if he hadn't thought I was

even capable of making an apology. Connar blinked, and a small smile crossed his face. Even though I'd been the hardest on him, he was willing to let bygones be bygones so quickly.

I'd better be worthy of that loyalty.

Naturally it was Declan who got down to the practicalities. "Does that mean that your whole campaign to knock Rory down a peg is over?" he asked, his tone as even as ever. He hadn't fought with me over the feud, but he'd tried to steer me onto a different course. And I'd ignored him. He deserved the apology as much as the other two did.

"No more fighting," I said. "It wasn't helping anything. I should have seen that sooner."

Connar allowed himself to sink onto the sofa. "I don't think Rory ever wanted to fight," he said quietly.

I could believe that. Her stance on the boathouse floor hadn't been that of a predator readying for the next lunge but a protective hunching in defense. Seeing her in that moment, the battleground I'd thought we'd been waging war over had crumbled away.

If I could have been that wrong, misread her that badly when I had a direct line into the fear I was provoking in her... how many more subtle cues had I missed from her along the way? Dad had been urging me on, and my pride had been stinging from the way she'd tried to cut me down that first day, and she kept singing the praises of those fucking joymancers—

I cut off that train of thought with a tensing of my jaw.

"I'll figure out how to address that with her, between the two of us," I said. "Right now—what do you need from me? I'm not going to assume saying I'm sorry is enough."

"I'm just glad you've thought this through," Declan said.

Connar looked down at his hands and then back at me. "You aren't going to be pissed off about me—or anyone else—spending time with her? I don't want to just not hassle her. She deserves to be a part of the pentacle."

"Cozy up to her all you want," I said, even though my stomach lurched all over again at the thought. That he would touch her—that she would welcome his touch in a way she couldn't mine—

Get back on track, Malcolm.

"And we'll get the pentacle business sorted out," I added. "It's going to be complicated. I made the problem, so can you let me worry about sorting it out?"

Connar nodded.

Jude slung his legs over the arm of the chair and ran a finger along his lips. "Since you're in such a contrite and generous mood," he said lightly, "I *have* always thought that Aston Martin of yours would fit perfectly in my collection."

I narrowed my eyes at him. "I'm not giving you my car."

He spread his hands with a wide grin. "Hey, it was worth a try."

There was something so perfectly Jude about the way

he'd said it, the expression on his face, and the fact that he'd tried it at all, that an unexpected laugh careened up my throat. I tipped back in my chair as it spilled out of me, and Connar started laughing too, and after a moment all four of us had cracked up, the sound bouncing through the room.

A good sound. A sound like a family back together again.

Something shifted in the air, and when we settled down, we fell into a natural conversation of trying to suss out what each other's summer project plans were and who'd gotten a scoop on future tests from which teachers, like old times. By the time we got up to head off to our dorms, I was breathing a little easier.

But not exactly easy. I caught Declan before he headed out after the others and waited until the door swung closed.

"What's the matter?" he asked, taking in my expression.

I grimaced and forced myself to spit out the question. "What exactly do you think my father did?"

I didn't need to tell him I was talking about our conversation at his house. Understanding lit in his eyes. I braced myself with the same sickening uncertainty that had been tugging at me since I'd left Rory in the boathouse.

If I could act like a monster... who was to say my parents had never crossed that line? And with far more resources than I had at my command.

Declan's shoulders had stiffened. "I haven't accused

any of the barons of anything," he said in a voice that sounded a touch stilted too.

"I know," I said quickly. "That's not what I meant. Just… if someone had taken down Professor Banefield on purpose… what would that have looked like? What would you have to look *for* to know?"

He seemed to work the question over. Then he sighed. "The best thing I can say to you is, if you want to know more about what your father is doing, you should ask him about it. Ask him, and really *listen.*"

That was less of an answer than I'd hoped for, but it might have been the most reasonable one he could give me.

He paused with his hand on the doorknob. "How are you going to approach Rory?"

Now that was *the* question. "I'm working that out," I hedged.

I was still a scion. I was still a Nightwood. Maybe I wasn't going to undermine her anymore, but I couldn't cut my own feet out from under me making amends either. It was… a delicate balance.

What would a Nightwood do with her? What would the mage I wanted to *be* do with her, after everything that'd happened between us?

I honestly didn't have a clue.

CHAPTER TWENTY-FIVE

Rory

Deborah scampered off my hand onto the roof of the Lexus. *Ready to stand guard! Do you think you have a better idea what you're looking for now?*

I peered around the shadowy expanse of the school garage, even though I'd just double-checked that I was alone here a second ago. While that hadn't changed, I kept my voice low anyway. "I'm not sure. But I've at least got a new angle to try."

She stayed perched on the roof as I pulled the box of Professor Banefield's records out of the trunk and brought it into the back seat, where I'd been conducting all of my searches through it. Her sharp mouse ears would pick up on anyone coming into the garage before I might notice, especially once I got absorbed in the task ahead of me. No one had come poking around my car yet, but they might if they noticed I was using it for more than just driving places.

I needed to look for a sign Banefield might have left just for me—something the average person wouldn't recognize the meaning of. But something that wouldn't stand out too much as unusual either, since that would draw attention too. I sucked my lower lip under my teeth as I considered.

He and I hadn't really had anything I could call an inside joke. There were things it was possible only the two of us knew about, like how he'd helped me get the hang of generating fear by having me protect a rabbit from a cat, but I wasn't sure how he could convey that in a simple notation somewhere in these documents.

If he'd even left a hint in these at all. Maybe I'd missed something in his office or his apartment that he'd meant to guide me instead. Although I thought I would have noticed a clue left on some random object... Records like these would be the easiest place to hide them.

There was of course the key itself. I dug it out of my purse and studied it. It was printed with a brand name that an internet search had revealed tons of keys had, as well as a few digits on either side that didn't appear to have any meaning. 1307 on the left. C95 on the right.

Generic might be good in this case. No one would know either of those sets of digits referred to a key. They could be just about anything.

I pulled out the first stack of records and started scanning them. Before, I'd focused on the official lists of charges and investments. Banefield had made notations on the edges of several of the papers that might have been references for tax purposes—just a few letters jotted here or there. I'd stopped paying attention to them after I'd realized they were so common.

Now, I focused specifically on the handwritten bits. What might BFR stand for? Or ZP? I still couldn't see how any of them connected to me or this situation at all.

I flipped through the first stack, set it aside, and pulled out a bunch more papers. More of the same, more of the same…

My hand paused over a bank statement from a few months ago. At the bottom, Banefield had written *C95* in faint pencil, followed by a street address.

My pulse stuttered. That had to be it. I moved to tear off the bottom of the paper, thought better of it, and took a photo of it with my phone. Then I tucked all the papers back in the box. All I needed to do was look up that address, and—

Deborah's voice carried faintly through the telepathic connection. *Lorelei, I'm not sure this is anything you need to worry about, but someone's yelling outside nearby. They sound rather distressed.*

I went still and then eased open the car door so I could hear better. When I strained my ears, I made out the voice but not the words, filtering through the garage walls. It sputtered something, fell silent, and then abruptly hollered something else.

No, I didn't like the sound of that at all.

"Come on," I said. I shoved the box back in the trunk and leaned close so Deborah could jump onto my shoulder. We hurried out of the garage.

Outside, the sound reached me more clearly. "There's no point," a guy was saying raggedly. "It's all so stupid."

There was something familiar about the voice. And it was coming from around Killbrook Hall—from the east field. I picked up my pace.

As soon as I came around the building, my heart sank. I had a view of the clubhouse now—the external frame complete and the roof just finished—and a figure standing on the peak of that roof. A figure I could recognize even at that distance as Benjamin Alvarez.

Several other students had gathered around the base of the clubhouse. "Come down, Ben," one of his classmates called. "Please."

The steel rungs of the ladder he must have climbed up gleamed in the mid-morning sun. He'd walked to the opposite end of the building though, teetering there on the edge like he was thinking of jumping. It wouldn't have been that far a fall, but he could still hurt himself badly.

My gaze darted across the grounds and settled on a head of ice-blond hair streaked with purple and pink. Cressida was watching the commotion from farther down the field, a small falcon-like bird I guessed must be her familiar perched on her arm. Her lips were curled with just a hint of a smile.

She'd done this. She must have cast some sort of persuasive spell on Benjamin to set him out of sorts and then pushed him toward the clubhouse. The building was protected from magic, but *he* wasn't.

Somehow I doubted he was even her assigned Nary. Everyone seemed to have figured out by now that this construction was my summer project. This was all part of the same campaign to mess with me.

The sight of her predatory familiar sent a flicker of caution through me. I veered toward Ashgrave Hall on my way over and touched the wall. "You can make it to my room no problem from here?" I whispered to Deborah. "I don't know if you'll be safe out here while I'm dealing with this."

Understood. I can find my way back. Take care of yourself too.

"I will." As much as I could.

"Why do you even care?" Benjamin was saying. "I wasted so much time…" He swayed on the roof, his arms whipping out for balance, and my stomach lurched. I had to get him down from there.

I stepped a little closer, but not so close that the gathered students would hear me casting. With my first tentative spell just to feel out his mood, the hum of my wards' magic echoed back at me. Shit. They were going to deflect any spells I cast in that direction as much as they would anyone else's.

Cressida had picked this set-up for more reasons than one. What better strategy than to cast her spell outside the wards and then send him behind them where he'd be harder to help.

But they were my wards, and they responded to my call. I could reach out to them quickly now after the practice I'd gotten. I extended my awareness to the one closest to me and murmured to it under my breath. Just a little opening, enough for me to send spells through without pulling down the defenses completely. Lord only knew what Cressida would do if I gave her that big an opening. Or her friends, if Victory or Sinclair were lurking around too.

With a gap opened in the wards' magic, my insight spell found Benjamin's mind. His thoughts were a storm of pain and shame, so fraught I could hardly focus on any one impression before it whirled away again.

"Calm," I whispered, willing those emotions toward him. "Steady."

He kept ranting, wobbling again on his feet. My attempts at soothing the desperate chaos Cressida had stirred up weren't penetrating the haze. I frowned and made another attempt, but that magic didn't have any noticeable impact either.

"Tricky situation."

My head snapped around at the voice beside me, my concentration slipping from Benjamin. Jude had joined me, his coppery head cocked as he took in the scene, his mouth set in a flat line. "And here our fellow fearmancers are proving just how much the Naries need that clubhouse of yours, hmm?"

"Yeah," I said. "But I'd rather they didn't end up proving it by having my guy break half the bones in his body."

Jude nodded. "Understandable. What have you tried?"

"His mind's all in turmoil. I tried to soothe it, to calm him down, but whatever spell is acting on him already, it's stuck in there pretty tight."

"You know… when a person's caught up in a mental spell like that, sometimes you need to take their mind off the pattern it's stuck in for a moment before you can get a real foothold. A brief distraction, not trying to change anything yet, just giving them a pause." He glanced at me. "Can I try something?"

"Please," I said. "As long as it doesn't involve rampaging bears."

He chuckled and lifted his chin toward the clubhouse. "I've got a lot more range than that. Be ready with your calming spell when he's open to it."

He made a subtle gesture with his hand by his side, speaking a few quiet words, and a form shimmered into being in the air just a few feet in front of us: a bright-feathered bluebird.

It fluttered its wings and flitted across the field, finding the gap I'd opened in the wards. With a cheerful chirp, it swooped around Benjamin.

Its colorful body caught his eye. His head turned, just slightly, following its path. The bird flew around him again and landed on the roof a few feet behind him. This time, Benjamin shifted around to study it with a puzzled look, probably wondering why it was being so friendly.

Well, puzzled was better than his previous state. I cast my calming spell again, finding his mind already less scattered when I touched it. I urged more magic from inside me to settle his thoughts, to wash away the hopeless gloom Cressida has filled his head with. He wavered and seemed to register where he was for the first time.

His hands shot out for balance. "I—what--?"

"Come back to the ladder," one of the Naries below said. "Just walk carefully. We're right here to help you."

I eased closer as he picked his way across the shingles. The other students congregated around the base of the ladder. A couple of them reached to help steady him as he made his way down.

"I don't know what I was thinking," he said. "Everything just felt so... dark for a second." An embarrassed flush darkened his cheeks.

I cast more calm toward the rest of the students, willing acceptance and reassurance. I didn't want this moment haunting Benjamin for the rest of his time here at school, tainting his friends' opinion of him.

One of the girls pulled him into a hug, and then they all drifted away from the building. "Let's go chill out for a bit," someone else said. "You must be putting too much pressure on yourself."

When I glanced Cressida's way again, the other girl had vanished. So had Jude's bluebird. He set his hands on his hips with a satisfied smile. "Nice job. Let's see this clubhouse of yours."

"It's more theirs than mine," I said as he ambled over to the doorway where no door had yet been attached. He stepped inside, his shoes echoing dully on the unfinished wood, and I trailed behind him.

The frame gave off a pungent pine smell that tickled my nose. Light streamed through the two raw windows. It was all one big open-concept room with a few cupboards where a fridge and microwave would be set up at one end and a built-in bench beneath one of the windows. Enough room for a couple dozen students to hang out here without it feeling crowded.

I hadn't seen the inside since the walls had gone up. Looking around, I couldn't help smiling.

Jude swiveled on his feet, taking the space in. "Nice job here too," he said. "Just for the Naries, huh? I'm feeling a little left out."

I smacked his arm. "Says the guy who has a whole basement entertainment room just for him and his three friends."

He shrugged with a grin. "My three friends and my girl. The lounge is open to all scions."

"Yeah, and I feel super welcome there," I said with a healthy helping of sarcasm.

"We'll work on that." He caught the hand I'd swatted him with and twined his fingers with mine as he turned toward me. "We made a pretty good team out there, didn't we?"

"We did." And when he beamed down at me like that, it made me want even more with him. But I didn't know —being with me meant *so* much to him—I couldn't give him the escape he wanted so badly. Not yet, anyway.

As I gazed up at him, I felt the need to say something to that worry, though. "You know that even if I'm not ready to commit to a whole future together, I'm going to do whatever I can to make sure your parents don't make you pay for their mistakes, right? If your dad's going to try to hurt you, or worse, he'll have to get through me first."

A pleased glint lit in Jude's eyes at the vehemence in my voice. He touched my cheek and drew his fingers along my jaw in a caress that sent tingles all through me. "He doesn't stand a chance, then, does he?" he said, and kissed me.

It was the kind of kiss that swept every other sensation away. His lips branded mine and his spicy smell filled my lungs, and everywhere our bodies touched, mine started to melt. I tucked my hand around his neck and tugged him closer. He wrapped his arm around my back with a little groan. It felt like being worshipped and claimed all at once, and I was totally on board with both.

Nothing stirred inside me except heat and wanting. Not a single shred of fear flickered in my chest this time. Maybe I wasn't ready to tie my life to this guy's in a permanent way just yet, but I believed in him. I believed he'd be there for me the way I'd just promised to be there for him.

Jude released my lips to trail his mouth down to the side of my neck, and a sigh quivered out of me. He teased his fingers down over my shoulder toward my chest at the same time.

Things might have gotten a lot more interesting if voices hadn't carried from outside. I tensed, and Jude lifted his head.

"Damned Naries coming to take back their damned clubhouse," he muttered, but with enough amusement in his tone to diffuse the complaint. He kissed me again, quickly. "We'd better give it back to them."

Benjamin wasn't in the group that was strolling over to the clubhouse, but a couple of his friends were, and some of the other Naries, including Shelby. They gave us an uncertain look as we stepped through the doorway. Jude made a grand salute.

"The inspection is complete," he said. "Continue onward."

I bit back a giggle. The other students still looked apprehensive as we passed them, but Shelby's voice reached my ears, bright and firm.

"You don't have to worry about Rory. She's okay— she's my friend."

I made a mental note to do something particularly nice for Shelby as soon as possible.

"Oh my god, this is seriously the best ice cream I've ever had." Shelby took an enthusiastic swipe at her cone as she, Imogen, and I came out of the shop. "Why haven't we ever gone in there before?"

"I think they just opened this year," Imogen said with a smile at the other girl's enthusiasm. "And I don't know about you, but ice cream during a New York winter isn't super appealing to me."

"If it's this good, maybe it'd be worth it."

I laughed and took a nibble from my own chocolate-banana-almond scoop. It *was* pretty damn good ice cream, creamily sweet with just a hint of salt from the nuts. Although… "There was this amazing place near where I lived in California, where they made their own flavors with fresh fruit in custom combinations…"

I trailed off as a punch of homesickness and grief hit me. The painful loss of my old life, of my parents, had started to numb, but it came back without warning at random moments like this.

Imogen shot me a concerned glance. Shelby only looked curious. She had no idea of the history there.

"I forgot you're from California. I guess it's ice cream weather there pretty much all the time. Must be nice!"

"Yeah," I said, forcing a smile of my own. "There's a lot of nice stuff back there."

Unfortunately, I couldn't say the same for this particular area of the world. Especially right now, when the two figures emerged from a car down the street and hustled over with expectant expressions. I stopped in my tracks.

"Persephone!" my grandmother chirped. "What a wonderful surprise. I'm so glad we happened to cross paths."

My hackles had gone right up. No way was this a coincidental meeting. Why on earth would they have been hanging around in this town other than to see me?

First following Declan to his workplace, then catching

me by surprise here—my grandparents were turning into total stalkers, weren't they?

"Good to see you too," I said stiffly. "We, ah, were actually just—"

My grandmother barrelled right over me. "These must be your friends from school! I don't think we've met." Her gaze took in Imogen and then Shelby, with a tightening of her mouth when it crossed the leaf pin on her blouse that marked her a Nary. "Well, it is wonderful to see you out enjoying yourselves. Stella Evergrist, and this is my husband Rupert."

She held out her dainty hand to Imogen, who took the whole thing in stride with a shake, and then to Shelby. As she gripped the Nary girl's fingers, I caught a movement of her lips with the intake of her breath.

A faint vibration shivered through the air—the impression of a spell deflected by the violin charm hanging from Shelby's neck. The taste of it prickled over my tongue with a tinge of queasiness and the flavor of vomit. My whole body went rigid.

She'd tried to make Shelby sick, probably so the girl would leave and wouldn't prevent us talking about any magic-related subjects. Fury rose up inside me so quickly I could barely contain it.

My grandmother's brow knit as she let go of Shelby's hand, realizing her spell hadn't worked, and I snatched her wrist. "You know," I said, fighting to keep my voice even, "there's something I really need to talk to you about now that you're here." I looked to my friends. "Give me a couple minutes?"

"Of course," Imogen said, frowning as she picked up on the tension. Shelby went back to her ice cream without the slightest idea she'd just been under attack.

I marched my grandmother several feet away, letting my grandfather trail behind us. When we reached their car, I stopped and spun on her.

"Don't you *ever* cast magic on any of my friends again," I said, quietly but sharply.

My grandmother's eyes widened. "She was just—she's a feeb. We can't—"

"*Shut up.*" I dragged in a breath and got a hold of my temper. "She's my friend. That's all you need to know if *you* want any part in my life at all. Got it?"

"Your grandmother didn't mean anything by it," my grandfather said, in such a remorseless tone that I wanted to hex them both halfway across the country right then.

"It still happened, and I don't want it happening again. And because it happened, I don't really feel like spending any time with you right now. Go home—and please don't drop in on me out of the blue like this again."

"Now, Persephone," my grandmother started.

"My name is Rory," I gritted out. "*Leave now.*"

I spoke the last words with the heft of a persuasive spell. It cracked right through the mental barriers my grandmother had in place, and she reached for the car door automatically.

"You really didn't have to go that far," she sputtered as she got in.

My grandfather hustled around the car muttering something about respect for elders, but my grandmother was already shifting in the passenger seat as if to move to the driver's side if he didn't get in there to fulfill my command quickly.

"I'll let you know when I'm ready to see you again," I said as he ducked inside, but as the rage continued to radiate through me, I wasn't sure that'd ever happen in my lifetime.

CHAPTER TWENTY-SIX

Rory

I'd been dreading my weekly sessions with my new mentor for most of the summer, and I didn't think Professor Viceport had been all that enthusiastic about them either. Most of the concerns I had, I wouldn't have felt comfortable bringing up with her anyway. I definitely wasn't going to discuss the problems of trying to give the Naries a better footing at the university. So the mentoring sessions had tended to consist of a quick check-in and a perfunctory suggestion or two.

Today, though, I had an actual goal in mind. I settled into the chair across from Viceport's desk, told myself the astringent whiff of herbs in the air was pleasant enough, and looked her straight in the eye. "I'd like to talk about my grandparents."

The professor blinked, clearly startled, before regaining

her cool composure. "That hardly seems like a subject related to your schooling."

I shrugged. "Our magical abilities are partly inherited. It seems to me that finding out more about my heritage could be useful. And I got the impression that you know at least a little about them, from the way you acted when we bumped into you in town."

Her jaw worked. "I still don't think it's entirely appropriate for me to discuss your relatives with you. If there's something you'd like to know about them, surely you can ask *them*?"

"Yeah, somehow I suspect I'd only get the answers they want me to hear, not what's actually true. They want something from me. Maybe lots of things. That much is obvious. It'd be really useful to know how much I need to worry about that. Like… am I in any actual danger from them if they don't get what they want?"

Viceport frowned. "Causing major harm to a scion or baron is one of the highest offenses in our society. They'd have to be insane to attempt it, and I haven't gotten the impression from them that they're quite so desperate as that."

"But they are desperate. Why?" When she hesitated, I leaned forward in the chair and played the last but possibly best card I had. "Let's say I'm not asking as your student. I'm asking as the heir and pretty much baron of Bloodstone. I've been out of the loop for a long time, and I need to know everything I can."

She didn't like me invoking my status. I could tell that

from the pursing of her lips. But she sighed and folded her hands on her desk, and I knew I'd won.

"I'm not sure there's a very concrete reason why," she said. "The Evergrists have always been a fairly powerful family, but from what I've seen, they're rarely satisfied with what they have. They're always seeking out more influence, more connections, more wealth."

"And they're willing to go to some questionable lengths to get that," I filled in, thinking of their blackmail attempts with Declan, the fact that they'd shouldered their way into my life in the first place.

"Well…" Professor Viceport looked at her hands and then back at me with a hint of a grimace. "There have been rumors. And occasional problems in the past. I would rather not say anything that could be construed as an attack—"

I waved off her concern. "It's fine. I'm sure I said worse things to them the other day than you'd even think of saying."

The corner of her lips twitched into something closer to a smile at that comment. "It was my impression," she said, "that their efforts at heightening their status escalated after your parents' marriage. And that they skirted the line of the law more than once, but the transgressions were small enough that the blacksuits ignored them in favor of avoiding conflict with a ruling family."

"They committed actual crimes?" I said.

"I don't know the details. I simply observed and overheard." Her expression turned grim again. "I trust these comments won't be repeated with my name attached to them."

"Of course." But her need to add that last remark told me a lot about the dynamics that could have allowed my grandparents to get away with who knew how many "transgressions." I wasn't sure how I'd go about finding out details of their crimes or what I'd even do with that information, but it at least confirmed that my instincts to avoid them were one hundred percent correct.

"Thank you," I added. "That's something I'll want to keep in mind."

"If you have any questions about your actual schooling…"

I shook my head and stood up. "No, I think I've got everything else under control. Unless you have any suggestions about my performance in Physicality?"

For a second, I'd have sworn she glowered at me before her face turned impassive again. "You've been doing quite well the last few weeks. Continue in the same vein, and I'll have no complaints."

I guessed that was progress.

I headed out of the staff wing and down the stairs to the main fore-room. I was just coming through the narrower hall between the two sections of the building when Malcolm stepped into view at the other end.

My legs locked automatically. Malcolm froze on the threshold of the hall. His usual expression of cool confidence came over his face, but his stance stayed uncertain.

"Bloodstone," he said in a tone I couldn't read.

"Nightwood," I replied tightly. The thought of squeezing past him, my shoulder nearly brushing his in the narrow space, made my skin shiver.

He wavered there a moment longer, and then he... backed up a couple steps. Out of the hall into the room beyond, so I could walk past with plenty of space.

For a moment, I was too startled to move. Was Malcolm Nightwood actually *giving way* to me? How was that even possible? Then I walked forward cautiously, every sense on high alert in case he tried some sort of magic on me.

He didn't raise his hand or cast a single spell, though. He just waited for me to go by. I slowed as I passed him, not really wanting to leave my back open to him while I walked on, and he cleared his throat.

"You might want to keep an eye out," he said brusquely. "Victory looks like she's on a rampage out there."

Without another word, he ducked down the hall and was gone.

I stared after him, letting the words sink in. He'd stepped aside for me, and he was also warning me about one of his biggest devotees? Had I stumbled into a parallel universe between Viceport's office and here?

Whatever was going on, I should probably go find out what the hell Victory was doing. I'd just proceed with caution, in case this was some kind of trick.

I passed a couple of professors in quiet conversation and slipped out of Killbrook Hall. It only took a second for me to spot my nemesis stalking across the other end of the green.

Victory's expression was taut, her hands moving restlessly at her sides as if waiting for the chance to cast. As I watched, lingering in the shadow of the broad doorway, she glanced toward Ashgrave Hall, then the field beyond where the clubhouse stood, then back to the hall. She stopped and brought her hands to her mouth. It looked like she murmured something into them, her eyes narrowing intently.

I didn't know what she was up to, but the vibe she was giving off and the direction of her attention made the hairs on the back of my neck stand on end. Whether Malcolm had hoped I'd clash with her or been trying to help me avoid a collision, he clearly hadn't been lying about her state of mind.

A couple of Naries left Ashgrave Hall, and Victory's gaze followed them while they gave her a wide berth, either from past experience or picking up on her current mood. They were heading toward Nightwood Tower, though. She made a face and folded her arms as she waited… for whatever she was waiting for.

After Cressida's assault on Benjamin the other day, I didn't think I wanted to give her the chance to act on her intentions. But how could I head her off? The second I started casting any magic on her, she'd notice, and the situation would only escalate.

Another few students came around Killbrook Hall—a couple of fearmancers walking together, and Shelby, trailing a careful distance behind them, clutching a bag of groceries she'd slung over her shoulder. I hurried over to catch her before she walked onto the green into Victory's realm of attention.

"Hey," she said. "What's going on?"

I tipped my head toward Victory. "One of our roommates looks like she's prowling for victims. Here, I'll walk with you over to the dorms. She's less likely to bother you if you're not alone."

"Okay, thanks." Shelby peered toward Victory and shuddered. "I don't know how people like her manage to get away with so much. She's got to be breaking some kind of school rule, the way she hassles people."

I paused, a spark of inspiration lighting in the back of my head. Victory *wasn't* breaking any school rules by harassing the Naries—she was doing exactly as we were taught. But there were other rules she'd be sanctioned for.

I didn't have to cast any magic *on* her at all. I just had to convince an authoritative witness that they had to intervene.

The plan unfurled in my head, but I couldn't do it alone. I touched Shelby's arm to stop her. Victory had noticed us skirting the green, but she hadn't left her spot at the far end. All we got was a sneer that looked way too self-satisfied for my liking.

"What if we could get her in the kind of trouble she deserves?" I said. "I think I can make that happen, if you'll help… but she might figure out it was us."

A slow smile stretched across Shelby's face. "What can she do that's any worse than how she already treats me? Of course I'm in. What do you need me to do?"

Her eagerness steadied me. I tipped my head toward Killbrook Hall. "Run in there and tell the first teachers you see that Victory's saying crazy things, you don't know what's wrong with her. I saw a couple of them talking in the fore-room—they're probably still there. I'll take care of the rest."

Shelby nodded with a sly gleam in her eye and jogged back to the hall. I drew farther back from the green so the buildings blocked me from Victory's view.

As soon as Shelby had disappeared through the door, I started murmuring a spell. An illusion, capturing Victory's voice. I'd heard that caustic tone when she was angry enough times to reproduce it pretty accurately, I thought.

I cast the spell toward the entrance to Killbrook Hall so it would echo through the door, projecting it only in that direction. If Victory heard what I was doing, she'd realize the trick in a second.

"*I can crush all of you feebs if I want to,*" I made her conjured voice screech. "*You think you're so special because you got to come here? You're nothing. We've got all the power. We can bend you to our will just like that. You want to see? This is what we call* magic."

I let the spell fade. At the squeak of the door's hinges a second later, I cast another, brief illusion—a thunderclap of sound intended to make Victory flinch and look unnerved.

The two professors I'd seen burst out of the hall and charged across the green toward her. "You need to come with us," one of them said.

"What the hell?" Victory said, out of my sight around the building. "What are you talking about?"

"The problem is what *you're* talking about," the other said. "A visit with the headmistress is in order, *now*."

I slunk even closer to Ashgrave Hall as they ushered Victory past, protests continuing to sputter from her mouth. Several seconds after they'd tugged her inside, Shelby emerged with a triumphant grin. She loped over to rejoin me.

"It worked, right?"

"It worked perfectly." I grinned back and raised my fist to bump it against hers.

Right then, it didn't matter that this girl had no magic and couldn't know about mine. She couldn't have been a better friend. And what were friends for other than conspiring together?

Glancing back toward Killbrook Hall, the ploy we'd just pulled off stirred another idea. We'd gotten ahead of Victory's scheming by pre-emptively bringing down sanctions on her.

What if there was another way that strategy could be put to use to save a whole lot more than one clubhouse?

CHAPTER TWENTY-SEVEN

Rory

It wasn't hard to pick the right time to drop by the teacher's aide office. I'd had enough sessions with Declan there last term that I was familiar with his hours—and which of those hours he usually had there alone.

At least, alone as far as other aides went. When I slipped into the office that afternoon, Declan was sitting at one of the tables in the large room, talking through something with another student.

They both glanced up at me, Declan's expression tensing for an instant and the guy he was tutoring only looking mildly curious. My first instinct was to turn around and hightail it out of there, but then I might as well hold up a sign declaring I was up to something untoward. So I gave a little nod in greeting and went to sit on one of the chairs near the door, as if I was there for the same reason the guy was.

"I can wait," I said.

Declan had a lot of practice at keeping a cool head. He returned the nod, his expression carefully neutral again, and turned back to his student. I tried to relax into the firmly padded chair as the drone of the air conditioner hummed in the background.

To my relief, the other tutoring session wrapped up quickly. Declan got up as the guy headed out. He didn't say anything until the door had closed solidly behind the other student.

"Rory…"

"I know," I said quickly, holding up my hands as I came over. "I just need to ask a couple of quick questions about the Insight work, and Professor Sinleigh is busy with classes this afternoon. It'll only take a few minutes."

I *had* confirmed that I had a good excuse for going to Declan instead of the professor, who'd been giving me some additional instruction as I asked for it during the summer. He made a bit of a face at the cover story, but his shoulders came down a little.

"Fair enough," he said, his hazel eyes intent on my face. "What's the problem?"

I inhaled slowly as I gathered my words. "It's more a possible solution than a problem. To the issue of my grandparents. I was talking to Professor Viceport about them yesterday, and she suggested they've committed some minor crimes in the past that were overlooked because of their connection to the barony."

"That wouldn't surprise me," Declan said. "The blacksuits are going to be a lot more hesitant to pursue leads involving one of the ruling families, in case it turns out they're wrong and there's backlash from the baron."

Or backlash even if they were right, I suspected. "Well," I said, "I know you've studied the laws backwards and forwards to make sure your aunt can't trip you up, and you're obviously good at doing that research… If you looked, you could probably find one of those crimes and some evidence for it, don't you think?"

Declan gave me a puzzled look. "And I'd do that because…"

"Because then you could see them *charged* for that crime, and that would get them off our cases. Or at the very least, once you've initiated that investigation, they can't make accusations about you and me without it looking like retaliation rather than a legitimate concern. *They* don't have any proof. And the only Bloodstone around who could get upset about them being investigated is giving you her blessing."

Declan's eyes had widened. "You really want me to try to get your grandparents arrested?"

An uncomfortable twinge ran through my gut. "Don't look at me like that. If they *have* committed crimes, it's their own fault. And they've proven they're dangerous while they're walking free. I'm protecting the people I care about."

Me. Shelby. And the guy in front of me, whose expression softened at the comment. "Okay," he said. "That's actually a pretty good plan. Having seen them in action, I'd be surprised if they haven't left a trail to one illicit dealing or another somewhere. Overconfidence can screw a person over awfully fast." He paused and gave me a little smile. "We'll still have to keep our distance from each other."

"I know," I said. "I just don't want them to be able to threaten either of us—or anyone else."

"Thank you."

I wasn't sure how he'd react, but I couldn't help reaching out to grasp his hand. That one small point of contact, his warm skin against mine while he gazed back at me with the affection he was trying to restrain, brought back the moment in his bedroom not that long ago when I'd gotten to be so much closer to him for the last time. He squeezed my fingers like a promise, and I eased back before he had to break the moment himself.

"You'll know when it's done," he said. "I'm sure they'll be harassing you for support the second they realize they're in trouble."

The corner of my lips quirked up. "And they're going to be so very disappointed."

My grandparents weren't my biggest concern. I still had the matter of a mysterious key to work out.

The traffic on the city street rumbled by as I sat in my parked car. I studied the building on the corner ahead of me, readying myself for what I hoped would be the last step in my quest for answers. A step I had to take completely on my own.

The back of my neck had prickled more than once as

I'd driven out here to this spot about halfway between the campus and Professor Banefield's home. Sudden worries about being followed had crept up through my thoughts. But I'd been parked here for several minutes, and I hadn't noticed anyone else stopping nearby. I hadn't seen any car behind me for an unusual amount of time during the drive over.

It was just hard not to be nervous when so much might ride on this moment.

I got out of the car and headed up the street to the post office the address in Banefield's note had led me to. It wasn't the only building with that street address in the whole state, and his note hadn't included any other details, but the others had been a daycare center and a bridal shop in other cities. This seemed to be the most likely of the possibilities.

A bell dinged over the door as I stepped inside. They had the air conditioning up high—my skin broke out in goosebumps within seconds. I resisted the urge to hug myself and veered around the line of customers waiting to mail something.

A wall of PO boxes stood at the far end of the space. And it *was* a whole wall—dozens and dozens of them, some small and some larger. I eyed them from the side of my vision, wandering over to the rack of envelopes and packing materials for sale nearby. My hand dipped into my purse to close around the key Professor Banefield had given me.

I couldn't go sticking the key in every box until I found a match. The post office staff would notice that weird behavior pretty quickly. They might have been able to look up the key in a database from the digits on it… but I wasn't sure what they'd do if they saw it was registered to an Archer Banefield who definitely wasn't me.

But I was a mage, so there had to be a better solution I could think up.

I ran my finger over the ridges on the key and considered the rows of locks. This felt like a physicality problem. Find the matching shapes among those holes.

After several sweeps of my thumb tip over the key, I had a solid image of the pattern in my mind. I reached to the magic thrumming behind my collarbone and molded it into an invisible copy of that pattern. Then I cast it off toward the rows of boxes with a murmured, "Fit."

An echo of sensation rippled over my skin as the spell slipped across the boxes. I felt it twitch into each opening and jerk back out when the grooves didn't match.

Halfway across the second row, a little jolt hit me and the rippling stilled. I stepped toward the wall of boxes with a skip of my pulse.

The spell tugged me toward the right one. I pushed the key in. It slid into place without any resistance, and the lock clicked over with the twist of my fingers.

A large envelope sat inside the box—nothing else. I grabbed it, shoved it into my purse, locked the box up again, and hurried out as quickly as I could without looking frantic.

I scanned the street again as I headed to my car. No one around me looked shady, but it wasn't as if I knew for sure what to look for. All of my enemies had magic too.

I set my purse carefully onto the passenger seat and started the engine. I'd noted a good pull-off spot on my way here. About a half hour outside the city, there was a little diner that appeared to have been closed for years, given the amount of rust on the drooping sign. It wouldn't look too strange for me to be parked in the lot out front, and the open fields all around gave me a good line of sight if anyone approached.

Despite those benefits, after I'd pulled into the parking lot, I also cast a few temporary wards on the ground around the car. Better safe than sorry, especially with the kind of enemies I was clearly up against.

My mouth went dry as I picked up the envelope. It was sealed, with a postage label and mark on the upper corner—Professor Banefield hadn't just stashed it in the box but mailed it to himself. Just before he'd gotten sick the second time, from the date on the mark. He'd been preparing, knowing he probably wouldn't be able to tell me anything useful directly because of the spell on him.

The seal tore easily at the tug of my thumb. I pulled out the sheaf of papers inside, many of them creased and different sizes. A hodgepodge of compiled records.

One of the first papers, lined and frayed at the top as if it'd been torn out of a notepad, held only a list of names, a couple of them crossed out, added to at various times based on the different shades of the ink.

Julian and Dahlia Nightwood
Edmund Killbrook
Marguerite and Quince Stormhurst
Wesley Cutbridge

Alice Villia

Roland Crowford

I paused over that one. Was that Professor Crowford? The professor who'd come up with our horrible summer project? I couldn't remember if I'd ever caught his first name. I'd have to check the plaque on his office door when I got back to school.

There were several more names on the list. I didn't recognize any of the others except *Pierce Darksend*, who might have been the junior Physicality professor based on his last name, and an Ilene Burnbuck, who might have been related to my Illusion professor. A few of the other last names sounded vaguely familiar, maybe from hearing the professors call on fellow students in class, but I couldn't connect faces to them.

Who were all these people? The barons were obvious —were the rest of them the "reapers" Banefield had mentioned? I set the list aside and dug deeper into the collection of papers.

A lot of them were what looked like rough meeting minutes. Last names and hastily jotted point form remarks that referred to ideas I wasn't familiar with: *Faraday transaction* and *Ulverton switch* and so on. The parts I did understand sounded like plans being made, resources shifted around. A few comments gave the impression of some sort of a bribe, promises made to ensure support.

Then there were articles, both newspaper clippings and printouts from online publications. Politicians announcing new undertakings or canceled projects, companies starting up ventures or adjusting old ones, things like that. Things maybe the people on that list had influenced?

At least some of the events must have been connected to those meetings, because I started seeing names I recognized. James Faraday, CEO of this communications conglomerate. Ulverton Pharmaceuticals. My body tensed as I flipped further.

If I'd had all the context, I suspected this collection of information would have pointed to fearmancers purposefully influencing various powerful Naries. I had no idea why, though. There wasn't any clear pattern I could see to the news articles. And I wasn't even sure using that kind of influence was against mage laws anyway.

A realization sank in slowly as I approached the bottom of the pile. There was something bigger than what I could find here that the barons and maybe some other people working alongside them wanted to accomplish. Something they couldn't accomplish without my agreement, either given freely or forced. If this stuff was all that mattered of them, they wouldn't be attacking me—or magicking the people around me into attempting assaults.

Professor Banefield must have been at these meetings. How else would he know so much about what they'd talked about and who'd been there? Had he *agreed* with what the barons were doing some of that time?

I flipped another page, and suddenly that question didn't matter anymore. Because the next article had a large photograph of a man in a suit surrounded by onlookers— and on the fringes of that crowd stood the barons Nightwood and Stormhurst. Behind them, her head just partly visible beside Connar's mother's, was the unmistakeable profile of Lillian Ravenguard.

A cold shiver crawled up my back. I set the papers down and closed my eyes.

Maybe it was just a coincidence? She was a blacksuit— she might have been assigned as a sort of bodyguard in the crowd.

I held onto that hope for a few minutes longer, until I came to another set of meeting minutes. The fourth of those pages had some discussion about the blacksuits. Something about them *coming on board* and *assisting with the transition*. And the initials LR were marked down here and there all through that section.

I hadn't trusted my mother's best friend to begin with. I wasn't even sure I could trust the person my *mother* had been. But Lillian had at least appeared to be kind to me. It would have been nice if she'd turned out to be an ally and not in cahoots with the people Banefield had desperately wanted to warn me about.

Maybe I didn't know what to make of everything here, but one thing was clear—I couldn't tell Lillian anything, couldn't ask her anything that might reveal my intentions. She might have been my mother's best friend, but she was no friend of mine.

CHAPTER TWENTY-EIGHT

Connar

The entire Stormhurst mansion was gloomy, but the hall outside my brother's rooms held so many shadows I felt them pressing against my skin as I walked to his door.

I wasn't supposed to be in this part of the house. Since the fight they'd provoked and his subsequent injuries, my parents had shut Holden away in a small section of the house with a few adjoining rooms. They'd hired a nurse to check on him and see to his needs. Now, they pretended he didn't exist, and they expected me to follow suit.

To care about the loser in our battle was weakness. They didn't want to see any weakness in their scion. But the truth was, it took far more strength for me to make this walk than it did to stay away and avoid the guilt.

I stopped outside the door and whispered to the air around it, tasting the spells cast there. My parents were talented mages, as all the barony families and their chosen spouses were, but I'd started to surpass them in a few areas. There was a ward meant to alert them if anyone other than the nurse crossed this threshold—I could shift it to one side so my coming and going wouldn't affect it. Opening the physical lock was a piece of cake.

The hardest part, really, was opening that door and stepping through it.

"Holden?" I called cautiously as I entered.

Classical music carried faintly from one of the deeper rooms: strains of flute and piano. The room I'd come into was sparsely furnished with a desk by the broad window, an armchair in the corner, and a couple of bookshelves along the walls. Holden had loved to read his whole life, and he still did. The brain injury he'd taken made it difficult for him to express much, both verbally or in writing, but he could still take just about anything in, as far as I could tell.

A sweet smell drifted from a few springs of lily of the valley arranged in a vase on the desk. He must have managed to communicate to the nurse that he'd wanted her to bring some up from the sparse garden on the west side of the house. They were just starting to droop.

"Holden?" I said again, and the music quieted. The whir of the electric wheelchair announced his approach before I could see my brother himself.

He cruised into the room and came to a stop a few feet inside with a tight smile. I couldn't read much into that, since from what I'd seen it was the only kind of smile his face was capable of now. His head always listed slightly to one side. He'd once been as broad in frame and features as I was, but the lack of exercise had slimmed him, turning him into sharper angles. His hair, a darker shade of brown than mine, fell in waves to the tops of his ears.

"Con," he said in acknowledgment. He hadn't been able to manage my full name since the fight.

"I'm just home for the weekend," I said, as if that mattered all that much to him. "I felt like it'd been too long since I came to see you. How are you doing?"

An awkward question, but I couldn't *not* ask it. He gave his closest approximation to a shrug and said, "Ar— Th—Same." Sometimes it took him a few tries before he hit on a word he could force all the way out.

"The nurse is keeping you well-stocked in new books?" I glanced toward the shelves.

"I," he said, the smile tugging a little wider and even tighter, and gestured to the tablet he'd tucked beside his paralyzed legs.

"Oh, you're lowering yourself to ebooks now, huh? I doubt you can get many fearmancer texts that way."

He made a snorting sound, but the flicker of his eyes made me regret the attempt at teasing. A lot of the books on the shelves behind me were magical texts. He'd kept studying them even after he'd lost any real ability to cast. He didn't need his limitations rubbed in, though, especially when I was the one who'd caused them.

"Sorry," I said. "I just—" I made myself shut up for a moment. I never really knew what to say to him. Sometimes I was sure I was only making things worse.

That feeling had lengthened the time between my secret visits more than once.

There was one thing I'd decided I *had* to say before I'd even come up here. I took a step toward him, my head bowing.

If I could talk to Rory about this—if I could beg *her* forgiveness for what I'd done to her—I should at least be able to say a few honest things to my own brother.

"I'm sorry for a lot more than that," I said. "We never talk about it, so I don't think I've ever really apologized. I never wanted to hurt you. I hate that I did. I—If I could give the barony to you and have you back the way you were, I'd do that in a heartbeat. You'd be better for it anyway. Our parents have messed up ideas about what makes a good leader. *You* were the one who was stronger. You resisted them longer—you had more self-control."

I braced myself as I raised my eyes again, half expecting anger or disgust on his face. Instead, Holden only looked sad. "There—" he said, and grimaced at the strain of trying to squeeze the words in his head up his throat. "See— Can't—"

With a frustrated sound, he directed the wheelchair past me to the bookshelves. He leaned forward to snatch up a volume he must have known well. After a few brisk flips of the pages, he held the novel out to me with his finger poised over one paragraph.

There was never any going back, not to the good or the bad. The best we could do was move forward carrying those lessons with us. It was hard to remember, but I returned to that thought whenever I drifted too far into regret.

A lump rose in my throat. "I know," I said. "I know I can't actually undo what happened. And I'm trying to do what's right going forward. It's still…" I trailed off, not knowing how to end that sentence.

Mom had brought in doctors to tackle Holden's injuries, but she said they'd declared most of them too severe to heal even with magic. He was never going to walk again. He was never going to be able to speak or write properly. He would never cast more than a hiccup of magic here and there. And there wasn't anything I could do to change that.

"When I'm baron, I'm kicking them out of the house," I said with abrupt certainty. "I'll put in an elevator and ramps and whatever the hell else so you can go wherever you want, when you want. They shouldn't keep you shut away like this."

He gave that sort of shrug again, as if to say he was used to it, which after nearly six years, I guessed he was. That only made the situation worse.

"I mean it," I said, holding his gaze. "That's a promise." Even if it was one I wouldn't be able to fulfill until years from now.

The highway-side restaurant a couple hours away from the university wasn't much to look at. "Dive bar" would probably have been the appropriate term. But that might have been exactly why the four of us scions had come to appreciate it as a stop-off and meet-up spot on the way back to campus.

After the stresses of a visit home, with all the expectations and emphasis on appearances, where better to unwind than a place where nearly everything on the menu was deep-fried and the only kind of button-up shirts the other clientele wore were printed with plaid?

It was usually Malcolm or Declan who arranged those meet-ups, though. I couldn't remember when Jude had ever reached out to me with a specific invitation. I hadn't even realized he'd gone home this weekend too. But he'd texted me while I was saying my goodbyes to my parents, and while I wasn't sure whether this was going to be a friendly conversation, I wasn't going to snub him.

It was easy to tell he was already there when I arrived. His Mercedes was the fanciest car in the lot by several degrees. I parked beside it and headed inside.

A country rock song was twanging over the speakers, and the air had its familiar salt-and-grease flavor. Jude had staked out a booth near the back, his dark red hair catching my eye even with the yellow lighting dulling its vivid color. I walked over and slid onto the opposite bench.

"You made good time," Jude said mildly, and beckoned for a waitress. He already had a drink in front of him, something dark poured over ice. Even when we'd been in our mid-teens, the waitstaff here hadn't given our enchanted IDs more than a cursory glance. Another reason we liked this place.

"I'll have the bacon burger with pepper fries," Jude said, and tipped his head to me.

"A New Belgium if you still have it on tap, and the barbeque wings." I'd been here often enough to skip a glance at the menu.

"I'll get right on that," the waitress said cheerfully, and sashayed away.

Jude tugged at the collar of his shirt as if he were too warm in it, even though the air conditioning blasting from the unit nearby was keeping the space pretty cool. He looked away from me for a moment, the corners of his mouth pulling down.

"Tough visit?" I ventured.

"Ah, I was prepared for that. It's never *fun*." He turned back to me with a wry smile. "As I'm sure yours wasn't either."

"Let's not get into that." The waitress plonked my beer on the table, and I took a large gulp. "Is there any specific reason you wanted us to grab lunch today?" The last time we'd talked one-on-one, he'd been telling me off.

"Can't I just want to hang out with one of my good friends?" Jude said innocently, and shook his head at himself. "I figured if Malcolm of all people can own up to his assholery, I should be able to too. I've been rough on you this summer, mostly because of my issues rather than any real issue with you. So, I'm sorry about that."

It took me a second to process what I was hearing. I'd have much sooner expected Jude to simply pretend any hostility had never happened than to apologize for it.

"It wasn't a big deal," I said by way of accepting the

apology, and let a wry note creep into my voice. "I learned a long time ago not to get too offended by anything you say when you're shooting your mouth off."

Jude sputtered with mock-indignation, but his eyes glinted with amusement. "Look at Stormhurst giving the verbal smackdown. Not your usual style. I guess Rory was right."

At the mention of the girl who'd taken up so much space in my head and heart over the last few months, my mood turned more serious in an instant. "Right about what?"

"Oh, don't worry. It was a compliment. She said the rest of us didn't give you enough credit for being more than the brawn. I'm willing to concede that may be true."

The thought of Rory speaking up for me that way sent a warm flush through my chest, only slightly moderated by Jude's cheeky phrasing. "May be true?" I muttered.

He grinned at me. "I'm not finished collecting evidence yet. That is the other subject I wanted to talk about, though. Rory—and our common interest in her."

I raised my eyebrows. "I hope you didn't apologize for laying into me only to warn me off her all over again."

He waved his hand dismissively. "No, no. Really the opposite. For reasons I'm sure no one would be able to fathom, she's clearly fond of both of us. And she's had a rather rough few months since she arrived at Blood U, I'm sure you can agree."

"Yeah." Not least because of our own initial treatment of her.

"So, I simply suggest that we should focus on making

the coming months more enjoyable for her, however we can. And if that means both of us fawning over her, well... In this particular case, maybe more can still be merrier."

I studied him. "Is this some weird way of giving me your blessing? Which I didn't actually need in the first place, by the way."

"Hey, you could give *me* the benefit of the doubt too," he said. "I'm just saying... Let's not fight about it. Let's not interfere with whatever she ends up having going with the other. We each do what we can to show her a good time, and she'll end up with double the good time. Maybe we can even make a joint effort of it now and then." His grin came back. "With both of us on a date, I'm fairly certain she'd at least never be bored."

"We'll see about that," I said, but as the idea sank in, my initial balking reaction faded. His main point was solid. Rory deserved better than having us squabble over her. And maybe... it would make her even happier to see we could not just tolerate each other's presence in her life, but embrace the fact. I wasn't sure what a "joint effort" would look like, but anything that'd make her happy, that'd offset the pressure she was under, I was all for.

"If you think of any possibilities along that line, let me know," I added, and Jude's grin turned into a full-out smirk.

"Oh, I'm sure I can come up with something without any trouble at all."

CHAPTER TWENTY-NINE

Rory

The central air in Ashgrave Hall was having some kind of technical difficulties. Even tucked away in a dim corner of the library, I couldn't escape the summer heat. Sweat trickled down my back as I flipped through one of the books I'd gathered. I swiped at my forehead.

The hardest part about researching anything to do with fearmancers was they didn't exactly broadcast their activities to the wider world. I'd tried digging around online for news articles or other records that might help me figure out the connections between the names on Professor Banefield's list and the Nary activities they'd apparently interfered with, but there hadn't been anything beyond the clippings he'd already collected, none of which mentioned the fearmancers themselves anyway.

I *had* determined that the Crowford on the list was my Persuasion professor, and the Darksend was the Physicality professor I'd only seen in passing. The fact that not just one but two teachers on campus were part of this group—the group that presumably had been responsible for Banefield's death—was far from comforting.

In my earlier searches of the university library, I'd discovered a small section that held volumes of fearmancer records: the lines of inheritance within the ruling families, significant events at the university, and other write-ups someone or other had decided were worth committing to paper. Sorting through those, I'd made a few more discoveries.

Lillian Ravenguard was married to Julian Nightwood's second cousin. Ilene Burnbuck was my professor Burnbuck's aunt and had come by the school for occasional special tutorials. Three of the other names on the list, people I hadn't recognized at all, had contributed funds to the restoration of the Killbrook Hall after a bad storm had caused a bunch of damage, which suggested they were fairly prominent and involved in fearmancer society.

So, basically, my enemies were a whole bunch of people with tons of power. Wonderful. I still didn't have any clue what they were after that had made it worth trying to crush me into submission. Or why they appeared to have eased back in their efforts after my mentor's death.

Maybe they were unsure of what Banefield might have managed to tell me, and they wanted to watch what I did next before deciding *their* next moves. Maybe they were worried that launching another assault so soon after his death would be too risky. There had to be people who wouldn't agree with what they were doing—enough people that they felt they needed to go about their attempts as surreptitiously as possible.

Knowing that wasn't much of a comfort either, though. It didn't mean they were done. It only meant I was getting a reprieve before another attack that might come at any time in any way. How could I prepare when I had no idea what was going to come at me or how soon?

I set down my current book with a sigh and picked up another. This one talked about various international tournaments and the winners who'd come from Blood U. I wasn't sure there'd be anything useful in there, but I skimmed the pages just in case.

I'd only made it a little way through when the floor at the end of my aisle of shelves creaked.

"Here she is," Jude said, with a fond shake of his head. "Hiding away in a pile of books. Typical."

Connar had come over with him. "Project research?" he asked me, looking at the stack.

"Something like that," I said. "Not that I'm getting very far." I paused. I didn't know how to broach the subject of the barons' hostility with either of them. Not that Jude or Connar seemed to really *like* the people who'd raised them, but I'd seen how difficult a fearmancer's sense of loyalty could be to shake. Look at how long Connar had ignored his conscience to support Malcolm's plans. And the barons weren't just family to them—they were the leaders of their entire society.

I'd have to talk to them about it at some point... but

maybe not quite yet. Not until I was sure it'd help me and not backfire in my face.

I tucked a damp strand of hair behind my ear, wondering what to make of the fact that they'd come looking for me *together*. Jude waved for me to get up.

"Come on," he said. "We're getting you out of this oven. I'm sure you need a break by now anyway. Go get your swimsuit, and we'll cool off in the lake."

The thought of the lake made my chest clench up. I hadn't gone in the water since things had gotten hot—and then chilling—with Malcolm. "I—"

"You'll be able to focus better if you give yourself a breather," Connar said, clearly anticipating my protest even if he didn't know exactly why. "Summer's almost over. You've got to enjoy it while you can."

He looked at me so hopefully that my resistance wavered. It *would* be nice to get out of the heat. And there was something incredibly sweet about the way the two of them had joined forces to rescue me from my study habits, even though they didn't always get along. Even though they had every reason to feel at odds while they were both vying for my affection. I didn't want to discourage that peacemaking.

I'd decided I wasn't going to let Malcolm ruin any part of my life. Why should I let one bad memory stop me from enjoying one of the few things I did actually like at this school?

"Okay, okay," I said, getting up. "I'm sold. I'll meet you down at the dock?"

Jude winked at me. "You'd better be fast about it, or I'll come and carry you over."

I made a face at him, and he laughed. But I did pull on my bikini as quickly as I could once I reached my dorm room, grabbing a tee for more modesty on the walk down.

When I reached the shore, Jude and Connar were already standing on the dock, Connar in swim trunks and Jude in a fitted Speedo that left very little to the imagination. Between that and the amount of toned musculature on display, a different sort of heat fluttered under my skin.

"Why are you two just standing around?" I teased as I dropped my shirt and towel on the warm boards of the dock. "Last one in's a rotten egg!"

I leapt off the end with that last declaration. The splash and surge of the cool water washed away all the lingering sweat on my skin. There was a shout as the two guys joined me, the water rocking me with the waves from them hitting the water.

"I think we can declare that a tie," Jude said, flicking his hair back from his eyes. Wet, it turned so dark it was almost black.

"If you insist," Connar said, smiling.

"The important part is that I beat both of you," I declared, and started swimming deeper into the lake with casual strokes. The vibe of the moment was already totally different from the previous afternoon. The memory faded more with each push through the water.

Jude dove down. A few seconds later, a tug on my

ankle nearly pulled my head underwater. I kicked out instinctively to free my leg, and the Killbrook scion emerged with a sputter.

"You almost broke my nose there, Ice Queen."

"A girl's got to defend herself." I arched my eyebrows at him. "You should be careful. I'm told I'm a very powerful mage."

He just laughed.

Connar swam past us, moving east. "Apparently we gave other people the same idea," the bigger guy said with a quick nod to the shore. A few Naries, none of them students I knew well, were heading down to the water in their swimsuits.

"There's a little bay over here that's nice," the Stormhurst scion added.

And a little more private, I guessed. I followed him, watching the rise of the shore from low rocky ground to nearly sheer gray cliff. Giggles and splashes carried from behind us, but the hiss of the waves against the uneven wall of stone gradually overwhelmed them.

Somewhere up there lay the little clearing where I'd first spoken to Connar, where we'd first kissed… Where we'd done a lot of first things.

Jude cruised after us, switching between a lazy front crawl and gliding along on his back, his pale skin stark against the dark water. For a second, with the sun shining off his boyish face, his lips curled into a smile of contentment so pure it made my heart ache.

Maybe he'd needed a break from reality too.

The shoreline curved, the forest peering over the edge

of the cliff high above, and the voices of the other students vanished completely. Nothing stirred in this alcove at the edge of the lake other than the leaves overhead and us swimming into the still water. I shifted onto my back like Jude had, staring up at the broad expanse of the blue sky. The same sky that had spilled out over me back in California. So much had changed, but some things I could count on.

Connar swam closer to the cliffside where he could stand on the bottom, the water rippling around his shoulders. "You like it?" he asked with a pleased gleam in his eyes as I joined him. The lake bottom was rocky too, but the stones pressed smoothly against my feet when I set them down to give my muscles a break.

"You know all the best spots, huh?" I said.

He gave me that glorious grin that had made me want him from the first time I'd seen it, and I had to bob up for a kiss. Connar steadied me in the water with an arm around my waist, his lips slick but still warm against mine. We'd only pressed together with this much bare skin once before. Desire shot through my body, sharp and heady.

Jude cleared his throat with a disgruntled sound where he'd come up behind me. I turned, and Connar's arm loosened around me without letting go completely. Before I could rethink the urge, I grasped Jude's hand and pulled him to me.

His mouth collided with mine, and oh Lord, I hadn't known it was possible to feel this much all at once. Jude kissing me, his hand cupping my face. Connar tracing his thumb over my stomach where he held me beneath the water. Both their bodies connected with mine with such delicious friction, turned slick by the lake.

There had better not be anything wrong with wanting two guys at once, because now that I was experiencing it, I couldn't imagine giving it up.

Connar ducked his head to press his lips to my neck. Jude claimed my mouth even more completely, his tongue tangling with mine. His fingers stroked down my side— and back up to the curve of my breast, shifting the current with the motion.

My breath hitched with a jolt of anticipation, but a thread of anxiety wriggled through the haze of pleasure. I drew back just far enough to speak. "What if someone else comes around this way?"

Jude met Connar's eyes over my shoulder. A sly smile curved his lips. "I think we can make sure there's no need to worry about that. A physical barrier to block off other swimmers and stop sound from traveling, and an illusion to prevent any glimpses from a distance?"

"Sounds like a plan," Connar said in a voice low enough to send an eager shiver through me.

Both of them spoke under their breaths as they cast. Their magic flitted through the air with a faint vibration I only picked up for an instant.

Jude turned back to me looking very satisfied with himself. "Now, where were we?"

"In the middle of making sure this is the best swim our Princess Bloodstone has ever had, I think," Connar said, and lowered his mouth to nibble my earlobe.

Jude kissed me again, teasing his fingertips along my

collarbone and then the edge of my bikini top. I gave an impatient hum that Connar responded to first. He slid his hands around me to caress both my breasts at the same time.

My body arched with the rush of pleasure, and Jude gripped my hip, aligning our bodies. If I'd had any doubts about how much *he* wanted *me*, the bulge that brushed against my core would have dispelled them. A hungry ache formed between my legs.

He didn't rush, though. He just held me against him and kissed me with so much passion my head spun, already giddy with the bliss Connar was working through my chest and with his lips along my neck and shoulder.

Connar released me for just a second to undo the clasp at the back of my top. The water glided up over my bare skin even more intimately as the fabric drifted free. Jude tugged it right off and, with a cheeky grin, hung it from a notch in the cliffside.

Connar palmed my breasts again, carefully and then with more assurance. He swiveled his thumbs over my nipples until they stood at throbbing attention and then rolled them between his fingers so firmly I gasped against Jude's mouth. The ache between my legs expanded.

With a rough breath, Connar shifted me higher against his frame, setting me in the perfect position for him to lavish even more attention with his mouth on the sensitive spot where my neck met my shoulder. My breasts broke from the water's surface with a fresh lick of pleasure. He tweaked the nipples again. Then, as Jude left my mouth to nip along my jaw, Connar slid his hand underneath one breast as if to offer it up to the other scion.

Jude let out a breathless chuckle. "Now there's a delicacy I can't resist."

He sucked the tip of my breast into his mouth, Connar worked over the other side even more enthusiastically, and all I could do was moan and be thankful their spells had covered any noises we made.

Pleasure rushed through me in waves of sparks. I tipped my head back, and Connar managed to capture my lips from behind, tucking his head over my shoulder. He teased my breast more tenderly and then pinched the nipple so I whimpered. My hips canted toward Jude.

Even as Jude swiped his tongue over the peak of my breast, he tugged me tighter against him. But that friction wasn't enough to satisfy me anymore. I gave Connar one more desperate kiss and then yanked Jude up so our mouths could crash together. At the same time, I ground against him. He groaned, his teeth nicking my lip.

"Are you sure?" he murmured in a strained voice. His hand came to rest on the waist of my bikini bottoms, his fingers hooking around them meaningfully.

I nodded. "God, yes."

He peeled the bottoms off me and tossed them over my top where it was hanging. With another tug beneath the water, the head of his cock traced over my clit. Connar had resumed his attentions to both my breasts and my neck, and for a few seconds that swell of sensation was enough. Then I growled impatiently.

"Jude…"

"Right here." He curled his fingers into my opening first with a quick murmur to make sure this encounter didn't end up with consequences more serious than any of us were prepared for, and then he was sliding inside me, one hot solid inch at a time. He clutched my thigh with a ragged exhalation as our bodies joined. The ecstatic burn of him filling me in combination with Connar's touch and the fact that this was happening at all nearly sent me over the edge right there.

"Fuck," he muttered. "You feel even better than I imagined."

Somehow the thought of him imagining this moment, of him dwelling in his desire for me, made me even giddier. I bucked my hips to encourage him, and with a shaky laugh he plunged even deeper. My head lolled back, which Connar took full advantage of. The other scion scraped the tips of his teeth over the skin along my throat to blissful effect.

I wanted to give him more too. If I could make him feel anywhere close to as good as I did right now…

Jude thrust into me again, and my ass brushed Connar's groin. I gasped as much from the thick erection that nudged my cheek as from the pleasure of Jude's cock lancing through me. It didn't seem Connar minded being a witness to his friend fucking me. He was nothing if not turned on.

I snaked my hand behind me and gripped his cock through his swim trunks. Connar's breath stuttered against my shoulder. He squeezed my breasts as I slid my fingers over him. After a few tentative strokes, partly rocked by the perfect rhythm Jude was setting, I slipped my hand right beneath the fabric to caress him skin to skin.

Connar pumped into my grasp with a groan. He trailed his fingers down my body and pressed them to my clit just as Jude drove into me.

I cried out, pleasure bursting through me, and Jude claimed the sound with a fierce kiss. He thrust faster, my hand tightened around Connar, and Connar kept working over my clit. The wave of bliss surged even higher and crashed over me all over again, in time with a choked breath from Connar.

Heat rushed past my palm as the Stormhurst scion reached his release too. Then it flooded me from the inside, Jude bowing over me with a shudder. He hugged me to him, tucking his head next to mine, and Connar held me too, nuzzling my hair on the other side.

I floated between them, adrift on ecstasy, too blissed out to even speak for the first few minutes. Then I managed to say, "Definitely the best swim ever. It'd be hard to top this."

Connar chuckled, and Jude pecked my cheek playfully. "That sounds like a dare, Ice Queen," he said.

I was a fearmancer, and I wasn't equipped to absorb any emotion other than fear. I'd have sworn in that moment, though, I could feel the joy radiating through all three of us.

Just this once, just for now, everything was right. Even if I knew it couldn't be more than the eye of a storm I hadn't seen the end of.

CHAPTER THIRTY

Rory

About a dozen of the Nary students were working together to lay the final coat of paint on the outside of their clubhouse. Watching them laugh and chatter with each other as they swiped their paint brushes over the wall, a sense of joy came over me for the second time in as many days. I smiled as I leaned against Ashgrave Hall in my usual vantage point.

The clubhouse was essentially done. The door was in place, glass in the windows, and the first batch of furniture had arrived this morning. Whatever my fellow fearmancers' projects had been, they hadn't managed to prevent mine from coming to fruition. And every word and gesture the Naries made showed how pleased they were with what they'd accomplished too.

This triumph wasn't the only one I had to celebrate. A couple hours ago I'd gotten a frantic call from my grandmother cajoling me to intercede on her and my grandfather's behalf in a "misunderstanding" that had brought the blacksuits to their doorstep. "I'll look into it," I'd told her blandly, which wasn't really a lie. I was curious to find out what Declan had dug up on them. But they'd face whatever their due punishment was.

He and his family should be safe from their machinations now. We'd see whether any sanctions laid were enough to get them off *my* back, but they had a lot less to threaten me with now.

"I need a top-up!" Shelby called, bringing around the tub she'd filled with paint for the students around the other side of the building. Benjamin exchanged a grin with her as he poured more in from the bucket. Was that a bit of a blush in my friend's cheeks? Maybe she'd found even more than I'd expected with this project.

"So, you pulled it off," a sour voice said.

My head jerked around. Sinclair had come up beside me, stopping a few feet away. She regarded the Naries with a frown. "Why the hell you want to do them all these favors to screw over the rest of us, I don't know."

"*They've* never been assholes to me," I said. No need to point out the other side of that fact—most of the mage students had been.

Sinclair shrugged. "You've spent so much time coddling them, maybe you haven't looked after everything else you really should have."

I looked at her more sharply. "What are you talking about?" I had no idea what punishment *Victory* had faced for my trick with the voice illusion or whether she'd realized I'd orchestrated it, but her eyes had narrowed every time she'd seen me the last few days. I'd suspected yet another retaliation might be coming.

Sinclair smiled at me—a thin, tight little smile with about as much warmth as an icicle. "Sometimes it's a trade-off. You can't save everything. Let's just say it's the cat's turn to play."

The cat. Panic shot through me, and at the same time, as my thoughts leapt to my familiar, a distant sensation prickled into my chest. Something small and frantic, tinged with the urge to flee.

I was picking up a hint of Deborah's feelings through the familiar bond. I spun around, my gaze snapping to my bedroom window high above us. What the fuck was Victory doing to my mouse now?

My legs tensed to run up to the dorm, but the vague impressions that reached me from my familiar gave me the sense that she was moving downward—toward me. Through the building? I stayed braced where I was, training all my attention on those clues, tuning out Sinclair's gloating presence completely.

At the front of the building, the door swung open. A snicker I recognized instantly as Victory's reached my ears. "Any second now," she said to someone.

I started to storm around the hall to confront her, but I'd only made it two steps before I felt Deborah's presence getting fainter. She was moving in the opposite direction. I backtracked and came around the other side of the building, my pulse thumping. What was going on? If she wasn't coming to me, where *was* she going?

Footsteps scraped the ground on the other side of the building. Then a small white shape sprang from a tiny opening I wouldn't have noticed otherwise between two of the hall's stones. Deborah dashed away across the field toward the garage, her pale body flashing amid the blades of grass.

"Wait!" I called after her—and another furry shape bolted in the same direction. A much larger, cream-and-brown colored shape that dashed after Deborah with a flick of its slim tail: Victory's cat familiar. With a few bounds, it was already closing the distance.

I had no idea how Victory had contrived to get Deborah out of the dorm—some sort of spell targeting her emotions, maybe, given the distress that had been thrumming off her before she'd even emerged?—but I had no doubt at all what she'd ordered her familiar to do if it caught the mouse. I threw myself after them as fast as my legs would carry me.

If casting magic on my familiar was fair play, I could do the same to hers. They were racing ahead of me so quickly, though, that I had to be careful to make sure whatever I cast hit the right target. If I slowed Deborah down instead, I'd be signing her death sentence.

I pushed myself faster, my legs burning. Thumps behind me told me I was being followed, but I couldn't spare the focus to glance back. I narrowed all my attention onto the larger furry shape charging ahead of me.

"*Stop*," I shouted with a surge of persuasive magic, but I mustn't have aimed well enough. The cat ran on. I groped for an alternate strategy. "Box."

Like the walls I'd used to protect me from Malcolm's persuasive designs in the past, the physicality spell was crude but effective. A transparent but solid structure snapped into place around the cat. It was racing along too fast to register the change in time—its face smacked right into one wall. It rebounded with a screech.

Deborah was still running. I could barely make her out in the taller grass behind the garage now, but I didn't want to shout out her real name. My enemies were smart enough to question whether I'd really have named a normal mouse "Deborah."

"Squeak!" I called instead, resorting to the name I'd called her by for the four years before I'd known the mouse contained a human's spirit. "Squeak, come to me!"

Either she'd forgotten that name belonged to her or she was too terrified to process anything. I was just coming up on the garage when her little white body scrambled up the concrete side of that building. Her claws scrabbled against the roughly textured surface, and she skidded halfway down again. I lunged forward and caught her in the middle of her second attempt.

My hands closed around her trembling body. She squirmed in my grasp. "Deborah," I whispered to her. "Deborah, listen to me, you—"

Terror coursed from her into my chest. She flailed around and sank her teeth into my thumb, so deep the spike of pain made me yelp.

I managed to keep my grip on her, but other voices started hollering from behind me. I whipped around to see not just Victory but Cressida and Sinclair loping toward me.

Victory had just reached her familiar. She grimaced and shattered the spell I'd cast around the cat with a snapped word and a jerk of her hand. Then she pointed toward me.

Cressida called out a casting word. I didn't know what her intention was until a bolt of energy smacked into my hands, heaving them apart. Deborah's panicked form plummeted back to the ground.

"No!" I leapt after her, and Victory said something else in a cutting tone. A force like a steel bar slammed into my shins. I tumbled forward onto my hands and knees, a rock scraping my palm.

Deborah was dashing toward the forest now. I didn't think she'd be all that much safer there, where she'd have other predators to contend with. Victory's cat barreled after her in hot pursuit.

I shoved myself back onto my feet, my thoughts whirling as I tried to think of a spell to stop the animal that wouldn't be easily shattered, a way to stop the three girls from stopping *me* yet again.

Too late. The cat coiled its muscles and threw itself into a pounce. A choked cry slipped from my lips—

—and a dark body hurtled out of the woods to slam the cat to the ground.

Malcolm's wolf pinned the Siamese under its heavy paws, its lips pulled back in a growl. Victory and her friends jarred to a halt around me. The cat yowled, the wolf gnashed its teeth in warning, and Malcolm himself stepped out of the forest.

"What the hell, Mal?" Victory protested, half pouting, half seething. "Get your familiar off of mine!"

"We're just making sure no one else's familiar meets an untimely end," Malcolm said, folding his arms over his chest. "Are you going to call off the cat?"

Now I was just as confused as Victory was. Stunned speechless might be more accurate. Thankfully, she had no problem asking the questions I would have for me.

"Are you serious?" my nemesis said, flinging her arm toward me. "I was messing with her. You should be *helping* me, not getting in the way."

"I don't think so." Malcolm stepped forward to stand beside Shadow. "From now on, scion business stays between scions. I don't want to see *any* of you hassling anyone in the pentacle, including Glinda here. Are we clear?"

Victory stared at him. "But— You said— This is fucking ridiculous, Malcolm. You know what she—"

Malcolm's voice cut through hers, cool and firm. "Are. We. Clear?"

There was so much menace in his expression that she faltered. Half of her interest in harassing me had come from wanting to make good with him, I suspected, at least to begin with. And he, for some bizarre reason, was pulling that rug out from under her.

"We're clear," she said tightly.

"And if I call Shadow off your familiar, where are you going to take him?"

"Back to my dorm." Her lips pursed. "Do you really—"

His eyes hardened even more. "Do I really need to remind you that arguing with me isn't a good idea?"

The other two girls stood silent, shocked or wary or both. In the midst of the tension, it occurred to me that while Victory was focused on Malcolm, this was the perfect time for me to remind her just how bad an idea coming at *me* was.

I fixed my gaze on her and rolled a persuasive spell off my tongue like the lash of a whip. "*You will not cast any more magic.*"

Her mental shields had wavered in her bewilderment, and she hadn't been paying attention to me anyway. I felt the spell spear straight through her protections into her mind. Victory flinched and jerked around to face me. "You—"

"Making sure you have to keep any promises you're making," I said as calmly as I could. My hands were still shaking where I'd clenched them at my sides. Deborah was out there somewhere, still in the grip of the magic Victory had possessed her with.

When Malcolm and the other scions had stolen my familiar before, they'd only tormented an illusion of her. Victory had meant to slaughter the real animal. I wasn't so self-confident I believed the all-encompassing spell I'd just cast with my still-developing talents would last very long, but long enough to make Victory regret what she'd done today was all I needed.

She opened her mouth, maybe to try to mutter a spell,

because her voice didn't emerge. She couldn't do it. She glared at me and turned back to Malcolm. "I'm going. If you want me to take my familiar with me, call yours off him."

Malcolm snapped his fingers. That was all the command the wolf needed. It bounded away gracefully, and the cat sprang up with its back arched. When Victory clucked her tongue to it, it streaked across the field to her side. She scooped it up with comforting murmurs, aimed one more glower at me as if this whole situation was somehow my fault, and stalked off with her lackeys flanking her.

"That was cold, Glinda," Malcolm said with an amused gleam in his eyes. "Slipping that spell in like that."

"She deserved it." And I didn't particularly want the Nightwood scion's approval. I let out a ragged breath and scanned the field. My thumb throbbed where Deborah had bitten it. I tucked it, welling blood and all, against my palm. "If you wouldn't mind going somewhere else with Shadow, I'd appreciate it. I still have to find *my* familiar and wake her up from whatever Victory cast on her."

"You should be able to get a sense of her through the familiar bond."

"I know. I don't need your help." I paused. "And if you're sticking around waiting for me to thank you for stepping in just now, don't think I've forgotten that you're the one who egged Victory on in the whole 'destroy Rory' campaign in the first place. I don't know why you're telling her off now, but you'll forgive me if I don't trust that it's from the goodness of your heart."

"Rory…" His jaw tensed. At the tap of his fingers, Shadow trotted to his side. "I meant what I said to her. Anyone who takes you on will have to answer to me. Whatever we still have to work out between us, that's between *us*, and we can do it like colleagues, no more campaigns of destruction."

Oh, he'd just decided that, had he? How wonderful for him. I didn't know what he thought we still had to work out. All I'd ever wanted was for him to stay the hell away from me.

"Great," I said. "Maybe next time a new scion turns up, you can follow that philosophy a few months sooner. Can you please leave now? I have no problem with your *wolf*, but I don't think my familiar is going to calm down while there's one around."

Malcolm looked as if he almost said something else, but whatever it was, he thought better of it. He dipped his head to me with an unreadable expression and strode away, Shadow following at his heel.

I took several slow breaths to steady myself, and a thin thread of emotion crept back into my chest. Deborah. I walked closer to the forest, calling out a little louder now that there was no one around to hear me other than her. "Deborah? Deborah, it's okay now. There's nothing hunting you. It's just me here. Rory."

I paced along the edge of the forest for a minute before the underbrush rustled. A little white head poked from between the leaves. Her voice traveled distantly into my head. *Lorelei?*

Relief washed through me. I knelt down and held out

my uninjured hand to her, and my familiar scampered onto it, trembling but still in one piece.

"There you go," I said softly. "I've got you. You're okay now."

I tried not to think about the fact that she might not have been if it'd come down to just me—that I might owe her life to the last guy on Earth I'd have wanted to owe anything to.

CHAPTER THIRTY-ONE

Rory

"You know," Jude said, "technically this competition is over. You can stop working on your project now."

I shot him a mock-glower where we were standing in the field outside the clubhouse. "*You* know I didn't work on this just for the competition."

The tang of new paint still hung in the air, but the building was completely finished. A couple hours ago, before the Nary students had headed home for a week's break before the fall term started, happy voices had been carrying through the windows. We fearmancer students had an assembly to announce the winner of the project competition in a few minutes, but I didn't need any official recognition to feel triumphant.

Jude grinned at me. "Yeah, well, it was worth a try. You push yourself awfully hard. I guess it's a good thing you have the two of us around to make sure you take a breather now and then."

"It is," Connar agreed with a chuckle. He straightened up from where he'd been kneeling a few feet from Jude. "I think that ward's completely solid. We'll still want to check on them periodically, but no one's taking this building down without a lot of concentrated effort."

I wasn't sure what warmed me more—his effortless use of "we" to mean the three of us or the memory of the treatment I'd gotten during the last breather these two had arranged for me.

Jude's eyes twinkled as if he knew what I was thinking about. He grabbed my hand and tugged me closer to him. "And I don't think Ms. Grimsworth will look kindly on that kind of destruction once this project is named the winning effort of the summer. Too bad none of the Naries know to thank you."

"I'm okay with that," I said. I wished I'd been able to do more. This was a step in the right direction, giving them an escape from the mage students who preyed on them, but it still gnawed at me that the school encouraged the rest of us to prey on them at all.

That would end once I could dismantle this place with the help of the joymancers. I had trouble picturing exactly what fearmancer society would look like in the aftermath, but at least I could now say there were people ready to lead who didn't prioritize cruelty. And the documents Professor Banefield had led me to would hopefully get me one step closer to *that* goal. We had a week off for the end of summer after this assembly, and I planned to spend all of it tracking down more information to better understand the pieces he'd given me.

Connar glanced at his phone. "We should get going if we want Rory at the assembly to receive her prize."

Jude sighed dramatically. "And here I was hoping we could take the opportunity to break in the new building with a little… action." He waggled his eyebrows at me.

I swatted his arm. "We're not going to go desecrating the place we just finished shutting people like us out of. We've got the whole rest of campus to make use of."

"Hmm. True." He kissed my cheek. "And what do you say we find some part of it to make use of before we all head home."

A flush spread all through my body. "I might be on board with that," I said, my pulse thumping even faster when I saw the hunger that had lit in Connar's eyes too. "But assembly first. We don't even know that I'm going to win."

Jude scoffed. "If you don't, I'll stage a protest. Let's go, then, Ice Queen."

Many students were already heading toward the Stormhurst Building. We merged with that current, letting it carry us along to the gymnasium where our summer project had first been announced. The platform was set up at the far end as before, Ms. Grimsworth standing near the podium speaking with Professor Crowford. At the sight of him, remembering his name on my mentor's list alongside the barons, my skin tightened.

As we waited for the rest of the students to trickle in, my phone chimed. I fished it out to see Lillian

Ravenguard had texted me. *I understand the summer project results are being announced today. Let me know how yours turned out!*

All of me tightened seeing those friendly words. I had no idea just how complicit Lillian might be in the horrors I'd faced since arriving here—and I sure as hell wasn't ready to take her to task. Since I'd retrieved Banefield's records, I hadn't spoken to her at all, and things could stay that way for the time being. I shoved the phone back into my purse without replying.

Ms. Grimsworth tapped the microphone, and the chatter around the room fell silent. "It looks as though we have everyone here," she said, gazing over the crowd. "To begin with, I'd like to congratulate you on a successful summer all around. We saw great efforts from many students and minimal overstepping of rules." Her voice turned wry with those last words.

I couldn't help glancing toward where I'd spotted Victory standing in the midst of her closest friends and a few other girls on the other side of the room. She didn't look my way at all. She'd completely avoided me since her attack on Deborah two days ago. I'd imagine my persuasive spell had worn off and she could use her magic just fine, but she probably wasn't in any hurry to risk losing it again.

I might not have exactly *won* there, and whatever success I'd achieved had been partly due to Malcolm's intervention, but if all she did was ignore me for the rest of my time here at Blood U, I'd consider that a real victory.

"I'm sure you're all impatient to hear which student's performance exceeded all others, so I won't leave you waiting," the headmistress went on. "I'm pleased to announce that our judges unanimously agreed this year's prize should go to a young lady who's not only achieved a remarkable goal but done so only a short time after discovering her powers: Rory Bloodstone."

My name rolled over me with a momentary jolt of shock. Jude whooped, and Connar let out a cheer, and that seemed to spur any students who might have been hesitant given the focus of my project into action. Applause echoed around the room.

Ms. Grimsworth beckoned me up to the platform, and I pushed myself forward to weave through the crowd. A smile stretched across my face as exhilaration bubbled up in my chest. I'd *hoped*, but I hadn't really been sure—hadn't known whether the professors judging our work might dock me an awful lot of points for helping the Naries rather than attacking them.

But they hadn't opposed that approach, at least not enough for them to deny how much I'd accomplished. That was a reason for a lot more hope, wasn't it? Maybe I had even more people here who could transform fearmancer society into something less horrifying.

When I stepped up on the platform, Ms. Grimsworth gave my hand a brisk but firm shake with a smile that was warm by her standards. Professor Crowford came up to me with a small gilded certificate.

"Congratulations, Miss Bloodstone," he said. "Have you decided on your chosen object and enchantment?"

Right—the prize. I'd gotten so focused on seeing the project through that I'd forgotten I'd win anything other than seeing it complete.

"I'm going to need a little time to decide," I said.

He nodded. "Whenever you're ready, bring that certificate to the professor you'd like to cast the spell, and they'll be happy to comply."

I turned back toward the room, and Ms. Grimsworth nudged me forward with her hand on my back. "Let's hear a little more appreciation for this year's winner," she said.

Another round of applause and cheers echoed through the room. My gaze found Declan standing off to the side, clapping hard and beaming like he'd never doubted I'd pull this off. If only I could have really celebrated with him too.

Malcolm stood several feet beyond him, clapping too, his own smile crooked. But it *was* a smile. I didn't know what to make of this apparent truce he'd decided on, but I guessed there'd be plenty of time to hash that out next term.

Before I got down from the platform, I scanned the crowd one more time for another familiar face framed by dark blond hair. I'd have liked to acknowledge Imogen— she'd helped me pull the clubhouse together too. She didn't appear to be in the room, though. Maybe she'd headed home early, she'd been so sure she wasn't in the running?

Shelby should have gotten credit as well—most of the Naries should have, really—but they had at least gotten their clubhouse as a prize. That'd have to do for now.

Several of the other professors came over as I left the platform, grasping my hand or patting my shoulder with enthusiastic congratulations. I tensed a little at Professor Viceport's approach, but her expression didn't look as stiff as it usually did.

"An impressive bit of work, Miss Bloodstone," she said, shaking my hand with her cool dry fingers. "I have to say I'm looking forward to seeing how far you can take these skills of yours in the months ahead."

That approving remark felt like a whole extra win. I restrained the urge to do a fist-pump in celebration.

After a few moments, I was caught up in the crowd of my fellow students, with more congratulatory gestures and remarks. I doubted most of them meant that appreciation all that genuinely, but fearmancers were nothing if not pragmatic when it came to sucking up to people. If it meant even fewer of them messed with me next term, I was all for it.

The maintenance staff set out platters of snacks and drinks on tables along one wall, and for the next hour or so, the gym turned into an end-of-summer party. Someone turned on an upbeat pop album that didn't sound fearmancer-y at all, and Jude twirled me around a few times in his approximation of dancing. Connar grabbed the last of my favorite kind of tart before it disappeared.

As people started to drift out of the building, the two guys each took one of my hands. "So," Jude said meaningfully, "about that 'action' we were planning…?"

I elbowed him, but a flicker of heat ran through me. "We could go for a little drive, get right off campus?"

"I'd go for that," Connar said.

"Let me just pop back into the dorm. These aren't the best shoes for driving." I'd worn heels to go with my dressy slacks, but I wasn't so confident behind the wheel I wanted to experiment with advanced types of footwear just yet.

"As you wish," Jude said. "We'll meet you at the garage."

We parted ways on the green. As I headed to the stairs in Ashgrave Hall, Cressida barged past me in the hall with a rigid expression and a swish of her braid, her shoulder jarring against mine. Apparently *she* was in quite a rush to get home.

I hurried up the stairs to the fifth floor, my mind riffling through the possibilities for a peaceful—and private—date spot. Maybe the place where Jude had arranged our picnic what felt like ages ago? Or we could go all the way out to my country property. That might take too long for us to make it home in good time tonight, though...

I pushed open the door to the dorm room and stopped in my tracks. Every thought in my head scattered.

A body lay sprawled on the floor just a few feet into the room. A body splattered with blood and unnaturally still. A body with blond hair held back by a silver clip that glinted beneath the flecks of red.

My stomach lurched, and a rush of images flashed in front of my eyes. Imogen's face, twisted with anger, yelling something at me. Her hand slashing out to slap my face, the impression so real my cheek stung. My throat vibrating with words and power. A hail of razor-edged magic cutting my friend down. *Her* throat, slit. Her chest and stomach gouged.

"No," I said, shaking my head as if I could force the images away. But they weren't coming from inside me. They had to be some kind of spell, an illusion. They started up all over again from the beginning, Imogen yelling at me even as she lay there lifeless on the floor.

I tried to spin, to grope for the door that had hung open somehow behind me. My legs jarred, refusing to budge. I sucked in a breath to scream, and that caught in my throat. Magic gripped me from head to toe as the illusion whirled through its violent imagery in front of me. I couldn't even force my eyes to stay closed. My eyelids jerked back open with every blink.

And Imogen just lay there, the blood seeping further across the floor...

I had to help her. If there was any way she was still alive—*please*, let her still be alive—

There was a gasp and a shriek in the hall behind me. A voice murmured frantically as it faded away down the stairs. The illusions battered me again. I strained at my legs, at my vocal chords. Come on, Rory.

Footsteps thundered up the steps, and just like that, the spell released me. I stumbled around with a ragged inhalation to see four figures in black shirts and slacks bursting into the fifth floor hall. They charged right at me. One of them caught sight of Imogen's body beyond me and grimaced as he nodded to the others. A woman dropped beside Imogen and held her hand over Imogen's chest with a murmur of a casting.

"My friend—" I started.

"She's dead," the woman said, looking up.

The man at the front of the pack wheeled on me. "Rory Bloodstone," he said in a hard voice. "You need to come with us. You're under arrest."

ABOUT THE AUTHOR

Eva Chase lives in Canada with her family. She loves stories both swoony and supernatural, and strong women and the men who appreciate them. Along with the Royals of Villain Academy series, she is the author of the Moriarty's Men series, the Looking Glass Curse trilogy, the Their Dark Valkyrie series, the Witch's Consorts series, the Dragon Shifter's Mates series, the Demons of Fame Romance series, the Legends Reborn trilogy, and the Alpha Project Psychic Romance series.

Connect with Eva online:
www.evachase.com
eva@evachase.com

Made in the USA
Columbia, SC
09 January 2020